where

i belong

Alabama Summer Series, Book One

New York Times bestselling author

J. DANIELS

To my family.

where

i belong

Alabama Summer Series, Book One

mia

BENJAMIN KELLY WAS the bane of my existence. His teasing was relentless, always making sure to point out each and every one of my insecurities whenever I was around him. And because I was best friends with his sister Tessa, I was around him all the time.

"You have food stuck in your braces. That's so disgusting. Maybe you should just stop eating since you're so fat anyway."

"Gross. What is that on your face? It looks like a second head."

"God, can you even see anything out of those glasses, nerd? How many times are you going to run into things?"

"Mia Corelli is the ugliest girl I've ever seen. Oh sorry, Mia. I didn't see you sitting right next to me."

I hated him with a fury. I was convinced that his sole purpose in life was to break me down to nothing. And he succeeded on more than one occasion. I never cried in front of him, though. I never gave him that satisfaction. I just stood there and took it, saving my tears for when I was alone. Tessa was always standing up for me, throwing every insult she could think of at him. And I was grateful for that, because I didn't have it in me to give him what he deserved. My bank of comebacks were pathetic compared to Tessa's. So I'd just sit back and let her handle it.

"You're just jealous that Mia's teeth are going to be

straighter than yours, loser. Why don't you go get that giant gap fixed before someone kicks a field goal through it?"

"What's that on your face, Ben? God, it's hideous. Oh, never mind. There's nothing on your face. That's just how you look."

"At least Mia isn't stupid like you, Ben. If you make it out of eighth grade, it'll be a miracle."

"Ben Kelly has the smallest penis in the world. He has to hold it with a pair of tweezers when he pees."

Her comebacks would shut him up temporarily, but when he found his voice again, it was frequently used to take a shot at me. I was his sister's nerdy, awkward best friend who became his favorite punching bag for five grueling years. I grew some thick skin and became used to the torment, but my insecurities were always there. He'd never let me forget about them. He was the spawn of Satan, the biggest jerk on the planet, and I'd hate him for the rest of my life.

Benjamin Kelly was the worst thing to come out of Alabama. And if I never saw him again, that would be fine by me.

mia

"I DON'T HAVE to go. If this is too much on you, I can stay here. It really isn't a big deal, Aunt Mae." Closing the door to my mother's bedroom, I walk down the hallway into the kitchen behind my aunt. "Really. I mean it. Just because she's doing okay right now doesn't mean it's a good idea for me to leave the state."

My aunt places her hand on my shoulder, squeezing it gently. "You need a break from all of this, sweetie. You've been taking care of her twenty-four hours a day for the past nine months. Everyone needs to take some time for themselves." She tilts her head, her expression softening with a smile. "She wants you to have fun, Mia. Go enjoy your summer and leave all of this to me."

Sighing, I shake my head, not fully committed to the idea of leaving. "What if she gets really sick and I'm not here? What if she needs me?"

The thought of my mother calling out for me while I'm four hours away is enough to cancel this whole trip. She loves my aunt, but I'm the one that's been here. I'm the one that's been doing everything for her since she fell ill. She's used to me, not Mae. I know the look she gets when she's really feeling bad, but won't admit it. I know how to get her to eat when she refuses. Me; I don't need a break, let alone an entire summer off from taking care of my own mother.

"If anything happens, even the slightest change in her condition, I'll call you." Her hand cups my face, her thumb stroking the skin of my cheek. "Promise me you won't let all of your worrying prevent you from having an amazing summer with Tessa."

"I just don't know if this is the best time. She hasn't had her strength back for that long."

Aunt Mae issues me a look, indicating that she's not letting me back out of this. "This is the perfect time. And like I said before, she wants you to go. If you try and stay home now, I'm afraid you won't only be getting an earful from me."

I smile and nod in agreement. My mom does enjoy laying into me when I deserve it. She's stern but sweet at the same time, always following up a punishment with a hug.

"All right, I'll go. But you need to promise you'll call me if there's any change. Even the slightest."

"I promise." She drops her hand and steps around the counter, digging into the pile of dishes that has accumulated in the sink.

I'll be staying with Tessa at her parents' house for the summer while she looks after it. I have a ton of memories at that house, considering the fact that I practically lived there for five years. I'd always go to Tessa's house after school, staying there until my mom would pick me up on her way home. Tessa was like the sister I never had, and when my grandmother got sick and we had to move to Fulton, Georgia the summer before ninth grade, I cried for weeks. We kept in touch over the years, and now I'll be spending the entire summer with her just like we used to. And as long as her pain-in-the-ass brother stays as far away from me as possible, it's going to be the best summer of my life.

Benjamin Kelly. World's biggest dickhead.

I head back to my bedroom, needing to finish up my last

bit of packing. Tessa is expecting me tomorrow afternoon sometime, but I'm not waiting until then to get into Alabama. There is something I want to do before I start my summer break. Something I've wanted to do for a long time. If I'm really going to enjoy myself this summer, I need to let go of all my inhibitions. This will not be the summer of hang-ups or shyness. I'm not the same girl that left Ruxton nine years ago. That girl has been gone for a long time. The braces came off first, followed by the weight and the glasses; which were exchanged for contacts. My hair is no longer a wild mess of curls now that I've learned how to manage it. My skin cleared up in tenth grade, and that wasn't the only big change to my appearance that year. My breasts came in overnight it seemed, and they are definitely my best asset, if I do say so myself. And with the help of the volleyball team I joined in high school, my body got tight and stayed that way. The new Mia Corelli is going to let loose and experience everything an Alabama summer had to offer. But in order to do that, I need to handle something first. And that thing is going to be handled tonight.

I grab my phone, falling back onto my pillow after pushing my suitcases to the floor.

Me: All packed up! I'll call you when I'm on the road tomorrow.

Tessa: OMFG I'm so excited! Your ass is mine for the summer! I have so much planned for us already. :)

Me: Yay! I can't wait to get there and relax by the pool for three months.

Tessa: That's not all we're doing. We're finding you a play thing for the summer. I'll surround you with penises if I have to.

Jesus, Tessa.

Me: Well there's an image. Speaking of dicks, any chance your brother will be out of the country for the summer?

Tessa: Don't worry about Ben. I don't even see him that much so you won't have to either. And besides, he's already been warned. If he bothers you, I get to kick him in the nuts.

Me: Only after I get the first shot at him. :)

Tessa: There's my girl. This summer is going to be amazeballs!!! See ya tomorrow!

Me: See ya!

I DON'T EVEN know the name of the bar I'm currently sitting in. But I doubt it matters. It was the first one I spotted when I got off the Ruxton exit and it looked promising enough. A bar seems like the perfect venue for what I am about to do, or at least attempt to do. I don't want to face another summer as a virgin, especially when my best friend isn't shy about her sexual conquests. If I am going to keep up with her this summer, I have to ditch my virginity, and fast. That's why I picked a bar. This doesn't need to be romantic. I'm not looking for a relationship. This is just sex. Get-it-over-with kind of sex, and hopefully with an orgasm in the process.

Tessa has no idea that I still hold my v-card, and I really don't want to show up tomorrow waving it around like some sort of abstinence banner. So, with the help of my most non-virginal outfit, I'm going to be giving away that card to one of the lucky men in this bar tonight.

"Here ya go, sweetheart," the bartender says, placing a bright purple drink in front of me. "From the guy with the black shirt at the end of the bar."

I wrap my fingers around the glass and glance down the length of the bar, meeting the eyes of the man that bought me the drink.

He's hot. Really hot. Insanely hot. The kind of hot that makes you think, there's no way in hell this guy is looking at me. He has short, dark hair and eyes that are bright enough to see in the dim lighting.

I send him a smile before looking away to take a sip of my drink. It tastes delicious, like raspberry and coconut. I take another sip and glance back down the bar, but the man is no longer there. A surge of disappointment floods my system.

"Crap. Where'd he go?" I utter under my breath as my eyes search the crowded bar. Who buys a girl a drink and then leaves before cashing in on the thank you? Didn't he see the giant florescent arrow pointing to me, flashing this chick wants to get laid by you? Damn it. That hottie was definite v-card redeeming material.

"Where'd who go, baby?"

Whipping my head around, I meet the eyes of my sexy little drink buyer as he claims the stool next to me. Gasping softly, I allow myself a moment to take in the hotness that is now brushing up against my arm.

His bright gray eyes are hooded by dark eyebrows, and my attention is drawn down to his lips as they curl up into a smile.

Those. Lips. Holy hell.

Full and way the hell inviting. If I had the nerve, I'd jump all over them.

I look back up into his eyes with a grin. "Oh, um, you actually. I wanted to thank you for my drink. It's really good.

What is it?"

"Purple passion. No, purple hurricane?" His eyebrows furrow as he thinks it over. I smile around my straw, taking another sip. "I don't know. Some purple, girly drink. You looked really thirsty from where I was standing, so I thought I'd help you out."

I arch my eyebrow. "Oh? And how long have you been watching me to make that observation?"

He chuckles one of the sweetest laughs I've ever heard before replying, "Long enough to see that you're also here by yourself, which surprises me."

I watch as he motions for the bartender, admiring the way the muscles in his arm flex as he reaches into his pocket and pulls out his wallet.

"Why does that surprise you? And are you here by yourself, or is your girlfriend in the ladies room?" My tone is teasing, and I see his lip curl up in the corner as he absorbs my words.

This guy better not have a girlfriend. He'll be wearing my delicious drink if he does.

He turns his body toward me, reaching his hand out to trail down my arm. "You're really fucking hot, that's why it surprises me. And I wouldn't be taking you back to my place if I had a girlfriend."

Old Mia would be shocked by his forwardness, but new Mia is looking up to the heavens, thanking God for putting this gorgeous man who doesn't waste any time on this planet and in this bar tonight.

His finger stops on the top of my hand and he begins rubbing my skin softly there. "That is, if you want to go back to my place. Or we could do yours. It doesn't matter to me. I'm game for any place that'll put me between your legs." His grin spreads and two massive dimples appear in each cheek.

Oh, good God. That's adorable.

"You certainly cut right to the chase."

He shrugs. "I just know what I want, and I've been staring at her for the past twenty minutes."

I like this guy. And not only because he's too good looking for words and blunt as hell. There's something about his playfulness that's drawing me to him. Plus, I feel hotter than I've ever felt; confident even. Which could be because of the one drink I've already downed before this hottie bought me another. Either way, Tessa would be proud of this Mia.

I cross one leg over the other, gaining his attention when the hem of my dress slides higher up my thigh. "Getting between my legs requires changing locations? You don't seem like the type of guy that shies away from public sex."

He definitely doesn't. He looks like the type of guy that would take me anytime, anyplace, and not give a shit what the consequences are. There's an edginess to him that is definitely hitting all my hot spots.

He smiles before he leans in and brushes his lips against my ear. "I'm not, but this bar will eventually close, and I don't plan on stopping what I'm going to do to you until your body can't take anymore."

I shudder at the thought and move my hand to his thigh, flexing my fingers and feeling his muscles contract against me. Turning my head, I put my lips right up to his ear and mimic his position. "Will you be gentle with me? I've never done this before," I whisper. "But God, I want this. I want you to make me come." I lean back and meet his bright eyes, noticing the specks of blue that stand out against the gray. His gaze hypnotizes me. "Do you think you can handle me?"

I swear I hear a growl rumbling in his throat as his hand trails back up my arm and grips the back of my neck underneath my hair. It feels possessive, as if he's claiming me right here in front of everyone. And I know it sounds crazy, but I want to be owned by this man. I want to give myself to him completely and a huge part of me doesn't want gentle. I don't care that it might hurt. I want him to take me and I don't want him to hold back.

He grabs my chin with his other hand and turns my head, bringing our lips together for the slightest bit of contact. I crave more instantly, whimpering when his mouth leaves mine. I see his lip twitch in response to my desperation.

He has me and he knows it.

"I'm going to fucking consume you," he says against my mouth, bringing his other hand around and raking his thumb across my bottom lip. I open my mouth and he slips it inside, his eyes watching with a new heat as I scrape my teeth along his skin and bite down with the smallest amount of pressure. The muscles in his neck twitch and he slides it out, dragging his now wet thumb down my neck. "Your place or mine, baby? I'm close to losing my mind if I don't get inside you soon."

I lick my lips, tasting the trace of whiskey that he left on them from our brief kiss. "Yours. I don't have a place."

"Just passing through?" he asks with raised eyebrows.

We're still sitting so close together, practically on top of each other, and I feel safe. Protected. Something about his looming presence makes me feel like I can trust him completely. It's unexplainable.

"Yeah, you could say that."

I finish off the rest of my drink and stand, indicating that I'm ready to take this where we both want it to go. I can't sit in this bar any longer with him touching me and not lose my mind right along with him.

He gets to his feet and my eyes do a double take.

Damn, he's gorgeous. I couldn't tell from his seated position, but the man has a torso that goes on for days. Broad
and built, he definitely works out–and often–with this type
of physique. His narrow waist is fitted perfectly in a pair of
jeans, and his legs are long and muscular. I can only imagine
what the back of him looks like.

I grab my clutch and look up, way up into his face. "I
could seriously climb you like an oak tree."

"Oh yeah? I think I'd like to see that." His playful response
makes me laugh, and I'm quickly being pulled through the
crowd and out the door.

The sweet Alabama air blows my hair off my shoulders.

"You wanna follow me or should I bring you back here
to get your car? It's up to you." He stops once we reach the
middle of the parking lot, my hand still firmly placed in his.

I don't want to pull it out of his to get in my car. I don't
want to be away from him for one second, because we'll only
have tonight. That's how one-night stands work, or so I've
heard. It's not like I know what I'm doing here. But it would
make more sense if we drove separately. Besides, if he's some
psycho, I'll need a getaway vehicle.

I squeeze his hand, looking up at him from underneath
my eyelashes. "I'll follow you, but I'm going to need to feel
those lips again first."

He doesn't waste any time. It's as if he's thinking the same
thing, because before I can move in, even slightly, to affirm my
desires, he's on me. His lips work mine, our tongues stroking
against each other's with purpose. These aren't teasing kisses.
These are *I want you right now, and if we don't get to a bed soon,
you'll be taken right here* kisses. I've never been kissed like this.
Never. I could do this for hours. Days even. I feel it radiating
throughout my body, pinging off every nerve ending. Our

hands are still interlocked; the pressure of his hold intensifies with the kiss. He licks along my bottom lip slowly, ending the passionate embrace our mouths are so happy to be in.

Well, at least my mouth, anyway.

"Coconut," he whispers against my mouth.

"Hmm?"

His lip curls up in the corner. "You taste like coconut. I fucking love coconut." I grin as he flicks his head toward a jacked up truck. "That's me. Follow close behind me, baby. I'd hate to lose you."

"That would be a shame," I tease, walking toward my cherry red Jeep that's parked only a few cars down from his. "I'd hate to have this night end after just one kiss."

His eyes narrow in on my license plate. "One hell of a kiss though, Georgia."

I can't keep the smile off my face as he pulls out of his parking spot and I follow closely behind him.

We are only on the highway momentarily before we hit the Alabama back roads that I used to be so fond of. Tessa and I would go 4-wheeling on back roads like this, and I spent a lot of summers walking up and down the dirt paths, picking wild flowers. But the girl that did those things all those years ago isn't currently following the black truck down these back roads. This is unfamiliar territory, completely new to me, and my stomach is beginning to do flips in anticipation of what is about to happen.

mia

HIS HAND FINDS mine again as I follow him into his house, and he wastes no time walking straight up the stairs and into the dimly lit bedroom.

I place my clutch down on his dresser, stepping out of my heels.

He isn't far behind me, and I feel him the moment I place my right foot on the carpet. His hands caress down my arms, rough against soft, as I stay turned away from him, feeling his breath in my hair. My pulse begins to thrum in my neck as he takes all of my hair over one shoulder. He presses his lips along the line of my neck and I tilt my head to give him the access we both want him to have.

Oh, God. I close my eyes and feel him. Everywhere. Even though he's barely touching me, I feel him all over my body. The junction where my thighs meet is pulsating and my nipples are so hard they might just rip right through my dress.

Jesus, this is intense.

His lips work up my neck to my ear and he licks it before biting it. I shiver and he does it again.

Who would have thought I'd like a little biting?

He turns me in his arms, latching his mouth onto mine. His tongue sweeps into my mouth and I groan, gripping his head to hold him to me. His hair is soft against my palms, and I run my fingers along the base of his hair line. I feel his desire for me pressing into my stomach, and it isn't a small desire.

Thank you, Jesus.

He moans into my mouth and sucks on my tongue, his hands roaming all over my back. Firmly planting them on my ass, he dips and lifts me off the ground in one quick motion.

My legs instinctively wrap around his waist as he carries me over to the bed, dropping me in the middle of it. I run my tongue along my bottom lip, tasting his mouth on mine. I'm ready. So ready. If he doesn't touch me again soon, I might just resort to begging.

He'd probably like that.

"Christ, you're so sexy. Look at you." He stares down at me, eyes blazing as I stretch out on the bed beneath him. "You've no idea how close I was to pulling over on the side of the road and taking you right there."

That would've been fun. Sex in a truck? A really bad ass looking truck? I'll have to put that on my to-do list.

"Maybe next time," I reply, but I know there won't be a next time. Not with this guy anyway. I'll probably never see him again, and I'm okay with that.

My eyes enlarge as he pulls his T-shirt off with one hand.

Oh, wow. His bare chest is a sight to behold; wide with a bit of dark hair in the middle. He's all man, and I don't feel a bit ashamed about the staring I'm doing. He should be on billboards all over the city.

He's muscular, every cut of him visible from my angle. His right shoulder is completely covered in tattoos, stretching down to his elbow. And trust me when I say that tattoos have never looked this good.

Six, no eight pack, maybe? The V. That freaking glorious V that leads to what I really want that's hiding beneath his pants.

He undoes his belt and his jeans fall to the floor, leaving

a very impressive erection pressing against his boxers.

My mouth waters instantly. I want to eat him up.

He drops to his knees at the foot of the bed. and I lean up on my elbows to see him better. I'm about to ask him what he's doing when my feet are grabbed and I'm pulled toward him. And now I'm very aware of what he plans on doing. I yelp and hear a small sound of amusement as my legs are dropped over his shoulders.

"I need to taste this pussy." His hands hike my dress up to reveal my lace panties. My favorite pair, actually. I felt losing my virginity warranted something besides my go-to boy shorts. "You wanna come on my lips, baby?"

Hell fucking yes, I do. Would anyone in their right mind say no to that?

"Uh huh," is all I can give him at the moment. My brain is having difficulty forming a complete thought as I anticipate his mouth on me there.

He groans, deep and guttural, sliding his hand up my thigh until I feel his fingers running up and down the length of the lace.

I'm shaking, fisting the sheets already and he's barely touching me.

"So wet and hot." He presses his face between my thighs and inhales, his moan vibrates against my body. "Damn, you smell good. I bet you taste even better, though."

My panties are removed and that first lick nearly rockets me off the bed.

"Holy shit. That's . . . oh, wow."

My thighs clamp his head so tightly, I'm surprised he's managing to move his head at all. But he manages, and he's eating me like this is all we're going to do tonight. Like this is the only way he'll get to experience my body. I can't take my eyes off him while he does it, and given the predatory look in his eyes right now, I'm not sure he'll let me look away if I tried. He's all over me, alternating his movements so I don't get used to anything. And he seems to be enjoying it as much as I am, going at it with such gusto and humming against me. The vibration moves through my entire body, pulsing, pulsing, until I'm so close I can't see straight. This is what oral sex is supposed to feel like. Raw. Uninhibited. Thank God, I left my shyness at the door because he's exploring every inch of my pussy. I'm tempted to lock him between my legs and never let him up for air. He's incredible at this, and I know without a doubt that given the chance, I would've never experienced anything even remotely close to this.

This man. Holy fuck. This man right here knows exactly what he's doing.

I don't want to come so quickly, but there's no way I can slow down my body's reaction to him. I arch my back off the bed, groaning loudly as my orgasm barrels through me like a shock wave.

He licks my length once, and then again, making sure to soak up every last drop of what he's earned.

"You're fucking beautiful when you come." He plants gentle kisses between my legs, his eyes glued to mine. "I need to see that again." He kneels in between my legs, dropping his hand to the spot he's just worked like the world was about to end.

I whimper as he teases me with one finger, slipping it inside as he keeps his eyes on me.

"When you get yourself off, do you just focus on your clit or do you fuck your pussy like this?"

Hottest. Question. Ever.

I swallow loudly as he slips in another finger, loosening

me, priming me for his cock. "Just my clit. I don't think I can come from," I gasp, "from that."

Holy mother of God.

His eyes sparkle with mischief. "Challenge accepted." He grabs my knee with his free hand and begins fingering me, ignoring my clit completely.

I'd protest if it didn't feel un-fucking-believable. I feel him curl them up inside me, as if he's beckoning me to come closer, to come all together. He's rubbing some glorious spot that I never knew even existed.

"What are you . . . oh, my God, I've never, is that . . . are you?" I'm panting and arching into his magical touch. If I begin speaking in tongues, I won't be surprised in the least.

"It's your G-spot, angel. I'll make you come in ways you never thought possible."

He presses up into that spot while his other hand pushes down on the front of my pelvis. I'm not sure if he feels the change that's happening to me or if he sees it. But he knows exactly when it happens.

"That's it. Give me another. I fucking need it," he growls and I obey, giving him exactly what he demands of me.

I lock eyes with him as my orgasm rips through my body, shredding me into post climactic pieces.

"Holy shit. Come up here."

I reach for him, seeing him stand and slip his boxers off as he sucks on the fingers that were just inside me. My eyes wander lower, lower, until I focus in on what might possibly split me in two. He's bigger than I thought. Way bigger.

"Oh, my God," I blurt out, causing him to glance over at me with a puzzled expression. We both laugh together and I cover my face embarrassingly. "Sorry. That was a good *Oh, my God*."

"Christ, I hope so." He slips on a condom and moves between my legs. "Let's see if you have anything for me to *oh, my God* at underneath this dress." His hands grip the hem of my dress and I sit up, granting him access. "I'm betting you're about to blow my fucking mind."

I blush crimson as my dress is removed. Lying back on the bed, I watch his eyes run all over my body, stopping and widening as they land on my chest.

Oh, God. I'm completely naked in front of this man and he's just staring at me.

I should let him stare though, after that mind-blowing orgasm. I should let him do whatever he wants with me. With a tongue like that and fingers I'd give my life for, I can't imagine how good the rest of his body is.

Speaking of the rest of his body.

My eyes drop to his massive erection and the need in me grows to a palpable hunger.

"Umm, is something wrong?" I whisper my fear, seeing his eyes jolt up to mine, finally leaving my breasts.

"Your tits are phenomenal." His hands squeeze them and I arch my back off the mattress, pushing them farther into his palms. "I want to slide my cock right here and come all over them." He trails a finger down the center, his eyes turning roguish. "I bet you'd look beautiful covered in me. I bet you'd like it too."

Jesus. This guy excels in the dirty talking department. And I never thought I'd be into that. But coming out of that mouth, from those lips, I'm way the hell into it. I've never been so turned on in my life.

He leans forward and presses my body into the mattress.

The sensation of him over me is perfect. Every part of his body is touching mine, and I never want him to move. His erection pushes against my clit, and I moan into him as his mouth collides with mine. His tongue twists and dips, licking and swiping into my mouth. God, he's so good at this. I feel like I'm just fumbling around but he isn't complaining. I run along the muscles of his back with my hands, feeling them flex against my touch.

His mouth breaks free of mine, and he slides down slightly. "I gotta suck them, baby." He flicks my nipple once, twice, and then draws it into his mouth.

"Oh, yes." I hold his head to my breast, not ever wanting him to stop this amazing sensation.

He alternates between them, giving each nipple equal attention as he sucks, twists, and bites. The pain is just enough that it blends into pleasure. Intense pleasure. It feels amazing. But I want more. I miss his cock already, now that he's moved down my body.

"Can you, oh . . ."

His head tilts up. "Can I what?" He keeps his eyes on me as he licks my left nipple. "I'm not doing anything else to this beautiful body unless you beg me to do it." His hands continue their sweet torture on my breasts. "You said back at the bar that you've never done this before. What did you mean exactly? Going home with a stranger? Or what you're about to beg me to do?"

I glance down and meet his smirk.

Christ, he's sexy as hell, and playful. Deadly combination. And he has every right to be cocky. I'm all for begging if it puts him inside me.

"Um, both actually. I've never done anything like this. I've kissed boys and they've touched me a little, but that's about the extent of my experience."

"Are you sure you wanna do this? You don't even know

me. I could eat your pussy some more or fuck you again with my fingers. It doesn't have to be my cock getting you off."

I bite my lip playfully. "Tempting. But I want this to be with you." Our eyes stay locked as he sits back between my legs. "I don't want to stop."

"Show me you want this." He holds me with his stare, commanding me to do what he's asking. "Show me you want me to be the one to take it."

I reach for his cock, sliding down the condom and rubbing his length. His groan vibrates through his entire body and I feel it tickling my palm.

"Do you think you can make me come with this?" I whisper my tease. "I'm betting you can. I'm betting you can make me come all night with it."

The biggest, sweetest grin spreads across his face and I swoon. I'm fucking swooning here.

"That's the plan, sweetheart. I'm gonna go slow, but I need you to tell me if it's too much for you."

He braces himself on either side of my face, taking his weight on his forearms. I feel him at my entrance and he gently places kisses to my lips as he slowly slides in with a muted grunt. I inhale sharply and clamp my eyes shut.

Holy shit, he's big. Really fucking big.

He stills, not all the way in, and I let out my air.

"Jesus. So damn tight." He groans and drops his forehead to mine. "Are you okay?" His concerned words blow across my face. "Do you want me to pull out?"

I open my eyes and meet his. I have to keep going. I know the pleasure will come after the pain. "No, don't pull out. I want you to fuck me."

His hand strokes my cheek in the most intimate way. "Baby, I can't fuck you until you're ready for me. It'll hurt if I try to do it right now." He reaches down and grabs my hand, moving it around him. "Grab me and pull me into you. That way you're controlling it."

I nod once, grabbing on to him with both hands and guiding him into me. The pain hits me again and I tense. Every muscle in my body contracts against his. I can't stop. I need to do this. I clamp my eyes shut as I pull him in.

Deeper. Deeper. Fucking hell. My nails dig into his skin and I sharply suck in my breath again.

"Oh, God," I pant.

The pain begins to shift, slowly disappearing into nothing. I lock onto his eyes and bite my lip, seeing his apprehensive expression.

He's just as tense as I am.

He doesn't want to hurt me.

I chose the right guy.

I relax my body completely and become familiar with the sensation. "I'm okay," I reassure him, seeing the tightness in his jaw disappear and his eyes light up.

He slowly pushes in all the way, gauging my reaction closely. Studying my face. His lips are parted slightly and his eyes are so bright, they seem to light up the darkness of his bedroom. A deep, guttural noise escapes his throat as I open up to him, spreading my legs as wide as they'll go.

"I'm all the way in you, baby, and it feels so damn good." He brushes his lips against mine. "Fucking perfect," he whispers.

"I'm ready for you to move," I say, assurance in my tone. I'm more than ready. I tilt my pelvis up and wrap my legs around his waist.

He slowly slides back out, keeping his eyes on mine and watching me closely. The pain is gone and the only thing I feel is pure ecstasy. Elation. Fucking euphoria. I moan and lift my hips, urging him farther.

Oh, yes. That feels good. Amazingly good.

"Holy fuck," he grunts, sliding back in slowly. He bends down and kisses the corner of my mouth. "Does it still hurt?"

I smile against his lips and shake my head.

"Good. I'm gonna really move now, pretty girl. I don't know how long I'll last though. You're squeezing me so God damned tight, angel." And then he picks up rhythm, his hips crashing against mine.

My breasts bob against his muscular chest and I kiss him deeply, exploring every inch of his mouth with my tongue. The room fills with our moans that are in no way muffled. I'm certain people in the next state over can hear us.

Thrust. Thrust. Thrust.

"Oh, my God," I say as he licks and sucks my breast. And I know I'm close. I'm familiar now with what he can do to me and there's no stopping it. The buildup is coming from deep within me, and it's coming quick. Like a wildfire spreading.

"You're right there, baby. Are you ready?"

How fucking hot is it that he knows when I'm about to come? I don't even need to tell him.

"Yes. God, yes," I answer.

He slides his hand between us and rubs against my clit. Thrusting harder and harder, deeper than I thought possible, and my orgasm rolls through me like a current.

"Oh!" I'm coming, clutching his body, and this is even more intense than the first two.

First two. How lucky am I right now?

My entire body trembles against his as I dig my nails into his back and rake them along his skin.

"Do that again," he demands urgently.

I repeat the action and he groans loudly, ramming into me and finding his release.

"Baby. Fuck!"

He twitches inside me and stills, relaxing his body against mine as we both slowly come down.

But I don't want to come down. I like this high. No, I love this high. This high is incredible. Now I understand what appeals to sex addicts. I'm elated and completely spent. I could actually die now and be okay with it. And I would like my tombstone to read the following:

Mia Blaire Corelli

Beloved daughter and friend.

Death by Orgasm. With a capital "O".

I HAD NO intention of falling asleep.

I had planned on surprising Tessa after my amazing night with my stranger, explaining that I was too excited to wait until the next day to leave. But after five orgasms, *five*, a girl can only take so much before she passes out.

After taking a small break to catch our breaths, he took me from behind, bending me over the bed, and then he asked me to ride him. I was embarrassed about that at first.

Me? Take charge?

Then I took him in and realized how deep he was that way. So incredibly deep. I think that's my favorite position now. Plus, it gave him unlimited access to my breasts, which he seemed to enjoy immensely. I believe his words were, "best tits I've ever seen." I'm still glowing from that compliment.

And then, to top off the best experience of my life, he held me. Like it meant just as much to him as it meant to me. Which is where we are now.

His arm is draped across my waist and he's breathing slow, steady breaths in my hair as I glance at the alarm clock on his nightstand. 10:14 a.m.

I can't believe I slept over. At a stranger's house. A complete stranger. Well, not complete. He's the only man that knows my body the way no one else does. And sweet Jesus, does he know it.

Plus, it felt natural to cuddle up next to him and fall asleep on his chest. It was almost intimate, our experience. It was hot as hell but also sweet. He was gentle with each new position, constantly asking if I was okay before he took me to that depth of passion and fucking owning me. And I felt his affection deep within me, but pretended I didn't. This wasn't supposed to mean anything other than a hot fling.

His warm body was pressed up against mine the entire night, our legs a tangled mess under the covers. The intoxicating aroma of his scent filled my lungs, and it was slowly becoming the only air I wanted to breathe. Nothing had ever smelled that divine. Complete manly deliciousness. I wished I could keep him.

I slip out from underneath his arm and scramble around the bed, picking up my dress and panties. After dressing and using the bathroom, I step into my heels and grab my clutch.

"Hey." His sexy morning voice grabs my attention as I'm about to sneak out of his room. "Come here, pretty girl." He props one hand behind his head, holding his other out to me. He looks positively adorable in that just-woken-up way—his hair sticking out a bit and his eyes still sleepy.

I walk over to the bed and take his hand, bringing it up to my lips for a kiss.

He smiles, weakening my knees with his dimples. "That's my move, isn't it?"

"I gotta go." I go to release his hand but he tightens his grip. "You're trouble, you know that? I have places to be."

His cell phone rings from the nightstand, forcing him to release my hand with a disapproving grunt. "Stay with me a little while longer. What's the rush?" The phone continues to ring in his hand as he waits for my response.

"I can't." I lean down and brush my lips against his, the ringtone finally fading out. And then I start toward the door, which is an extremely difficult task. Every ounce of my being wants to stay with this man, if only just to talk to him.

"Wait, damn it. At least tell me your name."

His phone starts ringing again, having been ignored the first time.

I silently contemplate his request, but decide against names. The old Mia would want a name. Not this new Mia that picked up a stranger in a bar and gave him her virginity. I'm a new woman and I'm doing things differently this summer.

I smile. "Thank you for last night. I'll never forget you."

I allow myself one last look before I slip out of his bedroom. His eyes are sad, pleading even, and I can't keep looking or I'm going to crack. I turn and leave before I weaken even more.

And I know I'll never forget him. He was amazing, and exactly what I wanted my first time to be like. A beautiful memory. That's exactly what he'll be.

ben

"JESUS CHRIST. WHAT?"

My voice gives away my mood, and I'm hoping this phone call is brief. I need to get some sleep. I barely got any last night, but that was well worth it. Really fucking worth it.

"Well good morning to you too," my sister snaps. She's my only sister, but she's all over the place sometimes with her personality, that it feels like there's twenty of her. "What are you doing right now? You busy?" Her voice softens, the snippiness gone and quickly replaced with the tone she uses when she wants something.

"I could've been if you wouldn't have interrupted me." I grab the pillow my nameless angel used last night, bringing it up to my face.

Christ, she smells good. Like berries and cream.

"What do you want, Tessa?"

"Can you come over here and clean the pool? Every time I try to use that stupid vacuum thing, it always jams up on me." I hear her breathy pause, knowing that the begging is about to start. "Please, Ben. It's hot as hell outside and when Mia gets here, I want to be able to spend the rest of the day in the pool with her. Please, please, please."

Mia fucking Corelli. The most annoying girl that's ever lived.

I completely forgot she was spending the summer with Tessa. Last time I saw her, she was an irritating fourteen-year-old. She and Tessa followed me around like damn puppies, always wanting to do what I was doing. And the fact that she practically lived at my house didn't help much. She was always around.

I toss the pillow I've been inhaling to the end of the bed. "Why the hell don't you just stay inside with her? I'm not in the mood to spend an hour cleaning out a damn pool."

"Oh, come on, Ben. You owe me and you know it. Besides, I'd rather have you and Mia get your awkward greeting out of the way so she can relax a little."

"What does that mean?" I get up and start getting dressed, holding the phone between my ear and my shoulder.

I don't know what awkward greeting she's referring to. It won't be awkward. It'll be brief. Really brief. I have no desire to spend any time with that train wreck.

"You know exactly what that means. She's nervous as shit about coming back here because of you." The sound of the sliding glass door opening and closing comes through the phone. "Christ, it's already a thousand degrees out here." Tessa sighs and it's dramatic, even though it doesn't have to be. I know what she's getting at. "If only I had a big brother who did nice things for me. Nice things that are well deserved after all the last minute favors I've done for him over the years."

"All right. Jesus." I zip up my shorts and grab a clean T-shirt from my dresser. "I'll be over there in an hour."

Her shriek causes me to move the phone away to a safer distance. I return it to my ear after her excitement dies down.

"You're the best brother ever. But can you be over sooner? She's on her way over here now."

"An hour. I've got my own shit to do today too, you know."

A particular girl to track down, and hopefully get her name.

I don't miss the slight grunt Tessa gives me before responding, "Fine. Thanks, Ben."

Hanging up the phone, I tuck it into my pocket and grab her pillow one more time.

Wait. *Her pillow?* Christ, get a hold of yourself.

I've had my fair share of one-night stands and never, never, let the girls spend the night. But this one was different. I was prepared to tie her to my bed if she tried to leave last night.

I inhale and let her scent run through me, feeling it hit me deep in my gut.

I've never taken a girl's virginity before. That was intense. I really didn't think she was one, not with a body like that and the way she was flirting with me at the bar. Sucking and biting my thumb like a fucking temptress. But her reaction to the sex we had and the blood stain on my sheets definitely confirms that she was, in fact, a virgin.

Tossing the pillow to the floor, I wrap up my sheets and walk them into the laundry room.

I like the stain. No, I fucking love the stain. It was proof that she gave me something that nobody else will ever have—a part of her I can hold on to since she didn't give me anything else. Not even a fucking name.

I walk back into my room to slip on my shoes.

Why wouldn't she tell me her name? What's the big deal? I get the whole casual hook up thing. No strings. No expectations. But I always know the name of the chick I'm banging, or at least the name they give me. It could be made up for all I know, considering that I've never pursued anything else with them after we've had one night together. But this chick, hell, I'd like multiple nights with her. Weeks even. She wasn't just an amazing lay, the best I've ever had, with a pussy I could eat for hours and tits that'll occupy all my fantasies until the day I die. She was more than that.

She was sweet and funny, with this laugh that I wanted to hear more of. Her whole face lit up when she laughed. I wanted to make her smile again, to see those full lips part and spread across her face. And the way she looked at me with those big brown eyes, so dark I could get lost in them. Plus, she fucking knew what I wanted last night without me having to ask. I need control and she gave it to me, but she also pushed back when I pushed her.

When I bit her body, she cried out for more. When I fucked her until I thought my spine was going to snap in half, she demanded harder.

She met me in the middle and gave as well as she took. It was wild perfection. A beautiful chaos. She was my match in the bedroom and I let her slip away without giving me a name.

The fuck? I should've spanked her and demanded she give it to me.

I inhale the pillow that's been pressed to my face for a good several minutes. Next to her pussy, it's the best thing I've ever smelled. It dulls my senses like a drug. I'm high on her and I'm pissed that it won't last.

I grab my keys and toss the pillow onto the bed.

I'm never washing that pillow case. Never.

The back roads leading away from my house are empty, which disappoints me. I was hoping her car would've broken down or, by some miracle, she would've gotten a flat tire and not known how to change it. Most girls don't, my sister included. But knowing my luck, she can probably change a tire faster than me and went on her way back to Georgia or wherever she was headed. Just passing through were her words.

To where? She's obviously from Georgia, and I have to hope she'll be making her way back through Ruxton when she's ready to return there, or if she's already headed that way that she'll want to pass through here again. And if there is a God, I'd see her again. And I will get that fucking name if it kills me.

I pull up around back at my parents' house and park my truck in the hardened mud.

Nobody parks back here besides me, but that's only because my truck is the only vehicle that won't get stuck. Tessa's car has had to be towed out of the muddy terrain back here several times when she's tried to prove that her Rav 4 rallies my truck in off-roading capabilities. She's smartened up and wisely parks on the driveway now.

Walking through the grass, I spot two pairs of legs bent on lawn chairs next to the pool, both forming an upside down V.

My sister's are a dead giveaway, considering she tans out here daily. The other pair contrasts against hers like the dark hair against my sheets last night.

Fuck. Not the time to get a hard on. Don't think about her.

I stroll around the pool and over toward the two girls, stopping next to Tessa. Both girls have their faces covered with beach towels, but that's not what I'm looking at. My eyes are glued to what can't possibly be Mia Corelli's body.

No fucking way. So much for not getting hard.

"Ben! Jesus Christ, you scared the shit outta me." Tessa sits up and drops her towel onto her lap, and I notice Mia's body tense up in her chair. She holds her hands in fists on the towel she's lying on like she's ready to knock my ass out at any second. "I thought you said an hour? I just got off the phone with you twenty minutes ago."

"Yeah, well unfortunately, my plans escaped me." I turn my attention to the tight little body wrapped so perfectly in that yellow bikini. "Mia, it's nice to see you again."

"Humph," she replies.

I chuckle. *Damn. Okay, if that's how she wants to play this.* "You look a lot different since the last time I saw you. Still wear those nerdy glasses?" Tessa's foot connects with my thigh and I grunt. "Ow. What?"

"You're an asshole," Tessa snaps. "Mia, ignore him. He's just mad that he hasn't gotten laid in three months."

I move in front of the chairs, giving myself a better view of Mia but making sure to keep my eyes on my sister's at the moment.

"Fuck you. I just got laid last night for your information. And she was incredible."

"Humph," Mia mumbles again.

I step to the side of her chair, putting her gorgeous body right under my nose.

Her tits are insane, full and barely wrapped up in the tiny piece of fabric. I want to shake the man's hand that created this bikini. It was meant for this body.

"Is my sex life amusing to you, Mia? Because if you'd really like to see what I can do, I'll take you right here on this lawn chair. I'll make you scream until your voice breaks."

"No thanks. I, like you, got laid last night and am good for several months. Years even. My pussy is still humming after getting worked with that mouth of his."

Her response is muffled by the towel but I definitely hear the word pussy. And my cock hears it too.

"Dayyyyum," Tessa chuckles.

I place my hand on her knee, gripping it softly. She tenses. "I bet I can work it better than him." My hand slides down her thigh, painfully slow, barely moving at all. Her skin is smooth and warm. She stops me with hers when I reach mid-thigh.

"I'll make you ride my face until you're begging for my cock."

"Jesus Chr . . ." She sits up mid-sentence, the towel dropping somewhere that I can't seem to focus on. Because I can only focus on the face that can't possibly be Mia Corelli. "You? Ben? Ben! Oh, God. Oh, my God."

"Holy shit." I'm shocked. Completely shocked. It's her. Mia Corelli is *her*. What the fuck are the odds? "Mia, I . . ." She quickly gets to her feet, her hips swaying as she storms toward the house. "Mia, wait up!" I yell, starting after her until Tessa puts her tiny frame in front of me and blocks me.

"What the hell was that? Did you really just tell Mia that you'd make her ride your face? You're lucky she didn't deck you."

My sister is small, so I can look over the top of her with no problem, and doing so, I see Mia slide the door shut behind her. "It's complicated. Move so I can go after her." Not that I couldn't move her myself, but if that happened, she'd just climb onto my back like she liked to do when I shoved her out of the way, and I needed Mia alone.

Her hands curl up into fists at her hips. "How is it complicated? You made her uncomfortable, like you always do, because you're an asshole."

I'm getting impatient. I grip Tessa's shoulders and firmly plant her in her lawn chair. "Give me a few minutes with her. I'm not going to hurt her, I promise. I just want to talk to her." My voice is sincere and Tessa knows it.

Her shoulders relax and she scoots back on her chair, resuming her favorite tanning position. "Five minutes. And if she's crying when I come in there, I'm keying your precious baby."

Nice threat. Keying my truck would be a way to cut me deep, but there'll be no need for that. Mia won't be crying. I'd never make her cry; if I could fucking find her.

I'm roaming the house, listening for any clues of where she might be, but dead silence fills the space. "Mia? Baby, please let me talk to you."

I hear a door open, and she emerges from the hallway, her eyes reddened and streaked with tears. "Don't call me that. How dare you say those things to me out there?" Our legs bring us together but she pushes against my chest, not liking the closeness our bodies seem to crave. "I can't believe this! I can't believe it was you last night. This can't be happening." Tears run down her face, and I wipe them away before she can reach up and stop me.

"I can't believe it either. But fuck, Mia, if this isn't the luckiest day of my life." I bring my hands up to her face and hold her there, feeling her shudder against me. "I haven't been able to stop thinking about you all morning. Last night was—"

"A mistake," she interrupts curtly. Her hands pry mine from her face and she turns her body, staring out the window. "A huge mistake. If I'd have known it was you, it wouldn't have happened. I'm sure you know that by now."

"It wasn't a mistake." I move closer to her, bending to put my nose into her hair. *Fuck.* Nothing smelled this good. I'll never get enough of it. "Something like that could never be a mistake. What you gave me. What we shared . . . Mia, I've never . . ." I pause, needing to choose my words carefully. "I felt it last night. Tell me you felt it too." My hands run down her arms, and the fact that she is still in her tiny bikini is making my dick harder than it's ever been. "Baby, please."

Please back up into me.

Please move my hands to your breasts.

Please turn around and beg me to fuck you right here.

I've never felt so completely geared up and so ready to

unravel at the same time. But that's definitely how I am feeling right now. Like I could snap at the slightest crook of her finger.

She moves quickly out of my grasp toward the hallway she just emerged from. "I didn't feel anything. And it was a mistake, Ben. A huge mistake." Her eyes reach mine with regret once more, and I swear that there are tears in them again. "You can't stop ruining my life, can you?"

I watch her disappear, unable to reply.

Ruining her life? Fuck me.

A door slams down the hall just as the sliding glass door opens. Tessa looks at me with raised eyebrows and I motion toward the direction Mia fled to.

"I have a feeling that I'm going to want to punch you, so you might want to leave before your face *and* your truck get mangled."

Instead of responding, I walk past her and make my way back out to my truck.

My mind is scrambled and my heart feels like Mia has taken her keys to it. The girl of my dreams turned out to be Mia fucking Corelli. What the fuck? She's not just passing through. She's here.

My angel is here for the whole summer, and she wants nothing to do with me.

mia

"WELL, I DID not see this coming. Not in a million years."

Tessa slumps down on the bed I've been curled up on after I shared my naughty little secret with her.

She paced during that run down, her jaw hitting the floor the moment I said I lost my virginity to her brother.

"This. Is. Crazy. I mean, first of all, I had no idea you were still a virgin. Fuck you very much for not telling me. Although, I'm not sure I would've believed you, considering what you look like."

I smile weakly at her compliment. "Yeah, well, I wish I still was. I can't believe I was stupid enough to not ask his name last night. This shit could've been easily avoided."

Because there's no way I would've went through with it if I'd have known that mouth belonged to Ben fucking Kelly.

The boy that made me cry daily for five years.

The boy that made me feel insignificant.

The boy I hated.

"I don't really see what the big deal is here. In fact, I think it's pretty fucking awesome." She moves up the bed and places her head on the pillow next to mine. "How was it anyway? Did you come?"

I roll my eyes at her bluntness. "You're disgusting."

"I'm nosy, and I can pretend it wasn't my brother." She

twirls her hair around her finger, smiling at me. "Spill it, Mia. I've shared all my sexcapades with you over the years."

"Without me asking. I'd love to be able to forget some of those horrific details."

"Oh, please. Like you haven't enjoyed living vicariously through my pussy. My very STD free pussy, by the way. You make it sound like I'm a hooker."

I cover my face with my hands, hearing Tessa laugh softly next to me.

If I am going to share how her brother got me off, I don't want her to see how much I enjoyed it. Because I didn't. I'd never enjoy anything involving him. And the tightness in my core that is forming at the very memory of last night has nothing to do with that jerk.

I grunt heavily before confessing, "It was beautiful. He was sweet and playful, but he also knew exactly what he was doing. I definitely came. A lot."

"How much is a lot?" I hold up my hand, hearing her soft gasp. "Holy shit balls. Ben can get it."

Dropping my hands, I roll over and face her. "But I don't want Ben to get it. I don't want him to be the guy that took my virginity. I hate him, Tessa. You know how much I hate him."

It wasn't a secret. I never hid my feelings for him years ago, and I wasn't trying to start now. As long as those feelings stayed familiar. I was used to hating Ben. Those feelings I could deal with. Not, whatever the hell it was that I felt last night. Or didn't feel. 'Cause I didn't feel anything.

"Mia, are you that same girl that used to live here? The girl that wouldn't dare say a cuss word or wear a bikini like the one you're currently rocking the hell out of?" She smiles and playfully wiggles her brows.

"No. I guess not," I reply flatly. I know exactly where she's going with this, and I don't really want to hear it.

"Well, Ben's not that same jerk-face loser that would pick on you every chance he got. He's actually pretty tolerable now." I try to roll away from her but she grabs my arm, keeping my gaze. "He's not that guy, Mia. He hasn't been for a while. And I think you know that deep down." She pauses, her lips turning up into a sassy smile. "There's no way that same guy would've made you feel the way you felt last night."

"Icky? Nauseating? Because that's how I felt."

"Yeah, okay. Tell that to your five orgasms."

She sounds as unconvinced as I feel.

Whatever. Even if he did own my body, I wasn't going to admit it to Tessa. Or myself, for that matter.

"This is so not the way I was hoping to start off my summer."

"I can't imagine starting it off any better. Hot sex that resulted in five glorious orgasms? I'll take, things I'd give my right arm for, for two hundred, Alex." She bumps her shoulder against me and slides off the bed. "I know two men that would help greatly in a situation like this."

"I'm not interested in your vibrators. We're close, but we aren't that close."

I hear her chuckle as she disappears down the hallway.

This is un-freaking-believable. The man I couldn't get out of my head since I laid eyes on him last night, turns out to be the asshole I longed to forget. It was Ben who made me feel hot and wanted for the first time in my life. It was Ben who ignited my skin and made my insides burn, and not in the STD kind of way. It was Ben who I screamed for last night and who I never wanted to leave this morning. Benjamin fucking Kelly. He made fun of my body for years, but last night, he worshipped it. Telling me how good I tasted. How amazing I felt. How he wanted to stay deep in my pussy until the day he died. And I was torn between wanting to take back everything that we'd experienced together not even twenty-four hours ago, and asking him to touch me again. Every time I closed my eyes, I felt his hands on me. His breath on my skin. His tongue on my clit. His cock in my pussy. He claimed me last night, and I hated that I loved it.

Tessa appears in the doorway, two pints of Ben and Jerry's ice cream in her hands. "I say we rent something nonromantic and devour the contents of these containers. You're in desperate need of a girls' night and I'm coming at you hard."

"Is that Half Baked?" *Damn. I haven't had that in years.* She nods and smiles wide. "You're awesome. I'm so in for girls' night."

"That's what I was hoping you'd say. Get changed and plant your perky ass in front of the TV."

She leaves me to do just that, and I don't waste any time. I throw on a sundress and meet her in the living room, diving into my ice cream as she scrolls the movie selections.

"Wolf of Wall Street or Captain Phillips?" she asks as she flips through the On Demand section.

"Wolf of Wall Street. I don't feel like crying, and seeing Tom Hanks held captive by pirates will probably wreck me. You know I love that man." I've been hooked on Tom Hanks' films since I watched Philadelphia. And don't get me started on The Green Mile. I cried like a baby when Tessa and I watched that together. The electrocution scene? I can't even.

She starts up the movie and we sit back, both digging into the meals that will surely ruin any appetite for dinner. We are halfway through the movie and our pints when Tessa's phone rings.

"You're interrupting girls' night, I'll have you know. And

the penalty for your crime is death by dick removal."

I giggle around my spoon, my eyes widening as Leonardo DiCaprio snorts coke off some chick's ass.

"Hmm, you're so hilarious. And that's none of your business. I think you've done enough damage to warrant a lifetime of therapy." I meet her eyes briefly before she turns her head. "Just leave her alone. If she wants to talk to you, she'll talk to you."

I don't need two guesses to know who she is talking to. And a part of me that I don't want to acknowledge, wishes she had been on a land line so I could pick up and listen in.

"I have no idea, but whatever it is, it won't be involving you. Now leave us alone so we can watch all this coke get snorted in a way that is definitely heating up everything south of my waist." She tosses her phone onto the coffee table. "Sorry about that. Apparently, you're hard to forget." She smiles coyly at me, and I brace myself for what she's about to say. "But that wouldn't affect you, because it's my brother we're talking about. Right?"

"Right," I affirm without hesitation. I'm not falling into that trap. I keep my attention on Leonardo and far away from thoughts of Benjamin Kelly.

"I mean, it's not like he was sweet and playful with you or anything."

"Nope. Not at all."

"And it's not like he gave you this beautiful experience to treasure for the rest of your life. That so wasn't Ben."

"It so wasn't."

"And he's *definitely* not the guy that, as you so sweetly put it, worked your pussy until you hummed between your legs for hours afterward." I hear her smile through her words, but I don't turn away from the TV. I don't want to crack.

"Definitely not him." I'm struggling, really struggling not to break. I feel keyed up all of a sudden, like my body is fully charged and ready to go. I'm beginning to fidget and it doesn't go unnoticed.

"Quick question. What did Ben call you when he fucked you, since he didn't know your name?"

"Baby. Angel. Pretty girl," I blurt out in the most crushing-on-a-boy sort of way. Even my voice raises an octave. *Fuck.* I turn toward her then. She won and she knows it, and the smile on her face only adds to my irritation. "I hate you."

"You put up an impressive fight, I'll give you that." She chucks a pillow at me, hitting me square in the face. "Just admit that you kind of like the idea of my brother knowing all the intimate details of your body."

"Never." I tuck the pillow she hit me with behind my head, taking a giant spoonful of ice cream into my mouth. I need a gag at the rate she's going with this conversation. I know the more we talk about this, the greater chance of me slipping up and saying something I don't want to reveal.

"This might seem borderline inappropriate . . ."

"Oh, God. Please spare me." I'm shoveling ice cream into my mouth at an impressive rate now.

Borderline inappropriate for Tessa means cover your ears and please escort all children out of the state.

She turns her body, tucking her legs underneath her ass. "Is he like, really big? Because I've heard rumors." She holds her hands out in front of her, measuring a distance between the two. "Nine inch rumors."

"Jesus Christ."

I shouldn't be surprised. I really shouldn't. This is Tessa Kelly we're talking about. She is comfortable enough talking about sex with anybody. Confessional priests included. I'm sure the number of Hail Marys she's been told to recite is in the hundreds.

I drop my spoon into my empty container and sigh heavily. "Why would you want to know that about your brother? That's incredibly weird."

"So I can high five you. Losing your virginity to someone as massive as he may or may not be is worthy of a damn award." She places her hand lovingly on my knee, but there is nothing tender about this chat. Her tactics are a ploy, a cover to make this conversation seem innocent. "And since your mouth was wrapped around his nine-incher, I'm figuring you'd be able to vouch better than anyone."

I push her dirty hand away. "For your information, my mouth was not wrapped around him. All of his nine inches stayed in between my legs the entire night."

"Ah-ha! So I *can* believe everything I've heard." She holds her hand up to me, and after several long seconds of debating her gesture, I oblige her with a high-five. "Fucking right. I'm jealous. Eight's my biggest number."

"How unfortunate." I grab the remote and turn up the volume. "Can we please watch the rest of the movie? I'm done discussing your brother's anatomy with you."

His damn fine anatomy.

"All right, all right. But answer me one last question before we finish this." I look over hesitantly. Lord knows what she could hit me up with next. She smiles. "How are you, anally speaking? Still virginal?"

"Very."

"Well, that's probably wise considering what he's working with."

The pillow that she used to hit me with is now striking her against the face. "You really should come with a warning label. *Please keep away from small children, the elderly, and anyone with a pacemaker."*

She chuckles, pulling her long, auburn hair back into a pony. "As should you. *Please keep all dicks less than nine inches away from this pussy, because the bar has been set."*

I feel my face heat up instantly.

Is it weird to agree with her on that assessment? I mean, surely there aren't many dicks out there that could compare to what Ben was so beautifully graced with. I've seen my fair share of pornos, and even those dicks couldn't hold a candle to his.

I slam my head back onto the sofa and stare at the TV.

Damn it, Ben. Not only have you ruined my life, but you've also ruined all average dick sizes for me. Now I'm going to compare each and every appendage to yours.

Thanks a lot, asshole.

I SHOULD BE sleeping.

But since I'm not sleeping, I should be reading a book, or watching TV, or doing anything besides what I am currently doing.

This is insane. I've never been pissed off and horny at the same time before, but that's exactly what I'm feeling right now. It's an angry lust and I hate it. I want to punch Ben in the throat and I want to fuck him all over the house. And I know for a fact, and I'm ashamed to admit, that I would thoroughly enjoy doing both.

It's 3:15 a.m., and while the rest of the Alabama population sleeps, my mind and fingers are very busy as I get myself off for the second time tonight with thoughts of Ben.

It doesn't take me long because he was that good and he

gave me a variety of memories to work with.

Earlier, I thought of him gripping my hips and slamming into me roughly from behind. He grabbed my hair and smacked my ass, and I came when I pictured his tongue licking up my spine and his teeth biting my back. But right now, he's devouring my pussy with that expert mouth of his. That smart ass mouth that I'd like to smack and then fuck. The one that he suggested I ride when we were out by the pool earlier. My legs are pinned against his head and I'm melting as if he were the sun and I was a popsicle. I come all over my hand, and I can't push aside the feeling of irritation that pours over me as I let Ben Kelly rule my body for the second time in one hour.

And I know without a doubt that he'll be irritating me again tomorrow night.

THE SMELL OF bacon hits me like a Mack truck, pulling me out of the Ben dream that I was annoyingly enjoying.

I'd usually be able to roll over and go back to sleep, but it's bacon, and I could eat my weight in that stuff, so the dreams can wait. I am surprised, though, that Tessa is up and making breakfast. She likes her sleep even more than I do and was usually the last one awake when I used to spend the night with her. Maybe she's just being a really good hostess. Either way, I'm all for getting woken up daily by this delicious smell.

I make my way down the hallway, pulling my wild, bed head hair back out of my face.

"Oh, my Godddd, that smells amazing. I'm so hungry right now."

I stop dead in my tracks as the kitchen comes into view.

Tessa is not the one cooking breakfast, and I suddenly want to hurl myself back into bed and go for round three with my favorite fingers. I bite back the shiver I feel run through me at the thought of doing just that.

Ben turns his head and hits me with a smile. "Good morning. What kind of eggs do you want?"

"What are you doing here?" I ask, crossing my arms over my chest and scowling in his direction.

Damn it. Now I suddenly don't just have a hankering for bacon. He's way too inviting this early in the morning.

Slight stubble. Check.

Hair sticking up a bit. Check.

Vagina awake and ready. Double check.

He's looking very fuckable right now and it irritates me to no end.

He laughs softly and grabs a plate out of the cabinet. "This is my parents' house. I eat breakfast here all the time." He holds the plate of bacon out. "Want some?"

"No."

He stares at me unconvinced. "Did I not just hear you say you're starving? And I know you want this bacon. We used to fight over the last piece all the time when you'd spend the night here." He places the plate on the island, which is already set for two people, and begins whipping up some eggs in a bowl. "Scrambled okay?"

"You don't know anything about me. Just because I used to like bacon, doesn't mean I want it now." I cross the room with an annoying scowl plastered on my face and open the fridge, pulling out the orange juice. "And I don't want any eggs."

"I know a lot about you," he says, his voice dropping to a low rumbled tone. I can't shake the way it ripples through my body, causing all my muscles to contract and my body temperature to spike. "Now sit down and let me feed you."

I take a sip of my orange juice and walk over to the couch.

"I told you. I don't want any breakfast." I begin flipping through the TV channels, trying to calm the hunger that is growing more and more persistent. I want that bacon.

And the man making it.

Shut up, vagina.

"Suit yourself," he says. The stool scrapes along the floor before the sound of crunching fills my ears.

And it's crispy bacon. Son of a bitch.

"Mmm. This is really good. Why don't you stop being stubborn and get your sweet ass over here and join me?"

I snap my head around and glare at him. "And why don't you stop being a creeper and eat breakfast at your own house. You can't honestly tell me that you're here just to raid your mom's refrigerator."

His lips curl up into a half smile. That cockiness pouring out of him that I want to not find attractive. "No, I can't. And you can't honestly tell me that you aren't at least a little happy to see me. Especially since I cooked your favorite food." He takes another bite of his bacon strip, smiling arrogantly. "Remember how mad you used to get when I'd steal pieces off your plate?"

I throw the remote down and stalk over toward the island, seeing him lean back in his chair at my irritated expression.

He wants to talk memories? Let's talk memories.

"No, I don't remember that. What I do remember is you calling me a cannibal, since I liked to eat my own kind."

His confidence quickly vanishes from his face, and he seems regretful now. Although, I'm not sure if he is regretting walking down memory lane or coming over here in the first place.

"It was kind of hard to enjoy my favorite food when assholes like you didn't let me forget how heavy I was. I went a couple days without eating one time because of shit you said to me. Did you know that?"

He drops his gaze from my face to the floor. "No, I didn't know that." He looks up again, begging me with his eyes. For forgiveness? For a pass on everything he's ever said to me? Fat chance. "I had no idea I got to you like that. I was a kid, Mia. I didn't really care about hurting your feelings back then. But Christ, it's been nine years. I'm not that guy anymore." He reaches out to stroke my arm but I back away before he can touch me.

I don't want his hands on me. I know exactly how much I'll like it.

His eyes shift and that mischievous glare of his that I am becoming familiar with, hits me. "You seemed to enjoy the guy I am now the other night. If I remember correctly, you enjoyed me five times."

"Wow. You just totally proved my point." I grab a handful of bacon and meet his confused gaze.

"What point is that?"

I glower at him before turning on my heel and walking back toward my bedroom. "That you're still an asshole," I yell over my shoulder.

Upon hearing the sound of the stool scraping again, I slam my door and lock it, backing away as the footsteps in the hallway grow louder.

They stop right outside my room and the doorknob rattles.

"Mia, come on. Just sit and eat some breakfast with me."

I sit on the edge of my bed and begin crunching on a piece of bacon. "Can you not take a hint? I'm not interested in eating or doing anything with you." I take another bite and hear some movement on the other side of the door.

He needs to leave. I really don't want to spend the entire day cooped up in my bedroom. And there is no chance in hell that I am slipping into my bikini in front of him again. Not after the lustful way he looked at me in it yesterday. I can't handle him looking at me like that again. Like he wants to eat me alive. Like he knows exactly what is underneath my bikini and exactly what to do with it.

"I'm persistent."

I look up at the door, imagining him standing on the other side. "What?"

The sound of a throat clearing comes before he speaks. "I'm a persistent guy. If you ask me to leave, I'll leave, but that's not going to stop me from trying to be around you."

Neither of us speaks for what feels like hours.

I don't want to like the idea of being pursued by Ben. My brain wants to hit him with some sort of stalker charge while my vagina wants to put him on lockdown for the summer.

"So, do you want me to leave?" he asks, and I can hear the anxiety in his voice. As if he already knows the answer to his question but is praying, by some miracle, he's way off.

"Yes," I quickly reply, without any indecision. I know if I allow myself time to think it over, my desire for a Ben-style orgasm will overpower any and all rational thought.

He doesn't say anything else before the sound of his footsteps fade into the distance.

After I hear the sliding glass door close, I fall back onto my bed.

Tessa had assured me that I wouldn't have to see much of her brother when I planned this trip, but that guarantee seems to be a distant memory now. I could be waking up every morning to the smell of Ben cooking breakfast if he decided to show me just how persistent he could be. I'm afraid to admit that a part of me doesn't hate the possibility of that type of wake up call.

And it has nothing to do with the bacon.

ben

'VE NEVER JERKED off this much in my life.

If my dick doesn't fall off soon due to the rough treatment it's been getting, I'll be shocked. I can't get her out of my head. Her lips. Her ass. Her fucking breasts. Every time I think I'm making progress, an image pops into my head or the memory of her noises fill my ears. Those fucking noises she made when I was inside her. When I licked her pussy. When I pulled her hair. I need to hear them again and I need to hear them soon. But she wants nothing to do with me. She hates me, and I can't say I blame her. I was a complete shit to her when we were younger. I made fun of her a lot. All the time, actually. But all guys are dickheads at that age. She has to know that. I'm not that same guy anymore, and she's definitely not that same girl.

And we fucking shared something, God damn it. She had to have felt it.

I had to see her yesterday, if only for a few minutes. I couldn't sleep anyway, so I figured I'd make us both some breakfast. Mia used to eat breakfast with us all the time, so I knew what she liked. I thought I could at least enjoy her company for an hour while she sat and ate next to me, but no. Apparently, I was a bigger asshole to her than I remembered. The thought of her starving herself over some dumbass comment I made, infuriated me. She is holding on to a deeper hatred toward me than I realized. But her pushing me away isn't going to stop me. I'm drawn to her, and not just because I want to be buried deep inside her at all times. It feels right being around her. Just fucking right. I want her. All of her. And I can be one relentless bastard when it comes to getting what I want. At least now, she is aware of that.

My phone beeps on my nightstand and I grab it with my free hand, taking the other off my dick. It's a good thing, actually. I'm about to rub myself raw if I don't get a fucking grip. Other than the one I've had for the last hour.

Luke: Everyone's going down to Rocky Point today. You in?

Luke is my best friend and has been since we met in the Academy. I'd usually be all for going to Rocky Point for the day with him. But I'm exhausted from another sleepless night of sexual activity, this time self-inflicted.

Me: Pass. I'm fucking exhausted.

Luke: Are you sure? I hear there's some hot piece of ass staying with your sister and they'll both be there. You know anything about that?

Fuck sleep.

Me: I'll meet you there. And don't call her that again.

Well, now my mind is made up. It really didn't take much persuasion on Luke's part. Or any at all. Where Mia goes, I'm going.

I hop out of bed and begin rummaging through my drawers for my swim trunks. I don't care that she most likely won't want me there. I am fucking going.

My phone beeps again as I'm walking out the door to

my truck.

> *Tessa: I must be delusional for giving you this information, or maybe I just have a soft spot for my big brother. We're headed to Rocky Point today, and I think you should be there. I don't think she'll hate you forever, Ben. But if you make her cry, I'll feed your dick to the gators.*

> *Me: I'm already on my way. Don't tell her I'm coming.*

> *Tessa: Do you think I have a death wish?*

She can't hate me forever. I'll spend the rest of my life proving myself to her if I have to. I've made a lot of mistakes. I've done things that I regret. But what Mia and I shared two nights ago, wasn't one of them.

I just need to somehow make her see that for herself.

I DON'T SEE Tessa or Mia's car when I park in the grass at Rocky Point. And I'm happy about that. I want to beat them here, that way Mia doesn't get to do anything without me. Even though I probably don't deserve it, I want all of her time. I am a greedy bastard when it comes to her and I'm not ashamed of it. I want everything.

Every smile, every orgasm, every fucking noise that comes out of that pretty mouth. And I'll need as much time as she'll give me if I'm going to make up for being such a shit to her when we were younger. She isn't going to easily let go of all the hate she has stored up for me. That hate runs deep.

Luke is seated at a picnic table with Reed, a friend of Tessa's. I walk over to them, throwing my stuff down on the bench and keeping my eyes out for a familiar vehicle.

"Why do you have two towels, man?" Luke asks as he searches through my stuff. "Oh wait, does this have anything to do with that hot piece of ass?"

I pick up my towels and move them out of his reach. "What the fuck did I say about calling her that? Her name's Mia, and that's what you'll call her. Nothing else. Got it?"

He holds his hand up, leaning away from me. "Sorry. Jesus."

I take a deep breath and let it out slowly.

I need to calm the hell down. I've never felt this anxious about seeing someone before. And for fuck's sake, I just saw her yesterday.

I scan the line of cars that head down the dirt path. No sign of them yet.

"This is the girl that used to live here, right?" Reed asks, moving off the bench to stand.

"Yeah," I reply, not prying my eyes from the vehicles. "She moved to Georgia a while back and is here for the summer."

I still can't believe it myself. This is the same girl that used to have sleepovers every weekend at my house with Tessa. I'd fucking kill for a sleepover with her now.

A red Jeep comes up over the small hill, and I suddenly find it difficult to take in a deep breath.

"I'll be right back," I choke out with a shaky voice. *Get it the fuck together, Kelly.*

"Fuck that. I'm coming with you," Luke states, getting to his feet.

We both walk toward the Jeep as it pulls in between two other cars. As soon as Mia locks on to me through the windshield, her jaw drops open and those chocolate brown eyes widen. I can see her hands tightening on the wheel as she leans over, saying something to Tessa with a tight jaw.

"She looks thrilled to see you." Luke laughs before walking over to Tessa's door.

I ignore him and the look Mia is giving me and open her door for her. "Hey. I'm really glad you came."

I feel calmer now, but my heart is still beating like I've just taken a shot of adrenaline. She is in a tank top, her bikini straps poking out, and tiny white shorts that barely cover the legs I want to be buried between. I pry my eyes off her lap to give her a smile.

"Someone failed to mention that you'd be here." She ignores the hand I hold out for her and steps out of her Jeep, pulling the seat back to get her bag.

I close the door and move to walk next to her. "I warned you of my persistence. This just proves that I'm a man of my word. If I find out you're going to be somewhere, there's a pretty damn good possibility that I'm going to show up."

She tries to ignore my comment, but I don't miss the way her cheeks flush at my vow. That has to mean something. Her mind, and its memories of the guy I used to be, might hate me, but her body doesn't seem to.

I take the duffle bag off her shoulder without a fight, slipping it on my arm. "I brought you a towel in case you needed one."

She stops in her tracks, causing me to double back. "I don't need you to do things for me, Ben. I don't need you bringing me towels and carrying my bags." She reaches for her bag but I step back.

Fuck that. I'm carrying her bag.

"Fine. Whatever. But just know that this nice act doesn't wipe out all the shitty things you've done to me." She steps closer, brushing her body against mine.

I freeze, completely unprepared for this type of contact

from her.

She tilts her head up and looks into my eyes while I use every ounce of strength in me to keep myself from getting hard. "That shit is still very raw. And no amount of bag carrying is going to make me forget it."

I watch her ass as she walks away, realizing now that I'm going to need to step up my game to knock down the walls she's building up around her. Which is fine. I'm all for a challenge. Especially one where getting close to Mia is the reward.

By the time I reach the rest of the group, Mia is talking to Reed while Luke and Tessa dive into the reservoir.

I place her bag on the bench, bunching up the beach towel I brought for her and stuffing it into her duffle. I walk up to the two of them, drifting in on their conversation and not giving a shit if I'm interrupting anything.

"You wanna get in the water with me, Mia?" I ask, pulling off my T-shirt and tossing it onto the bench.

I don't miss the way her eyes run down my body, and mine do the same to hers once she pulls off her top and slides down her shorts.

Christ, she is breathtaking. I can't get enough of her long, dark hair and the way it frames the delicate features of her face. That face—I can't get it out of my head. Deep brown eyes and full lips that'll form a knock-you-on-your-ass smile if you're lucky to see it. Then there's the curve of her breasts. Her tiny waist that leads to those hips that sway with each step she takes. Her perky ass and those never ending toned legs I want wrapped around me at all times. I've never seen anything so beautiful in my life.

She glances from Reed to me, not taking nearly as long to look at Reed as he shrugs off his shirt. "I want to get in the water," she replies curtly. She leaves off the "with you" part, but that's fine. I watch as she dives into the reservoir and I don't take long to jump in after her.

The water is warm as it always is, but too cloudy to see her swimming ahead of me. Luke and Tessa have climbed up onto one of the floating piers and are talking closely, but Mia doesn't seem to be headed for the pier. She's headed for the cliffs. I know for a fact that she was always too scared to jump off of them when she was younger. I did it a lot, and it scared the shit out of me every time.

It's high, really high, and I'm not about to let her do it alone.

I swim faster, pushing myself to get up next to her, and within a few strokes, I succeed. We both reach the rock ledge at the same time, and she looks at me once she wipes her eyes. I smile at her and I swear I see the slightest twitch in those perfect lips of hers, but I can't be sure. She struggles to pull herself up onto the rock, slipping every time and falling back into the water.

My girl needs my help and I'm going to give it to her.

I quickly climb up onto the rock, staring down at her and offering my hands. "Come on, pretty girl. Let me help you up."

"I don't need your help." She continues struggling, each attempt making her more exhausted. "There should be a freaking ladder here or something," she scoffs under her breath, and I have to resist the smile that's tugging at my mouth.

"Do you want to jump off the cliffs or not?" She looks up at me and shrugs once. "Give me your hands. I promise I won't bite." I smirk at her and she catches it, rolling her eyes. "Unless you want me to."

"Funny." She grabs my one hand and I motion for her to grab my other. She does, not before giving me an annoyed look, and I easily lift her out of the water and stand her up next to me. "Thank you." Her hands leave mine instantly and she looks up into my eyes. And fuck, I want to kiss her, right here. And I would if I didn't think she'd cut my nuts off if I tried.

"You're welcome." I place my hand on her lower back, moving her toward the rocks ahead. We have a ways to climb to get to the top and she will definitely be making that trek in front of me. "Go on. I'll be right behind you."

"Try not to stare at my ass too much."

Damn. Is she flirting with me?

I catch the smile she is trying to hide from me and I decide to give her one better. "Oh, I don't need to stare, baby. I memorized every inch of your body the other night."

She flicks her head back and spots my grin, her hands braced on the rocks above her. "Where's my birthmark?" she asks, challenging me. There's zero playfulness to her tone. She's testing my knowledge of her body, and by the look on her face right now, she thinks she's got me beat. But I fucking own that body and know it better than she does.

"On the inside of your right thigh. It sort of looks like a peanut."

She opens her mouth to speak, but closes it before turning back around. "Lucky guess."

I laugh and nudge her with a hand on her calf. She begins to move faster. "Luck has nothing to do with it. Fate, maybe. Putting us both in that bar the other night was more than some coincidence. But knowing that you like to watch me eat your pussy, or that you have to be digging your nails into something when you're coming, has absolutely nothing to do with luck." She glances over her shoulder at me with a staggered look. "I pay attention to every little thing about you."

She doesn't linger on my face, nor does she give me a response. But I think I may have impressed her. Maybe. Mia's difficult to read lately. She's definitely not sending me clear signals like she did the other night at the bar.

She turns her attention back to the rocks above her and makes her way up the side of the cliff.

I'm close behind her, keeping an eye on her footing in case she slips and I have to catch her.

We make it to the top and she moves to the edge, apprehensively glancing down. "Holy shit." Her wide eyes blink rapidly and she turns them on me. "This is really high. It didn't look that high from down there."

I stand beside her, brushing my hand against hers. "It is high. I do this all the time and I still get nervous up here." I run my finger down her arm, feeling her skin tingle against mine.

She seems completely unaffected by it and keeps her focus on the water.

How can she ignore that? How can she pretend her body doesn't respond to my touch?

"Want me to jump with you? It isn't so scary if you do it with someone." I try to grab her hand, but she pulls it away from me.

"Jump, you pussies!" Tessa yells, standing on the pier and waving at us. Reed and Luke are watching in amusement and Mia laughs next to me. And it is fucking beautiful. I'd give anything to hear that laugh every day for the rest of my life.

"I love that sound," I say, completely unashamed of my infatuation.

She looks at me with confusion. "What sound?"

"Your laugh. Your voice. Hell, all your sounds." Her lips part slightly, and a shaky hand comes up and tucks some hair behind her ear. "I can't get them out of my head."

She purses her lips, dropping her gaze to the water. "Stop it, Ben." Her voice is an intense plea, like she can't possibly handle another word coming out of my mouth.

Which is too fucking bad, because I have a lot to say right now.

"Stop what?" I bridge the gap between us and grab her hips with such blunt force my fingertips ache. I know she likes it like that, so I don't let her stunned look slow me down. She gasps softly as I turn her toward me. Her body is tense, fearful even, but she doesn't try and get out of my grasp. I hold her gaze, daring her to look away from me as I continue. "Stop telling you that I want you? Stop telling you that I've been going mad since you walked out of my bedroom?"

I reach up and brush my thumb across her bottom lip, wanting more than anything for her to pull me into her mouth like she did the other night. I need some part of me inside her. She allows me to touch her without giving me an inch. I move closer, pulling our bodies together so that they're perfectly aligned.

"Stop telling you that you're so incredibly beautiful, I'm having trouble remembering my own name when you're around me?"

She shoves against my chest, hard, causing me to stumble back a bit. "Stop it! You can't say things like that, Ben. Do you know what that does to me?"

"I know what being around you does to me." I grab her hand and place it against my chest, my other hand reclaiming its spot on her hip. Her eyes dart from my face to where her hand is, and I see her eyes react to the effect she has on me. "Do you feel that? That's what you do to me. Every fucking time I'm near you."

I can hear her heavy breathing while her eyes stay glued to her hand. I don't say anything else. I just let her feel it. *You own this part of me. Take it.* The magnitude behind that admission doesn't faze me. I don't care how crazy it seems to be this obsessed with someone after one night together. I've never felt like this.

She seems hesitant but she stays right there with me, her breathing filling my ears and her fingers moving against my skin. Tentatively. Just the lightest brush of her fingertips, but I swear to Christ, she leaves burn marks on my chest. Scorching me. Branding me with her imprint. And then I see it, the very moment a memory of our past washes over her. Breaking our connection. She blinks several times, her face falling before yanking her hand away from me as if I'm the one burning her. She looks quickly from my worried face to the water, and without a second glance at me, she jumps.

"Mia!"

I move to the edge and see her disappear. I don't waste any time before I jump in after her. My body hits the water hard, my back stinging at the awkward angle I land in. But I wasn't concerned about form when I jumped.

As I come up to the surface, I see Mia wincing in pain as she treads water. I swim over to her and hear her gentle whines.

"Where are you hurt? Let me see." I wrap my arm around her waist to help keep her head above water.

We are chest to chest, and I expect her to push me away but she doesn't. She keeps her eyes down, looking at the way our bodies come together. Her hands are gripping my arms and she slides them higher, grazing my shoulders until settling around my neck. She closes her eyes as I hold her to me, the pain-stricken expression vanishing and replaced with a look of contentment. She moans as I tighten my grip on her waist, bringing us closer.

Fuck me. *Yes, angel. Let your body feel it.*

A minute ago, she jumped off a cliff to get the hell away

from me, and now she's making those fucking noises that drive me insane.

She whimpers, raking her teeth along her bottom lip.

I press my lips to her ear and feel her shudder in my arms. "You're killing me, baby. Do you have any idea how badly I want to take you right here?"

I shouldn't have spoken. I should've just enjoyed the moment she was giving me and let her direct what was happening.

Her eyes shoot open, tears filling them instantly, but she doesn't look sad. She looks enraged. And I don't know if it's because of how blunt I was with her just now, or if she is remembering some asshole thing I did to her years ago. Hell, she could be angry at herself for letting her body take over and actually enjoying being in my company. But I don't have time to ask before she pushes against me with the same hands that were just holding on to me like she needed my contact.

I'm frozen in place as she begins frantically swimming toward the pier.

"Mia! Hold up a second."

I start swimming faster than I ever have, wanting, no, *needing* to get to her before she gets to that pier. I want her alone, especially if she is upset. But she beats me to it, and I get to the ladder as she places her feet on the wooden planks.

"Nice choke, Benjamin," Luke jokes as I get up on the pier. "Were you trying to break your back?"

"Fuck off." I move closer to Mia but Tessa once again puts her tiny body in between me and what I want. "Move, or I'll toss you into the water."

She pokes my chest with her finger aggressively. "Once again, you're upsetting my best friend." She leans closer to me. "What the fuck is wrong with you?" she sharply whispers her question, and I know it's because she's secretly pulling for me. My eyes register that no one's heard her but me.

"I didn't mean to." I look down at her and then over her head. "Mia, come on. How long are you going to be pissed at me for shit I did when I was a kid? That's not fair."

Her head snaps in my direction, and I want to jump right in the water myself with the look she is melting me with.

"Not fair? You wanna know what's not fair, Ben?" She steps behind Tessa, bringing us face to face. Mia towers over my sister as well, so it's as if Tessa isn't even between us. "It wasn't fair the last time I came here, when you told me that I couldn't try the rope swing because I would probably snap the branch it was tied to. It wasn't fair the time before that, when you begged me to keep my shirt on because I would blind you if you saw me in my bathing suit." Her eyes well up, and I want more than anything to shove Tessa off the pier and wrap my arms around Mia. "It wasn't fair when you . . ." she bites her lip to stop the tremors and turns, her shoulders beginning to shake with her cries.

Reed comes up and wraps his arm around her shoulder, doing the consoling that I should be doing.

"Baby, please don't cry. I was the biggest asshole back then." I step sideways to bypass Tessa, but she moves with me like a shadow. I meet Mia's eyes as she finally turns to look at me. "I hate that I said those things to you. I fucking hate how much I've hurt you. I'm so sorry, baby." I grab Tessa and shove her into Luke. She goes willingly with a slight grunt. "Please, just hear me out."

Mia shakes her head as she moves behind Reed, allowing him to put himself between us.

He blocks Mia entirely, and the protective vibe he's giving off blinds me with an overwhelming urge to knock his ass out.

"I think you've said enough, Ben. Why don't you just

leave her alone."

I step closer to him and he surprisingly doesn't step back. "Back the fuck off before I beat the shit out of you."

I mean every word of my threat. He is out of his fucking mind if he thinks I'll let him move in on my girl.

Luke grabs my shoulders and pulls me back. "Easy, bro. You need to calm the fuck down. Nobody needs to threaten anyone."

"Jesus, Ben," Tessa shrieks, wrapping her hand around my elbow. "Don't threaten Reed. He didn't do anything."

"She's mine, Reed," I declare, loud enough so there's no disputing what I've just said. Loud enough so everyone at Rocky Point is now aware who Mia belongs to. Everyone on the pier reacts to my words with the biggest eyes I've ever seen.

"Excuse me?" Mia wipes her face and steps in front of me. "I am not yours."

I shrug Luke off my back. "Yes, you are. You just aren't willing to admit it yet."

I move toward the edge of the pier and look over my shoulder at her.

She isn't crying anymore, the expression on her face has shifted into something I can't decipher. I see that familiar struggle in her eyes. The way she tries to ignore how I can make her feel. And that resistance is my fucking motivation to keep pressing her. To keep pushing her to where I need her to be.

Without giving her a chance to argue with me any further, I dive into the water and begin swimming toward the drop off.

Mia is mine. And I don't care if it takes weeks for her to realize it. Not only am I a greedy bastard when it comes to her, but I'm also determined as hell. I'll do anything for her forgiveness. Hell, I'll do anything for her. I see my future with her, and I'll stop at nothing to get her there with me.

mia

I STARE UP into his eyes as he enters me, so slowly that it is almost unbearable.

I want him to take me right now, to use my body for his pleasure, and I don't want him to be gentle about it.

Reaching down, I grab his ass and urge him deeper, harder. But he ignores my request and shakes his head, resting his hand on my cheek.

"No," he says, his word a breathy pant as he drives into me. "If you want me fast and hard, baby, you're going to have to give me what I want."

Anything. I'll give him anything right now.

I pull my legs up, giving him deeper entry. But he doesn't take it. He teases me with his cock and it is the greatest torment of my life.

I feel a brush along my nose, but his hand stays in place on my cheek. Confused, I ignore it and focus on him.

On the way he looks at me, his gray eyes so bright it's almost blinding. On the way his other hand grips my ass, fingers digging into my skin.

I feel another brush and shake my head, needing him to give me what I want. I try to urge him deeper again but his will is stronger than my desire. He keeps up the long, slow drags of his cock. It's a blissful torment that rocks me straight to my core.

"Please. I'll give you anything," I beg, digging my nails into his back. I feel another brush down my nose and grunt it away, not wanting anything to pull me out of this moment.

"You. I want you, pretty girl."

I close my eyes and feel his words run through me.

He wants me, but can I give him that?

"Are you a wheal pwincess?"

Another voice enters my head, along with another brush down my nose.

I shake my head, not wanting to hear anything but the man above me. But I can't hear him anymore. I can't hear his soft moans. I can't feel his skin against mine. Flesh to raw flesh. And when I open my eyes, I realize why.

My eyes focus on a tiny face that is staring at me, with wild brown hair and big gray eyes. He smiles, brushing his finger down my nose, and I don't miss the two massive dimples that appear in his cheeks.

"I woke the pwincess."

His little voice is husky and deep, like he's just had his tonsils removed. He climbs up onto the bed, holding a wooden sword in his tiny grasp.

I rub my eyes and sit up a little, propping myself up on two pillows. Smiling at him, I run my finger down his nose, and he giggles the most infectious laugh I've ever heard. "Hi, cutie. What's your name?"

"Nowwllaann." He drags out his name, jabbing his sword into the bed with three enthusiastic thrusts.

I laugh. "Nolan. That's a cool name." I touch his sword and he holds it up in the air, swinging it around his body. I notice the dragon embroidered shirt and patterned socks he's wearing, sensing an interest. "Did you slay all the dragons for me?"

His eyes go wide and he shifts to his knees before nodding frantically. "Daddy said I had to save the pwincess."

Daddy? Does Ben have a kid?

"Did he? How many dragons did you slay, noble knight?"

"One Fousand!" He jumps to his feet and holds his sword above his head.

I think I've just met the cutest kid that's ever existed.

I hold my hands around him in case he gets too close to the edge of the bed. "My hero. How old are you?"

"This many." He holds up three fingers and falls to his belly, sliding off the bed and swinging his sword all around him. He stops and moves closer to me, running his finger down my nose again. "What's your name?"

"Mia."

"Pwincess Mia," he corrects me with a crooked grin. "Daddy said that you might need to be kissed to wake you up."

"Oh, you're right. How silly of me."

I slump back down in the bed and close my eyes, feeling the weight of a small body next to me. I try not to smile as his lips touch my cheek, prompting me to pop my eyes open.

"I see you found the princess, buddy." Ben leans against the door frame, smiling at me with the same dimpled grin that just saved me from the dragons. "But didn't I say that if she needed to be kissed to come get me so *I* could do it?"

I sit up against the headboard, pulling the covers up to my chest. I slept in a tank top and tiny shorts, and I am definitely not wearing a bra. I smash the covers to my body, suddenly feeling incredibly shy around the only man that's ever seen me naked.

Nolan hops off the bed and walks over to him. "Can I go swinnin now?"

"Yeah, go get your bathing suit from the bag."

"Wait," I say, sitting up and motioning for Nolan to walk over. He quickly scrambles in front of me and smiles. "Your sword, noble knight." I hold out my hand and he gives it to me without question. "Look down at the floor." He does and I place the sword on his left shoulder. "I dub you, Sir Nolan, slayer of all the dragons in the kingdom." I move the sword to the opposite shoulder. "And protector of the realm."

He looks up at me with sheer exhilaration as I hand him back his sword. "Daddy, I'm a wheal knight!" He runs over toward Ben, jumping up and down enthusiastically.

Ben drops his smile from me to Nolan.

"I wanna go swinnin now." He runs out of the room and Ben rustles his hair as he passes by him.

"It looks like another Kelly boy has a crush on you," Ben states, crossing his arms over his chest.

He looks incredible in just a T-shirt and shorts, and my mind is suddenly flooded with images of the dream I was awakened from. Him above me, naked, driving me toward my pleasure at a punishing pace. I shake those thoughts out of my head and focus on him, which doesn't help me in the slightest. The way his muscles stand out, stretching the thin material of his shirt that I want to shred to pieces, is currently making me clamp my legs together underneath the sheet.

I try to keep myself from blushing, but I feel the warmness spread across my face. "He's so cute. I had no idea you had a son."

"I've been told that we look alike, so I guess that means you think *I'm* cute, right?"

I look away from him with a slight smile.

"Yeah, that's what I thought."

I turn back just in time to see his grin turn cocky, and I'd like to say that it doesn't do anything for me, but it does.

Damn him and that face.

"Daddy! I wanna go swinnin." Nolan's tiny excited voice comes calling from the hallway.

Ben turns his head to look down the hallway, straightening up before he looks back at me. "The next time you need to be woken up, it won't be my son kissing you, Princess Mia." His words are a promise that I don't want to react to, but I can't deny the shiver that runs through me. He has all the confidence in the world that he'll be the one to wake me up with a kiss. And I want to tell him that I'll never let that happen, but I can't seem to find the words.

I scramble out of bed once Ben leaves. As I'm slipping my favorite summer dress over my head, my mind begins to wander to memories of the old Ben. The boy I remember that never willingly stepped into any room I was in. The same boy that freaked out when he caught me in his.

"You wanna listen to music while we lay out?" Tessa asks as she skims the pool for bugs with the net.

"Yeah, definitely." I stretch out on my lawn chair, shielding my eyes with my hand.

"Well don't just lay there, goof. Go get the stereo."

I sit up and smile. "Where is it?"

"Ben's room. I think it's on his desk."

I lay back down. "Forget it. I'll just hum to myself."

She giggles softly. "He's not home. Just go in there and grab it really quick. I wanna listen to my new Justin Timberlake CD."

Okay, I can do that. He won't even know I was in there.

"All right. Be right back." I swing my legs off the side and stroll into the house.

I stop outside Ben's room and hesitantly turn the handle, pushing it open. I've never seen the inside of his room. It's off limits, which is fine with me. I don't want to be in here so I'm going to make this quick. I spot the stereo on the desk and run around his bed to get to it.

"Oh!" I trip over something, falling into the desk and rattling everything on it. Including the stereo. "Oh no." I reach for it but it's too late, and I watch with a sick feeling as the stereo hits the hard floor. I clamp my eyes shut, but I hear the damage I've done. "Oh no," I whisper.

"What are you doing?"

My eyes shoot open and I spin around, coming face to face with a very angry Ben. "Uh, I'm sorry. I was just borrowing your stereo. I didn't mean to . . ."

He pushes me out of the way and bends down, picking up the scattered pieces. "What did you do?" I open my mouth to speak, but he cuts me off. "You broke it. It's ruined. Why are you even in here? I've told you never to come in my room."

I step back, holding my hands out in front of me. "I'm so sorry. Tessa asked me to grab it and I tripped."

He throws the pieces of the stereo against the wall. "Stay away from my stuff! Get out! God, I hate you! I hate you!"

I dart out of the room, through the house, and back outside. Tessa sits up and studies my empty hands, tilting her head.

"Where's the stereo?"

"Your brother's home. I broke it. He's really angry."

Her mouth drops open. "Uh oh."

"Tessa!" Ben's voice booms out the sliding glass door I haven't closed.

We both wince and run for our lives.

I sigh, clearing that God-awful memory from my head. That was the last time I stepped foot in Ben's room. I understood his anger at the time, but it was an accident. And I felt so bad about it; I saved up my allowances and used the money to buy him a new stereo. But that didn't matter. Not to Ben.

He still acted like my very existence pissed him off. And that attitude continued until I moved away nine years ago.

My existence doesn't seem to bother him now.

I make myself a cup of coffee, moving to stand in front of the sliding glass door as I stir in my creamer.

Ben is in the pool with Nolan, pushing him around on a boogie board. He seems like a natural father, and seeing him with Nolan does things to me. Things that I try to ignore. He holds on to Nolan's hand so he can stand up on the board and pretend he is surfing. They are both smiling at each other, and watching him share this moment with his son, shows Ben in a completely new light. It distances him from the Ben I remember from years ago even more. I don't want to be intrigued by this Ben, but I am. My brain is screaming at me to stay away from him, but the way my body reacts in his presence is becoming harder to ignore. Hell, I practically came in his arms yesterday at the dam. That would've been slightly embarrassing. He was barely touching me and I was whimpering like I'd actually die if he stopped. Thank God, he spoke and snapped me out of my pathetic state. I really didn't want to fall apart like that. I wanted him to keep his distance from me. Being in his presence felt dangerous. I didn't trust my body around him. It seemed to betray me every chance it got. He didn't even have to work to get me close to orgasm. Just stick him in my general vicinity, and I'm immediately firing on all cylinders and holding the starter pistol in my hand with my finger on the trigger.

Just pathetic.

I don't even resist the urge to stare at him while he's in the pool. It's a battle I know I'd lose anyway, so I might as well save my energy.

The sun beams off his chest, and as he turns in the pool,

I watch as the muscles of his back ripple with his movements. The dark ink of his tattoo seems to stand out even more in the sun, and I want to be close to him. Close enough to study the design and read the words that are etched on his skin. His hair is wet and sticking up a bit, reminding me of the way it looked the other morning after our night together. There is no ignoring how attractive Ben is. And Nolan does resemble his dad, but I'd never label Ben as cute. He is ridiculously handsome, almost too good looking to be real. His words to me from yesterday keep playing on loop in my head. *You are mine.* He was so sure of himself, so certain that I found myself considering the possibility of actually being his. But I've hated him for so long, it seems impossible to let go of that emotion. Desiring someone and actually liking them are two completely separate things. And I can't deny that I desire Ben.

It is the whole liking thing that I'm having trouble with.

"Enjoying the morning view?"

I nearly drop my mug as Tessa comes barreling into my inner thoughts.

"Jesus. You scared the crap out of me." I glance over at her teasing smile, ignoring it as I take my first sip of my now cold coffee.

She waves at Nolan who does the same, smiling wide as he does it. Ben seems to only notice me, and I try to ignore that also.

"If I were to ask you how wet you are right now, what would you say?" Tessa inquires.

"My God. Is there any topic that's off limits to you?"

She thinks it over for a moment, twirling her hair around her finger. "Nope."

I step away from the door and sit down on the arm of the sofa. "Why didn't you tell me Ben has a kid?"

She shrugs once. "I told you he isn't the same guy he used to be."

"Just because someone isn't the same guy, doesn't mean they have little dimpled lookalikes running around. Did you really think that was how I'd interpret that?"

She moves to the chair next to me and slumps down in it. "I figured you'd find out eventually, especially if you give Ben a chance and actually hang out with him, Little Miss Unwilling to Let Go of the Past."

I ignore that last dig. "Where's the mom in all this? I'm assuming, considering what's transpired over the past several days, she isn't in the picture?" I take another sip of my coffee, contemplating the idea of Ben being married to someone. My stomach rolls at the thought.

"Ugh, don't get me started on that bitch." Tessa gathers her hair off her neck while I wait for her to elaborate. "She's so bitter about not being with Ben that she uses that against him. They were never together. It was just a drunken hookup that she's tried to make into something more, but because Ben isn't interested, she gives him as little time as possible with Nolan. Shit is fucked up."

"That's horrible. She shouldn't be able to keep his own son from him."

"Yeah, well, tell that to the freaking judge that gave her primary custody. Ben still gets to see him but not nearly as much as she does. And he should definitely get him more. He's the better parent." She pushes to her feet and pulls her phone out of her pocket. "I'm gonna run to the hospital and drop off the transcriptions I did for Doctor Willis this week. Wanna come?"

I stand and glance once more out the sliding glass door. "Nah, I'd better give my mom a call. See how she's doing."

Tessa looks at me knowingly, silently communicating that she is here for me if I need her. I've never kept any of the details about my mom's illness from her, and she and I spent several nights on the phone together, while she just listened to me cry.

I walk back into my room and set my coffee mug on my dresser, swapping it for my phone. After three rings, my aunt's voice comes through the other end.

"Hello?"

"Hi, Aunt Mae. How's everything going? How is she?"

"She's fantastic, Mia. Here, I'll hand her the phone."

I wait anxiously for my mother's voice, and after only a few short seconds, I'm rewarded with it.

"Hi, sweetheart. How are you?" Her voice is strong, and I can hear the smile behind it.

I can't help the tears that fall down my cheeks, but I keep my voice steady. "I'm so good, Mom. I miss you, though."

"I miss you, too. How is everyone there? Are you and Tessa staying out of trouble?"

"Yes, of course. We haven't done anything illegal yet."

My mom's laughter fills the phone, a sound I went several months without hearing when she was at her worst. "And her brother? Is he behaving himself around you?"

I hesitate, not really knowing how to answer that question. "He's . . . different. I don't know. It's strange getting used to this Ben when I was anticipating the old one."

"Well, time changes people," she states obviously. "It's certainly changed you over the years. My little girl became this beautiful young lady."

I smile and lie back on the bed, playing with the hem of my dress. "You sound really good. How is your strength? Are you eating? Are you having any more of those dizzy spells?"

"Oh, honey, I'm perfect." More tears fill my eyes, and I sniffle quietly away from the phone. "Your aunt and I went for a walk yesterday at the park. It was too nice of a day to stay indoors. I fed some ducks for you."

"Oh, the duck pond. I love that place." I sit up when I hear crying coming from down the hallway. Little, dimpled look-alike crying. "Hey, Mom. Can I call you back?"

"Sweetheart, enjoy yourself. Don't worry about me. I'm feeling great, okay?"

I swing my legs out of bed and stand up. "Okay. I love you."

"I love you, too."

I smile and toss my phone on the bed, walking toward the cries that seem to get more hysterical the closer I get. Nolan is sitting on the kitchen counter, wrapped up in a towel and trying to pull his knee away from Ben.

"Ahhhh stop! No, Daddy!"

"Buddy, let me look at it. I need to clean it out."

I walk over to them, and Nolan's eyes turn toward me. "Oh, no. What happened, Sir Nolan?" I place my hand on his shin, wrapping my fingers around his calf. He tenses a bit but doesn't pull away from me. "Brave knights don't cry when they get boo boos, do they?"

He dries up his tears and shakes his head at me, his tiny lip trembling. His knee is scraped up and a bit of blood is pooling on the wound.

"I fewl." He sniffs. "Daddy's gonna huwrt it."

I look up at Ben, meeting his gaze that I didn't realize was already fixated on me. "Daddy's not gonna hurt it. Are you, Daddy?" I don't mean for my tone to sound seductive, but given the intensified stare that shifts in Ben's eyes, I'm guessing it comes off as that. He blinks rapidly, dropping his gaze to Nolan's. I do the same. "You know, some princesses carry magical powers. And guess what?"

"What?" His eyes go wide and his voice becomes a fascinated whisper.

"I'm one of those princesses."

I disappear down the hallway and retrieve a small medicine bag that I carry with me out of habit. And this medicine bag just so happens to be covered in glitter. Very magical.

"What is that?" Nolan asks, the fear completely wiped from his voice and replaced with wild curiosity.

"This," I open the zipper and begin rummaging through it, "is my magic bag. It's filled with stuff to make knights feel better." I pull out some disinfectant spray, a few pieces of gauze, and a band aid. I place the bag on the counter next to Nolan, seeing his eyes broaden as he tries to see down into it. "Look in the bag and tell me what you see."

He becomes distracted, rattling off the list of items and allowing me to spray the gauze and apply it gently to his knee. Ben watches me intently from the side, my eyes meeting his every few seconds. I want to focus solely on my task, but my eyes betray me, and I allow them to wander. I blow softly on the scrape, but Nolan doesn't notice.

"What's this?" Nolan pulls out an ace bandage, unraveling it to the floor. "Whoa!"

I giggle and apply the band aid to his knee. "That is for brave knights that endure dragon injuries." I raise an eyebrow at him and he grins. "Do you have any dragon injuries?"

He nods anxiously. "I got hit by a tail wight hewre." He points to the invisible injury on his head, and Ben and I chuckle.

"Well, if it's okay with your daddy, I can wrap you up with my magic band."

"Pwease, Daddy?"

Ben picks up the ace bandage and holds it out to me. "Well, I can't have you bleeding all over my truck with that massive head wound." He winks at me, placing the bandage into my hand.

I wrap up Nolan's head as he adorably giggles. "Sir Nolan, you look ready to take on a land of dragons."

Ben picks him up, kissing his cheek before placing him on the ground.

I am about to turn when two tiny arms wrap around my legs. He smiles up at me before running toward the couch, picking up his sword and commencing the battle he seems to be constantly fighting in.

"That was amazing," Ben states, causing me to turn and look up into his eyes. We are standing inches apart, close enough to touch each other if we want to. "I couldn't go anywhere near his scrape, and you cleaned it out and stuck a band aid on it without him even flinching."

"Everyone forgets their fears when they're distracted. And a magic bag to a three-year-old is very distracting."

He moves in closer to me, his eyes flicking toward Nolan momentarily. His hand brushes against mine before he grabs it, interlocking our fingers. I try to pull mine out of his, but he holds it tighter.

"How am I supposed to make you like me if you won't let go of who I used to be?"

I pull harder, but he moves closer, eliminating all space between us. "I'm . . . not ready to like you yet."

He smiles, and it is so unexpected that I actually giggle like a complete fool. I slap my free hand over my mouth.

"Yet," he echoes. His eyes do a quick sweep down my body. "You look really pretty, by the way."

I swallow loudly, almost uncomfortably, as I drop my

hand. "Thanks."

It's suddenly feeling a thousand degrees hotter in here, and I need to back up. I need to put some space between us. I need to pull my hand out of his. But for some stupid reason, I can't. I want to yank my hand away. I want my feet to move. My brain is screaming at me right now to do the right thing here, but my body is overpowering it.

Goddamn it. Why does it have to feel good to be this close to him? Why can't he have halitosis or be all fluffy instead of a mountain of muscle with inviting breath? I may not have control over my body right now, but I still have use of my mouth.

Shit. And now I'm thinking about what I could do with my mouth. Shit!

I take in a deep breath and clamp my eyes shut, needing to at least take away the visual of him. "Ben, please back up."

He laughs softly above me. "Why are your eyes closed?"

"They just are. Can you please back up?"

He laughs again. And damn it, I love his sounds too. "Do you really want me to back up?"

"Ben."

"I'm just making sure." I feel his thumb brush along the skin of my hand. "You look really pretty, Mia."

"You already said that."

"And I'm going to keep saying it."

I open my eyes and stare up into his. There's nothing but kindness in them. No underlining lust. No hidden motives or agendas behind those crazy gray eyes. I suppose they've always been this amazing to look into, but nine years ago, I avoided them at all costs. Of course, nine years ago, he'd never have put himself this close to me. And he definitely wouldn't have given me a compliment.

He smiles, dropping my hand after giving it a light

squeeze. "I mean it. I'm going to keep telling you that. You might as well get use to it."

I look down at my feet, concealing my flushed cheeks. "Okay."

He finally steps back and I peek up, seeing him turn away from me. "Come on, buddy. Say goodbye to Princess Mia."

"Bye, Pwincess Mia." Nolan waves, tapping Ben's legs with his sword.

"Bye, Sir Nolan. If I see any dragons, I'll send them your way."

I turn and head toward the bedroom. And I know I shouldn't, I know I've had enough of him today, but I look over my shoulder anyway and lock on to Ben's eyes.

It's as if he is waiting for that last glance, because as soon as he gets it, he's out the door.

ben

"**G**OODNIGHT, BUDDY. LOVE you."

I squeeze Nolan against my chest, hearing his sleepy yawn. He rubs his face against my shirt before looking up at me, reaching his finger toward my face. I smile as he runs his finger down my nose, and he giggles when I do the same to him.

"Nighty, Daddy." He scrambles down the hallway, Angie following close behind him.

I hate sharing custody of my own kid. I want Nolan with me all the time, not just on days a judge allots. The system isn't fair to fathers. Angie is a mediocre mom, at best, and she gets primary custody just because she gave birth to him. I hate leaving Nolan with her. She isn't very attentive to him and that shit eats away at me. She never takes him anywhere, not even outside. Nolan is an easy kid. It doesn't take much to make him happy. And the thought of her not making him happy nearly kills me.

Now that he's getting older and figuring things out, he's beginning to ask questions. Questions I don't want to answer yet. He wants to know why he can't spend the night at my house every night, or why I don't live with him and his mother. I know I'll eventually have to answer them, but for right now, I am able to get away with changing the subject to something that catches his attention. Like dragons.

And now when I think of dragons, I think of Mia.

She was amazing with him today, and he took to her like she was Tessa, who he also adores. I've never been so completely captivated by someone. She knew exactly how to handle Nolan, and God, she was sexy doing it. The way her tongue rubbed the corner of her mouth while she cleaned out his cut. The way her lips rounded out when she blew on his knee. The way her hair fell past her shoulders, tickling her breasts while she wrapped the bandage around his head. She calmed him down immediately, and she'd only met him an hour before. And the whole knighting thing? Christ, if that wasn't the sweetest thing anyone's ever done for him.

I had to touch her; it was killing me not to. So I took her hand and held it like I had that night at the bar. That slight bit of contact was enough for me. Then she gave me a *yet*, and I felt as if I'd been holding her for years. Pure euphoria washed over me. Adrenaline pumped through my veins, and I finally had hope. Hope that I was slowly tearing down her walls. Hope that she'd eventually come to like me, and maybe even more than that. I could work with a *yet*.

"Who the hell is Princess Mia?" Angie asks, walking into the kitchen with an irritated expression. "Nolan went on and on about some Princess that he killed dragons for today."

I climb off my stool and grab my keys, keeping my smile hidden. "She's Tessa's best friend who's visiting for the summer. Nolan met her today when I took him swimming."

I could've saved my explanation, because Angie doesn't care for it. She's too busy rubbing me through my shorts.

I grab her hand and remove it with a disgusting grunt. "Get the fuck off. I'm not interested."

"Oh no?" She reaches for me again, but I grab her wrist, pressing it against her body. "Jesus. What's your problem?"

Her forehead creases as she stares at me, but her face relaxes with her next question. "Does this have anything to do with Princess Mia?"

I don't answer, because Angie doesn't need to know about my personal life. It's not like we are friends and I can share shit with her. We aren't anything. I brush past her and move toward the door. "Tell Nolan I'll see him soon."

"Are you really going to leave with a hard on?"

"What hard on?" I turn, stopping at the front door. "My dick doesn't want you, Angie. Stop kidding yourself."

"Well it wanted me last week, when I sucked you off and swallowed what you gave me. Or what about the week before that when I jerked you off on the couch?" She stands with her arms crossed over her chest, trying to come off as cocky and strong, but her face is giving her away. Angie hates rejection more than anything, and I've been rejecting her for years. "We can make this work, Ben. You know we can."

"There is no *we*. There never was. You've sucked my cock when you wanted to. I've never asked you to do that. I haven't even touched you in three years." I open the door and move out into the hallway of her apartment building.

"What about Nolan? Why can't you at least try for your own son, Ben?"

My blood boils. I grip the doorframe until my hand stings. "Don't ever use Nolan against me. How the fuck would seeing his parents at each other's throats every second benefit him?"

"You won't even give us a chance," she pleads, her eyes glistening over with tears.

"Enough with the bullshit. I won't pretend to have feelings for you just because you're my son's mother. I won't lie to him. Ever." I exhale roughly as her face saddens. "Make sure you tell Nolan I'll see him soon."

And I don't give her a chance to respond before I close the door behind me.

"SO, LET ME make sure I've got this straight," Luke says behind his beer.

We decided to grab a few after our shift ended, and I've just made him fully aware of everything involving Mia. Everything except the fact that I took her virginity.

"You tormented the hell out of this girl eight years ago—"

"Nine," I correct him. Not that one year really matters one way or the other. But I feel putting the most distance between my old asshole self and my current self helps my cause.

He waves me off with his free hand. "Whatever. You used to be a little dickhead, and now you're kicking yourself because she's smoking hot and the lay of your life."

I write her name in the condensation on my glass, but wipe it off before Luke sees it and gives me shit about it. "It's not just about the sex. I could listen to her talk for fucking hours if she'd let me." I sigh heavily, meeting the eyes of my very amused best friend. "Fuck you. Like you aren't completely whipped over my sister."

"I'm not." He is, he'll just never admit it. "And if you ask me—"

"I'm not."

He flips me off before continuing. "I think you're going about this the wrong way. You can't expect Mia to just jump into a relationship with you when she's hated you for years."

"Why not?"

"Because she's hated you for years," he reaffirms. "She'll just keep telling you to fuck off." He states his argument as if it is obvious, which I suppose it is. Even though I have undeniable chemistry with Mia, she isn't going to acknowledge it herself while she still hates me. "Why don't you try to be friends with her first? Let her see that you're interested in more than just fucking her."

I contemplate his advice in silence. That could be a better way to go about this. Winning her friendship means gaining her trust, which would surely grant me forgiveness. And friends do spend a lot of time together, and that definitely appeals to me.

"Nolan's crazy about her, and she's amazing with him. Would I be a complete shit to use my kid as an in?"

"You are a complete shit." He motions for the bartender. "Two Sam Adams, and did you card those fuckers at the end of the bar?" I follow Luke's finger and notice the two kids he is referring to.

And they definitely are kids. No fucking way are they twenty-one.

"Yeah, of course I did. Their ID's said they were twenty-two." The bartender gives us both another beer.

"Grab their ID's for me," Luke insists. The bartender returns seconds later, and I don't miss the uneasiness in the eyes of the two kids. "These are fake. How the hell did you miss this, Ray?" Luke is on his feet and I'm right behind him. He holds the ID's out in front of him, showing them to the kids. "You morons do realize that using a fake ID is a felony, right? How old are you?"

Both of them stand up straighter. "What's it to you?" one asks with snarky confidence.

Luke and I both pull out our badges, flashing it in front of their faces and seeing the panic set into their features. Luke steps closer. "You're making me repeat myself. I don't like doing that. How old are you?"

"We're twenty-two," the one who is apparently doing all the talking states, trying to sound as convincing as possible. His smugness alone makes me want to throw him out on his ass.

I move closer now, no longer in the mood for this kid's shit. "Answer my partner before I make you call your parents and I explain to them that their sons are getting arrested."

"We're nineteen," the meeker one answers urgently. His friend starts sweating, his hands shaking at his sides. "Please don't make me call my dad, officer. Can't you give us a warning or something?"

I narrow in on the honest kid. "Get out now before your friend screws you both."

He moves quickly and his friend tries to follow, but Luke shoots his arm out to stop him.

"Don't lie to a cop, asshole. Especially when you're dumb enough to use your real name on your fake ID, Parker Lance."

"How do you know it's my real name?"

Wow. This kid is asking to get locked up.

"Because you're too stupid to memorize any information that isn't really yours. And no one would willingly pick the name Parker. I'd feel sorry for you if you weren't such a lying piece of shit." The kid opens his mouth to argue but smartly decides to shut it. "Get out."

His now panicked face disappears out the door, and we reclaim our seats at the bar.

"Fucking prick. I should've made him call his parents just for being an asshole," Luke says.

I nod in agreement as I stare at the bottles of alcohol on the shelf in front of me, taking generous sips of my beer. My mind is elsewhere at the moment and Luke notices.

"Damn, man. I've never seen you this obsessed over some chick before. What the hell are you going to do when the summer's over and she goes back home? You know that long distance stuff doesn't work. Ask Reed."

I rub my temples with my fingers. "I don't know. I can't worry about that right now when I'm still trying to get her to tolerate being around me."

"At the rate you're going, you might not have to worry about it."

I ignore him and down my beer.

I can't think about three months from now, and not just because I'm not anywhere near where I want to be with Mia. The thought of her not being five minutes away from me forms a knot in my stomach and a tightness in my chest. I hate the idea of not being able to see her on an impulse. What if I have a sudden urge to kiss her, touch her, talk to her, or breathe the same air as her and she lives four hours away from me? The thought is maddening. I know I'll never survive that kind of distance from her.

The girl I once couldn't get far enough away from has become the woman I can't get close enough to.

LATER ON THAT night, I grab my phone and open up a new text message.

I only have three months with Mia, and I want to get the whole friendship thing rolling. The sooner she likes me as a friend, the sooner she'll see me as I see her.

Me: Can I have Mia's phone number?

Tessa: Why? Are you changing it up and trying to make her cry via text message?

Most days I love my sister. Most days.

Me: Look, I fucked up when I was younger and I'm trying to make up for it. You know I care about her, so would you please help me out here? I fucking gave Luke your number.

Tessa: I'll give it to you, but you need to know that Reed got her number too. I don't know if she sees him like that, but heads up. He's a nice guy and he's never made fun of her. He'd be good for her.

Fucking Reed Tennyson. I should've knocked his ass out when I had the chance.

Me: I'd be good for her. Reed can go fuck himself.

Tessa: Easy, tiger. I'm secretly pulling for you if it helps. 205-555-7991

Me: Thanks. I owe you.

Tessa: I know.

I've never been nervous about anything involving women. Never. But right now, a simple text message is terrifying me.

Me: Hey it's Ben. I was wondering if you wanted to hang out sometime this weekend.

Shit. That sounds like I'm asking her out. Which is what I really want to do, but that's not part of this new friendship route I'm trying to establish.

Me: Not like a date or anything.

Damn it. That just sounds shitty, like I need to clarify that I'm definitely not asking her out. Shit.

Me: Just as friends.

I chuck my phone to the end of the bed. I should just throw it outside to keep from making a further ass out of myself. It beeps and I dive for it like my life depends on it.

Mia: I don't know.

I half expected that type of response. And I am locked and loaded.

Me: A certain knight is requesting time with his favorite princess. You wouldn't want to disappoint him, would you? He'll probably cry for days when I break the news to him.

Mia: Wow. Did you really just use your son as bait?

Me: I did. I'm desperate.

One, two minutes go by and I'm starting to sweat.

Me: I just want to spend some time with you. I've made you smile a few times and I think I can do it again if you'll let me. I'm just asking for a chance, Mia. If you hate the guy I am now, then I'll leave you alone. I swear.

Fifty three seconds later, she responds.

Mia: Okay, fine. But I get to pick what we do.

I pump my fist into the air.

Me: Fine with me. What did you have in mind?

Mia: There's this medieval dinner show I passed on my way here the other day. I think it was off two exits before Ruxton.

Has Nolan ever been there? He'll get to see knights jousting and stuff.

Holy shit. Nolan's going to lose his mind. Why do I not know about this place?

Me: No, but that sounds awesome. Do I need to make reservations?

Mia: I'll take care of it. Saturday work for you?

Every day works for me. I'll rearrange my entire life at this point.

Me: Yeah. I'll pick you up. Just let me know what time.

Mia: Okay. I'll text you after I book it.

Me: I can't wait.

She doesn't respond to that, but I don't need her to. The only thing I need is the chance she's now willing to give me. I can finally show her the man I am now. I can make up for all the hurt I've caused her. All the pain.

I'll earn her friendship before offering her my life. It's hers anyway. She just needs to take it.

mia

Ben: I can't wait.

ME EITHER. I wanted to type, but I didn't. I wasn't just looking forward to spending time with Nolan, who just so happened to be the cutest kid on the planet. I wanted to be around Ben. I didn't want to fight it. I knew I couldn't keep shutting him out. I didn't want to hate him for things he did to me years ago. Not when he definitely wasn't that guy anymore. It'd be different if he was. That hate would be justified. But he's nothing like the old Ben. He doesn't talk to me like that same boy. He doesn't look at me like that same boy. And he definitely doesn't make me feel like that same boy. I'd be a total bitch if I didn't at least give this Ben a chance. So that's what I'm giving him.

Saturday wasn't coming soon enough for me. I've never felt anxious about doing something with a guy just as friends before. But this is Benjamin Kelly we're talking about. He's seen me naked. Completely naked. And now he wants to hang out like we haven't brought each other immense pleasure.

He came just as much as I did that night, so I'm taking credit for that.

How the hell am I supposed to navigate a friendship with a guy that I can't stop fantasizing about? I've had guy friends before. It's doable. But I've never gotten butterflies over those guys. I've never felt like I might actually combust just being in the same room as those guys. And I've definitely never wanted to bang the hell out of those guys.

Speaking of boys that want to be friends with me, I promised Reed that I'd meet him for lunch today. We've talked on the phone a few times since the day at Rocky Point. He was really sweet and funny, and when he asked me to hang out with him, I didn't hesitate to say yes. He picked a sandwich shop in town that I was familiar with. Tessa and I ate there several times with her parents when we were younger. I spent the morning in the pool with her, not being able to sunbathe because the heat was enough to make you pass out. After a quick shower, I drove into town and parked my Jeep next to Reed's truck. He was already seated at a table when I walked through the door.

"Hey, how are you?" I ask, walking around the table as he stands up to greet me. He gives me a hug, which I'm not expecting, but isn't awkward. And it definitely isn't anything other than a hug you'd give a friend, which relieves me. I'm hoping this really is just a lunch between new friends and not anything more. I'm not interested in anything else with Reed, and I don't want this to become uncomfortable.

He ends our one armed hug with a pat on my back. Very non-date like.

"I'm good. I ordered you a shrimp salad sub. I hope that's okay." Reed smiles at me as he takes his seat and I take mine. He has the lightest blond hair I've ever seen, almost white, that falls in his eyes with a bit of curl.

"Yeah, thanks. That sounds delicious." I take a sip of the water he had also ordered for me. "So, you were off work today?"

Reed had mentioned a few days ago that he was a laborer

for his father's construction company.

He nods. "Yeah. Business is kind of slow right now. But it should pick up soon. We're usually slammed in the summer time." Our sandwiches are placed in front of us, and we both take a bite, chewing behind our smiles. "What town in Georgia are you from again?"

"Fulton. Smallest town in the world." I swallow my bite and take a drink. "It's a military town. The air base is really the only thing in it besides a Wal-Mart."

"Have you ever been on the air base? I bet they have some really cool planes there."

I shrug. "I've only been on it a few times. They'll show movies there at the theatre for a dollar, but it's always like, three months after their original release date." I take another bite of my sandwich. "I don't think given the choice, I'd choose to live in Fulton. It's mainly a lot of old people that are retired," I pause and grin slyly. "And Marines."

He laughs behind his drink. "I could totally live there. I'm a sucker for girls in uniforms and military planes. My grandfather was a pilot and used to take me to the air shows when I was younger." The chimes on the door ring when it opens, and I watch Reed's eyes react to whoever walks in. "What the hell are the odds," he mumbles before fixating his gaze on me.

I turn in my chair and nearly fall out of it.

Sweet mother of all that's holy. Ben stands frozen just inside the shop door, his eyes shifting between mine and what I'm going to assume are Reed's. But I can't turn around to be sure. I can't do anything besides stare at the glorious sight of him in a cop uniform.

He's a cop? I had no freaking idea. What the hell else is Tessa keeping from me?

My chatterbox best friend seems oddly tight lipped on

everything involving her brother.

"Well, look who it is." I'm broken out of my trance and glance up to see Luke's amused grin. "How are you, Mia?"

Movement comes from my left, and I turn to see Ben walking over.

Oh, Good God. He's right next to me. He's right next to me and he's got handcuffs.

I swallow heavily and pry my eyes from his to look at Luke. "I'm good. Great. I'm . . . I'm good. Or great. Both. I'm both." And I've apparently forgotten how to hold a conversation.

Luke muffles his laugh.

"Hey," Ben greets me with a smile. I'd usually be able to react like a normal human being and say something, anything in response, but considering the fact that he paired that knock-me-on-my-ass grin with the uniform he's rocking, I'm pooling in my chair and unable to do anything but continue breathing. He shoots a glare at Reed, one that I wouldn't ever want directed toward me. "Reed," he practically growls, and I think Reed says something in return, but at the moment, my entire body is completely focused on Ben's, including my ears. He looks back down at me and grips the back of my chair. "Are we still on for Saturday?"

"Hmm?"

His lips move, parting sensually, but I've no idea what words, if any, just came out of them. I know exactly what those lips are capable of and that's the only thing filtering through my mind at the moment.

My God. Those lips are orgasmic.

"I'm sorry, what?"

He laughs and looks over at Luke quickly before returning to my stunned face. "I asked if we're still on for Saturday."

I nod. A lot. My head might have fallen off if I hadn't

forced myself to stop. "Yup. I made reservations for the five o'clock show." I clear my throat and take a sip of my water before continuing. *Christ. It feels like I swallowed super glue.* "Um, we have to be there fifteen minutes before showtime. I arranged for Nolan to get his picture taken with the King."

His eyes light up and his cheeks hollow out with his dimples. "Oh man. He's going to freak out over that." We smile at each other. The other two guys could probably catch on fire and I doubt either one of us would notice. I definitely won't notice. "Good idea, Princess Mia."

"Yeah, I can be pretty awesome sometimes."

Luke slaps Ben's back, and the sound snaps me out of my obsessive gazing. "Well, as much as I'd love to stand here and listen to you two not flirt with each other, I'm starving and we need to get back out there." He smirks at me. "You know, bad guys to catch and all. Protect and serve. That whole thing." He turns his head toward Reed. "Sorry to interrupt your date."

"It's not a date," I blurt out, immediately regretting the hidden implication that I'd never actually be on a date with Reed. I look over at him, silently pleading for him to agree with my statement and not make this any more awkward than I've just made it.

Help a girl out. Don't leave me hanging here.

He cocks an eyebrow at me. "Well, that's the last time I service you with my free hand underneath the table. You've broken my heart, Mia."

My jaw hits the table I definitely was not recently serviced under. Is he nuts? "What?" I manage to choke out.

"What the fuck did you just say?" Ben questions with a tone that no man in his right mind should challenge. "Say it again, asshole, and see what happens." He moves closer to Reed but Luke steps between the two.

"I'm gonna let him punch you if you say something stupid like that again," Luke states, straining his head over his own shoulder to connect with Reed.

Ben and Luke are roughly the same size, so Luke doesn't have any difficulty in holding him back. Reed, on the other hand, is more leaned out than muscular, and probably wouldn't stand a chance against Ben.

Luke turns back toward Ben, who is still looking ready to kill. "Not a date, man. Just relax." His words are barely audible, but I hear them. And Ben seems to calm down as he processes them himself.

Reed holds up his hands in surrender. "Kidding. Jesus Christ. You used to have a sense of humor, Ben. What the hell happened?"

Ben places his hand on the back of my chair again, hovering over me in a very possessive way. If I'm not mistaken, it's as if he's staking his claim in front of Reed, just like he did the other day on the pier. But this time, I don't object to it. This time, the very thought of being Ben's doesn't infuriate me. It intrigues me. I want to know what that feels like. But he asked me out for Saturday as friends, and friends don't act like that with each other. So that can't possibly be what he's doing right now. He's probably just looking out for me. So I push those thoughts to the back of my mind and watch his eyes shift back to mine. He hasn't said anything else to Reed but I don't think he needs to. His actions and demeanor are speaking loud enough for him.

"I'll pick you up at four o'clock. I figured we'd surprise Nolan so I'm not going to tell him where we're going." His tone is friendly, all edginess and agitation gone, as if he didn't just have a pissing contest with the guy that I am not on a date with.

I tuck my hair back behind my ear. "Make sure he brings his sword. He's gonna need it."

I feel his thumb brush along my back, and that slight bit of contact sends my lower half into a frenzy.

"Ben. Get over here and order," Luke calls out, having moved to the counter. He must have thought it was safe to leave his friend alone with Reed. That or he was too hungry to care anymore.

Ben lets go of my chair with a grin and brushes against my shoulder with his hand. These tiny touches are going to kill me.

"See you Saturday."

"Okay," I choke out with a shaky voice.

He turns and shoots Reed a scowl, before walking over to the counter. And now his back is to me. His shoulders in that shirt. His ass in those pants. Someone may have to scrape me off the floor.

"You're hilarious." I glare at Reed, accomplishing the difficult task of prying my eyes off the glorious body standing no more than fifteen feet away from me. "I think I'd remember getting fingered underneath a table, ass."

"I'd hope so." Reed grins before shrugging. "It's all good. I've never seen Ben get all *I'm caveman, this my woman* before. He's fun to rile up."

I roll my eyes before giving in to the temptation standing at the counter.

I don't want to stare, but given the fact that Ben's back is to me and he'd never know I'm drooling down the front of my shirt, I allow it. I hear Reed's voice as it enters my ear, and it would be rude of me not to answer him. Besides, I'm perfectly capable of answering one person while I'm glued to someone else. I'm a woman for Christ's sake. We can multi-task the shit out of stuff.

"Hmm mmm. Yeah, me too," I reply.

Ben pulls his wallet out of the back of his pants. Where his ass is. That. Ass. It's this perfectly sculpted entity in and of itself. There should be internet sites dedicated to it. Fan clubs. Parades, even.

"Oh wow. That sounds really fun. I'd love to do that," I respond.

Ben reaches over his shoulder and scratches his back, pulling his shirt tight across his muscles.

My God.

"That's crazy. I hate it when that happens." I have no idea what Reed just said to me. No idea. His chuckle catches my attention and I whip my head around. "What?"

His eyes drift from the men at the counter back to me. He grins amusingly. "I just asked you how your sandwich was, and you answered me with 'that's crazy. I hate it when that happens.'" His body shakes with silent laughter.

I slap my hand over my eyes and bow my head in embarrassment. "Oh, my God. I'm so sorry, Reed. That was so rude of me." I drop my hand and turn my body toward him completely, granting him all my focus. "I'm paying attention to you, I swear."

He tilts his head. "So, when should I set us up for sky diving?"

"Huh?" *Sky diving?* Hell no. I'd never agree to something like that.

"You said it sounded really fun and that you'd love to do it. Remember? Just two minutes ago when you were paying attention to me."

I open my mouth to apologize when the door chimes, causing me to whip my head around. Ben smiles at me before he walks out, and I wave like some obnoxious fan girl trying to flag down her favorite celebrity. *Real smooth.* I turn back around and see how much this is entertaining Reed. "Did I mention Ben and I are trying out this whole friends thing? I don't have the slightest idea what I'm doing." I filled Reed in on mine and Ben's history at Rocky Point the other day, leaving out the small detail of the mind blowing five orgasms he gave me. Five!

"Clearly." He smiles and throws his crumpled up napkin at me. "It's not gonna work."

"What?"

"Friends. You and Ben. I'll bet money on it." He crosses his arms over his chest, leaning back in his chair. He is grinning at me like he has it in the bag. Like he is already holding my money and counting it arrogantly in front of me. Oh, the smugness.

"Why are you so sure that it won't work? I can be friends with Ben." I mimic his appearance and lean back in my own chair. "We can totally be friends. It'll work."

"It's not going to work, and I'll tell you why."

"Okay, smart guy. Why?"

Don't ever tell a woman that we can't do something, because we'll die trying to do that very thing that you're so sure we can't do. I think the female race is stubborn as a whole. Maybe it's a design flaw, but whatever. I'm here to prove a point.

"Because—" he sits forward, pulling my half eaten sandwich in front of him before he picks it up "—I don't know about you, but I don't usually eye fuck my friends."

"Who's eye fucking?" I half yell. Thank God, we are the only two people currently in the sandwich shop. But it doesn't save me from getting a stern look from the owner behind the counter. "I was not eye fucking," I harshly whisper.

"And I'm not about to eat the rest of your sandwich." He grins condescendingly before taking a huge bite of my sub.

I roll my eyes, the eyes that were so not eye fucking anyone, before I respond. "What's your opinion on him anyway? Do you think he's a good guy?"

He nods and swallows his bite. "Yeah, when he's not threatening to beat the shit out of me." We both laugh, and I take a sip of my water. "He's really good with his kid. Even when Nolan was a baby, he just knew what to do with him. And he wasn't even nervous about it. I'd be scared shitless if someone threw a baby at me."

I giggle and watch him pop the last bit of my sandwich into his mouth.

I could tell just from being around them once that Ben was amazing with Nolan. They were so sweet together, and Ben seemed like the type of dad that would do anything for his kid, which is exactly how it should be.

"Well, I think anyone would be scared if babies were flying at them," I counter, getting rewarded with a sneer and another crumpled up napkin tossed at my head. We both stand up and push our chairs in. "Thanks for lunch. It was memorable, even without the finger fucking." He winks, unable to form any words with a full mouth. "You're a really good friend, Reed."

He grimaces and swallows his massive bite uncomfortably. "Friend zoned like a boss." I buckle over at his statement, laughing so hard my eyes filled with tears. "No worries. You're not my type, anyway. I prefer really dumb girls with low self-esteem and daddy issues."

I shove him in the direction of the entrance. "Oh that's nice. Daddy issues? Really?"

"Hell yes." He holds the door for me and we both walk

to our vehicles. "Girls with daddy issues are always looking for a new daddy." He throws his head back, cracking up at himself and the disgusted look I'm currently giving him. "See ya later, Mia."

I shake my head disapprovingly. Men.

ben

FUCKING REED TENNYSON.

I didn't know what he was playing at, but I was sure as hell going to find out. And I couldn't waste any time doing it either. Not when he was taking my girl out to lunch and shit. I was not okay with that. I didn't know what his intentions were. If he just wanted a friendship from Mia, fine. Anything more than that? Fuck no. She was mine, and apparently, he might need a reminder.

I know where Reed lives, so I stop by his house later on after work. We never really hang out that much, but I used to pick Tessa up from his house all the time before she could drive.

His truck is parked in the driveway, which is a good thing. I really didn't feel like driving all over the place looking for him, but I would if I had to. This shit needs to be cleared up tonight.

After parking behind him, I knock on his front door and see his head peer out the small window next to it. I hear a soft "fuck" before he swings the door open and greets me with raised eyebrows.

He studies my uniform, keeping his hand on the door-knob. "Are you here to arrest me for taking Mia out to lunch yesterday? Because if I have a choice, I'd much rather have you lock me up than beat the shit out of me."

I lean against the railing, ignoring the smart ass undertone that all of his words seem to be laced with. "What the hell do you want with Mia?"

He chuckles then, and I straighten up, causing him to wipe the smile off his face.

I really don't want to hit him, but he isn't making the decision easy on me. I'll deal with the ramifications later.

"Nothing. I mean, she's a cool chick and I like hanging out with her, but just as friends. Maybe if you hadn't marked your territory, I would've tried something, but I'm not stupid. I don't think she's interested in me like that anyway."

"She's not a fucking fire hydrant for me to piss on, dick. Don't refer to her as territory." I step closer to him, remembering what he said yesterday in the sandwich shop after Mia insisted the two of them weren't on a date. "And if I ever hear you joking around about touching Mia again, it'll take a lot more than Luke to stop me from tearing you apart."

He runs his hands down his face before letting out an exhaustive sigh. Turning around, he starts back into his house.

"Where the hell are you going?" I ask, stepping forward and grabbing the door. This conversation isn't over until I fucking end it. I follow him inside, stopping at the end of the hallway that dumps out into the kitchen.

He emerges from the fridge with two beers. "Here. I sure as hell need one of these, and maybe if you have one you won't be so inclined to murder me on my porch." He places my beer on the counter and leans against the fridge, taking a swig of his. "Actually, if you are going to kill me, do it outside so I at least have witnesses. And avoid messing up my face too much. I'm sure my mom would prefer an open casket."

"I'm not going to kill you. I might make it so you can't walk for a few days, but you'll still be breathing. And you can't blame me for wanting to find out what the hell your motives are with my girl." I walk over to the counter and grab my beer, keeping my eyes on him as I take a drink.

"Look, man, I'm not moving in on Mia. I swear. But I would like to keep being friends with her, and I don't fucking think I should have to ask your permission to do that."

I grin and take another sip of my beer. I have a good amount of muscle on Reed, so the fact that he has the balls to talk to me like I can't wipe the floor with him, earns my respect. "No, you don't have to ask my permission. I'm fine with you being friends with Mia. I just wanted to make sure that you weren't trying to be anything else with her. I'm fucking crazy over that girl."

He arches his eyebrow at me. "Really? I had no idea." We both laugh, and he pushes off from the fridge and moves across from me. "You're fucking crazy over a girl you're trying to be friends with? That makes a hell of a lot of sense," he states sarcastically.

I grimace. "I'm doing what's necessary. The torture I'm going to endure by not acting on my feelings will be worth it if she lets me in." He looks at me with a perplexed gaze, like I've just explained myself to him in another language. I take another sip of my beer and frown. "When you meet a girl that gets to you the way Mia gets to me, you'll understand. Friends genuinely like each other and I need her to like me. She'll never love me if she doesn't like me first."

He places his beer down with a shake of his head. "I had a girl get to me like that, and she completely fucked me over. I don't see how any of it is worth it. That's why I'm just with girls for one night. They can't rip your heart out if you don't let them anywhere near it." He smiles. "I hope it works out for you though. I think you have a pretty good shot with her from what I've observed."

"Why do you think that? Did she say something to you?"

If Reed and Mia are friends, she could've shared things with him like she does my sister. And I am suddenly all for their friendship if it helps my cause.

He regards me with a smile like he knows things. Things I desperately want to know.

I place my beer down and leer at him. "You're not going to tell me shit, are you?"

He smiles again, more cunning this time, after taking a huge chug of his beer. "I don't have much to tell. But a fucking blind person could've seen the way you two acted around each other yesterday. I could've burned the place down and I doubt either one of you would've noticed. You flustered her so bad she could barely speak, and she definitely wasn't paying attention to a damn thing I was saying once you stepped in the shop. I could've asked her to carry my children and she probably would've agreed without knowing it." He shakes his hair out of his eyes and registers my annoyed expression. "Not that I would've asked her that. I'm sure you've claimed that uterus."

I wave him off dismissively, holding the neck of my beer bottle with my free hand. "I'm glad I make it difficult for her to form a sentence, but I don't need to convince her body that we should be together. I've proven that point already."

He grabs another beer, tossing his empty bottle into the trashcan and offering me one.

I decline it.

"I just need her to see me as the guy I am now and not the shithead I used to be. And being friends and showing her that I'm not just in this for pussy seems like the best option for me."

"Unless she keeps your ass permanently in the friend

zone. This whole plan could blow up in your face if you aren't careful." He walks around the counter and sits down on the couch, turning on the TV.

I haven't thought about the possibility of that happening. But I highly doubt Mia can ignore the chemistry we have and only see me as a friend. The spark between us is fucking palpable. The air seems to crackle when we're in the same room. There is an energy to it, a dynamic that you can practically see rippling between us. Drawing us together like charged particles. There's no denying it. And once she only sees me as the man I am now and not the boy I used to be, I'll make it my life's purpose to never again let her feel the type of pain I once caused her.

"Hey, man, I'm gonna head out and go see my kid. Thanks for the beer."

Reed acknowledges me with a nod before I walk out of his house.

I feel better now that I know for sure he isn't trying to get with Mia. And I don't have a problem with him being friends with her. He's a decent guy. He's always been good to my sister.

But if he ever steps out of line with my girl, I won't hesitate to put him back in it.

I PARK OUT front at Angie's apartment complex and take the stairs quickly to her floor.

I want to tell Nolan that he'll be spending time with Mia on Saturday night. I know he'll look forward to it as much as I am once I break the news to him.

I knock on the door, hearing his gruff voice singing aloud somewhere in the apartment. The door opens and Angie stands there, looking less than pleased to see me.

"Great. Now I'll never get him to go to sleep." She steps aside and motions for me to walk in. "He's been fighting me for the past hour and my nerves are shot."

I can hear Nolan's voice coming from down the hallway where the bedrooms are. He sounds very animated, but that's pretty standard for him.

"I'll put him to bed. I want to talk to him anyway."

She closes the front door and moves past me toward the couch. "Don't keep him up with another story. I've already read to him four times, and if he doesn't get to bed soon, he'll be cranky as hell in the morning." She begins flipping through a magazine, seemingly done with lecturing me, which is a good thing because I'm fucking done listening to it.

If anyone needs parenting advice between the two of us, it sure as hell isn't me.

I walk down the hallway and stop at Nolan's door, leaning against the doorframe.

He is trying to balance his stuffed dragon on the end of his bed, holding his sword in his free hand. I watch with a smile as he gets his favorite sleeping buddy to stand up on the wooden footboard before he strikes it down with a mighty swing.

"Aren't you supposed to be in bed, buddy?"

His eyes light up and he scrambles off the bed, running toward me. I scoop him up and plant kisses all over his face.

"Daddy! You'wre hewre!"

"Shhh," I say against his hair, carrying him over to the bed. He crawls under the covers and I lie on my side next to him, tucking him in. "Mommy said you were supposed to go to bed a while ago."

He tugs at the buttons on my uniform. "I'm not tiewerd," his voice breaks into a yawn, and I try to hide my laugh. "Can you wead me a storwy?" He looks completely exhausted, and

I know I'll never get more than a few pages into it before he passes out. He continues playing with the buttons on my shirt, his sleepy eyes falling closed every couple seconds.

"Not tonight." I lean off the bed and grab his stuffed dragon, handing it to him. He pulls it tightly against him, popping one ear of the dragon into his mouth like he always does. He falls asleep that way every night, and wakes up if the dragon falls off the bed in the middle of the night and he no longer has it in his grasp. I run my finger down his nose and he focuses on my face, repeating the gesture.

"Guess who's going to hang out with us on Saturday night?"

His mouth unlatches from the ear. "Who?"

I smile. "Princess Mia."

His dimpled grin lights his whole face up, and he immediately gets to his knees. "Pwincess Mia! Yayyayayayayay!" He bounces on the bed and I hush him again, tucking him back in. "I wike Pwincess Mia, Daddy," he says in a softer voice before tucking the dragon's ear back into his mouth.

I bend down and kiss him on his forehead. "Me too, buddy."

He closes his eyes and begins humming against his dragon.

I settle down on my side, watching his body relax completely and hearing the low sound he is making get softer and softer. When I know he is asleep, I sneak out of his room, leaving the door cracked open.

Angie is still on the couch looking at her magazine, but throws it onto the coffee table when I enter the room.

"You know, stopping over here during the week and putting him to bed only confuses him."

I'm walking toward the front door but stop and turn after her statement. "What the hell are you talking about?"

She stands, hitting me with her most irritated expression.

I brace myself for whatever bullshit argument she is about to start. It would be nice to go one time seeing Angie and not have it out with her, but she seems determined to bitch me out about something every chance she gets.

"He's going to start expecting it. He already wants us to be a family, and when you come over here and put him to bed, it's just going to make him think that we are one." She steps closer to me, dropping her gaze to her feet. I know this tactic. She does it when she wants me to feel bad about something. It never works and I'm surprised she keeps using it. She looks up at me with only her eyes, keeping her head down. "He'll probably wake up and wonder if you're still here, and then when you're not, it'll just upset him."

"You're wasting your time trying to make me feel guilty. If I wanna come over here and say goodnight to my son on nights that technically aren't mine, I'll do it. He knows that the three of us aren't a family. He has me and he has you, but he'll never have us together."

Her head snaps up, the wounded façade disappearing. "God, you're such an asshole. What the fuck was I thinking hooking up with you in the first place?"

I continue my walk toward the door. "Neither one of us was thinking," I counter. Because I wasn't thinking that night.

If I had been sober, I wouldn't have slept with Angie. After talking with her for a minute, I would've seen what type of person she was. A self-centered, conniving brat. She seems to get joy out of my misery, and I wouldn't have lasted more than a minute in her presence if I wasn't drunk.

I grab the door handle and look behind me where she has fallen back onto the couch, pouting like a kid who has just been reprimanded.

"I'd never take it back."

Her eyes meet mine briefly, before she drops them to the floor, nodding to convey her understanding of what I mean.

I hate Angie, but I love the gift she gave me. Nolan makes me a better man. It pains me to imagine not having him, and I'll always feel indebted to her for not going through with the abortion.

"I'll pick him up after work on Friday," I say.

She acknowledges me with another nod, but her gaze never leaves the spot on the floor she is boring a hole into.

I close her apartment door behind me and make my way out to my truck.

It'll always be like this with Angie. Even giving her what she wants, us, won't change the person she truly is. She's a bitch by nature, and I'm tied to her for the rest of my life. But I don't care how she treats me. She can spew all her poison at me and I'll fucking take it. She gave me my son.

And he's the only thing that matters.

mia

"WHAT'S WRONG WITH what I'm wearing?"
I direct toward my best friend who is currently
rummaging through my clothes.

For my date, no, friendly hang out with Ben and Nolan,
I pick a pair of skinny jeans and a white tank top. I think this
is very appropriate for going to a medieval dinner show as
friends, but Tessa has other ideas.

Articles of clothing are getting hurled into the air as she
stays hidden in the closet I'm occupying for the summer. I step
behind her and start grabbing clothes out of the air.

"Do you mind? You're going to be ironing all these after
you pick them up." I chuck the handful of clothes I've managed
to catch onto my bed.

Tessa emerges from the closet with my teeny tiny jean
skirt and a tube top. "Strip. You package yourself up in this hot
little number, and I guarantee my brother will be unwrapping
you with his teeth later on tonight."

My best friend has a one track mind. A very dirty one
track mind.

I snatch the hot little number that I am definitely not
wearing out of her hands. "This is not a date, so there won't
be any unwrapping going on." I toss the outfit onto the bed
and continue brushing my hair in front of the mirror. "I told
you, we're hanging out as friends. There's no need for me to

be wearing anything revealing."

She plops down on the bed, sighing dramatically, because this is Tessa we're talking about. "Who the hell goes from a night of unbelievable, nine inch, pussy humming sex to hanging out as friends? Did you both hit a large rock when you jumped off those cliffs last weekend? Is your brain currently swelling and causing you to act like a complete idiot?"

I pin half of my hair up before I turn and look at her. "I'm just now getting used to the idea of not hating Ben for the rest of my life. Do you have any idea how dead set I was on that game plan? I was close to having a voodoo doll made of him."

"And now you two have bumped uglies, and you're just going to pretend that you didn't."

I grunt my frustration and shoot her a stern nook. "No one's pretending anything. He asked me to give him a chance and I'm giving it to him. As friends. It would be really shitty of me not to." I turn back around and continue messing with my hair.

There's no way I could ever pretend that Ben and I didn't share that one night together. If it was possible to forget, I would've forgotten about it already. Lord knows I don't want to be reliving it every night alone in my bed. That memory is sticking around permanently. And what a memory.

"I don't see why you can't give him a chance while he's between your legs. You'd at least get some relief if he was fucking you into the friend zone."

"Pwincess Mia!" Nolan's husky voice comes echoing down the hallway.

"Hold on one second!" I snap my head around toward a grinning Tessa. "I really hope your nephew didn't hear that," I scold her, but she merely shrugs her shoulders in response.

I grab my phone and stick it into my pocket, stepping in

front of the mirror one last time.

My hair is definitely not behaving, doing this weird curl thing at the bottom that I am so not digging. And of course, the more I mess with it, the worse it gets. I grumble my irritation under my breath.

"Mmm mmm," Tessa teases. "Just friends, my ass."

I ignore her and apply some lip gloss. "What's up with you and Luke? Are you two serious?"

She rolls over onto her back, moaning playfully. "Luke is fun. Really fun. Tie me up and own my body fun."

I should be shocked by that description, but I'm not. Tessa is into anything involving men. Especially when it involves fun stuff.

"But not serious fun?"

"I don't know. I like him and he likes me. I don't need anything more than that."

We meet each other's eyes in the mirror.

She wants to tell me more, I can tell, but decides against it and gives me a sly smile instead. "How many condoms will you be taking with you tonight?"

"You are ridiculous." I flip her off over my shoulder, walking down the hallway and into the living room.

Nolan is swinging his sword in the air behind the sofa, slaying invisible enemies, but my eyes don't linger on him. They can't. Not when *he* is in the room.

All my focus is magnetically pulled in the direction of Ben, who is leaning against the counter. He straightens when he sees me, melting me with his smile that beams like a thousand watt bulb.

If I was wearing heels right now, I definitely would've stumbled.

"Hey," he says, twirling his keys on his finger. It's so casual, like any normal greeting between friends, but his greeting makes my spine tingle and my toes curl.

God, how does he do that? How does he turn a simple *hey* into so much more than that? I feel that hey settle between my legs and root itself there permanently.

"Hey," I reply, trying to sound as sure and steady with this whole friendship thing as he does. However, my hey comes out broken and weak, giving away my anxiety. Although, even if I wouldn't have spoken, I'm sure my body language would be displaying my nervousness for all to see. I am completely rigid, and the conversation with Tessa that just transpired moments ago, is playing on loop in my mind.

Pussy humming sex.

Fucking into the friend zone.

Condoms.

Oh, God, do not get wet right now.

I drop my eyes to Nolan, needing a distraction.

"Pwincess Mia!" He runs over to me and I bend down, bringing myself down to his level. My worries and desires are left above me as I focus in on his cuteness. "Daddy said we're going to a surpwise." He reaches out and runs his finger down my nose, and I do the same to him. His tiny face scrunches up afterwards.

"We are. But I have to ask you a question before we go." His eyes get even larger, grayish blue just like his father's, as he waits for me. "Have you ever been to a real castle, Sir Nolan?" He shakes his head and his mouth drops open. "Would you like to go to one right now?"

I've never seen anyone go from one emotion to another so quickly. If I blinked, I probably would've missed it.

He begins jumping up and down, almost knocking me onto my ass in the process. "A weal castle! Daddy! Pwincess

Mia said we can go to a weal castle!"

Ben laughs as I stand up. "You ready to go, buddy?" He picks a squirming Nolan up and smiles sweetly at me. "Are *you* ready, Princess Mia?"

Am I? For friendship with a man that I can't stop thinking about? Pussy humming sex. *Shit.* I force a nod and swallow down my fear.

"Lead the way, noble knights."

NOLAN'S EXCITEMENT WAS infectious, and it grew as the evening played out.

When we pulled up in front of the castle, he couldn't get out of the truck fast enough and practically sprinted toward it. When he got his picture taken with the King, he couldn't take his eyes off him, even when Ben and I told him to look at us so we could take pictures of him with our phones. He stared at him with eyeballs the size of dinner plates, his mouth forming a tiny O. It was the cutest thing I've ever seen. And when the actual show started and Nolan got to see the knights in action, jousting and sword fighting right in front of him, I don't think he blinked even once.

And then there was Ben.

I kept catching glances from him the entire night, meeting his eyes every few minutes when I couldn't keep myself from looking at him. I'm sure my struggle was obvious, considering he caught me each and every time I gave into my temptation. But the look he shot back at me wasn't the one I was used to. It wasn't the look he gave me when I knew he was thinking about doing things to my body. I was familiar with that look. The greedy shift in his eyes, the tightness in his jaw, the way his nostrils flared like he was a caged Pit bull. But I didn't get that look tonight.

Instead of the raw thirst I had seen in his eyes on more than one occasion, I saw tenderness. A friendly affection. He regarded me sweetly, but there was nothing behind it. No underlying hunger.

And God, I wanted to be devoured by him.

"He is completely passed out." I observe, walking next to Ben and focusing on Nolan's exhausted face. I reach up and brush his wild brown hair off his forehead, smiling at his sleepy state. "I don't even think an actual dragon could wake him up right now."

Ben opens up the back door of his truck, laughing softly at the sight of Nolan's face as he peels him off his shoulder. "I figured he'd crash hard after all of this." He buckles Nolan into his car seat, closing the door and grabbing the passenger door handle. "I may have withheld his nap from him today in hopes of getting to talk to you alone on the drive back. My son likes to monopolize the conversation, as you witnessed on the way here."

I smile, climbing up into the truck after my door is opened for me.

Nolan talked nonstop on the drive to the dinner show, and every time Ben tried to talk to me about something other than dragons or knights, Nolan would adorably cut in and change the subject.

I'd be lying if I said I'm not grateful for Nolan's missed nap.

I settle into my seat and buckle up. "I can't say I blame him. Dragons and knights are way more exciting than what Tessa and I did today."

He closes my door and gets in on the driver's side, starting up the truck and pulling away from the castle.

I inhale, taking in Ben's scent that has completely filled the space between us. He smells like pure Ben. No cologne, just him. Like a man that knows exactly how to please a woman.

Shit. Don't go there.

"How's your mom doing? Tessa mentioned a few months back that she was really sick. Is it breast cancer?"

I cross one leg over the other, angling my body toward him.

His one hand stays firmly planted on the wheel while his other relaxes on the console between us. I'm glued to his fingers, the fingers that I moronically doubted that night. I didn't think there was a chance in hell he'd get me off the way he did. And now that I know what those fingers are capable of, I'm fascinated by them. I actually can't stop looking at them.

The length, the thickness, the fucking tips of them that played me like a record. I want him to turn his hand up so I can straddle his fingers and ride out my pent up orgasm right now, but that's not going to happen.

He clears his throat, gaining my attention, and I'm quickly reminded of the question he hit me with before I wandered off into finger fucking la-la land.

I paint on my most convincing I-wasn't-just-fantasizing-about-what-you-could-do-to-me face and answer. "Yeah. She's doing great right now. The treatments aren't making her nearly as sick as they did in the beginning. It was awful when she first started them."

He glances over at me and gives me a sympathetic smile.

"She wouldn't eat anything and she didn't have the strength to get out of bed. I couldn't leave her side for more than a few minutes at a time because she was constantly getting sick."

"But she's doing better now? Does she still have it?" he

asks, turning onto the main highway that leads to Ruxton.

I nod once. "Yeah, she still has it, but I guess the treatments are working because she's doing so much better than she was. I think she's gotten most of her strength back." I lean my head back against the seat rest, shifting my eyes from Ben's profile to the road in front of us. "I just, I don't know what I'd do if something happened to her. She's the only family I have left besides my aunt."

The hand that I had longed to mount reaches over and grabs mine. He squeezes it gently, comforting me. "Nothing's going to happen to her. And she's not the only family that you have. Tessa would kick your ass if she heard you say that."

I laugh and he smiles at me. His eyes shift to our conjoined hands. After one gentle squeeze, he lets mine go. I hold in my disappointment and rejoin my own hands together in my lap.

"So, Officer Kelly."

My God, does that have a ring to it or what?

Images of him doing things to me in that uniform flash in front of my eyes too fast to focus on. I blink rapidly as his eyes meet mine and darken. And that look, the look that he's hitting me with is directly connected to the pulsing spot between my legs. I clear my throat and the dirty thoughts from my mind.

"Do you like being a cop?"

Good save.

I hide my heated face behind the strand of hair that fell out of my clip, shifting my attention to the road in front of us. My body goes rigid when his hand brushes my face, tucking my hair back behind my ear.

"I do," he replies coolly, as if he didn't just touch me. As if he's completely unaffected by that touch. His hand returns to his lap before he continues, his eyes returning to the road as mine neglect it completely. I am entirely too focused on him and his smooth voice. "It's never boring, that's for sure. Plus, Nolan gets a kick out of it." His lip curls up into a smile, as if he's thinking of some memory. "What about you? What were you doing back home?"

"I was taking classes at the local community college, but stopped when my mom was diagnosed. I'd like to eventually do something with kids, I think. Be a teacher or guidance counselor or something."

"I can see that," he says. "I'm sure you'd be awesome at it."

I look to the back seat at a very sleepy little boy whose head is slouched against his car seat. "He really is the cutest kid I've ever seen." I pry his wooden sword out of his hand and place it onto the seat next to him. "You've raised this incredible little boy, Ben. If I ever have kids of my own someday, I hope they turn out as awesome as this one."

Our eyes lock.

"If there was any woman that was born to be a mother, it's you."

He means what he says. I can feel it. I settle back into my seat and stare at his profile. "Really?"

I've never given much thought to having children, mainly because I've never pictured the person I would someday have them with. When you've gone twenty-three years without a boyfriend, it's hard to imagine having a husband.

He looks over at me like I've just asked him the most ridiculous question—deep crease in his forehead and a curious frown. "Are you kidding? Look how you are with Nolan."

I shake my head in disagreement. "Nolan's easy, though. He'd probably love anybody that played knights and princesses with him."

"You're not just anybody. You knighted my son, which he hasn't stopped talking about. You gave him this amazing memory tonight, and he does the nose thing with you."

I furrow my brow, confusion setting in. "The nose thing? Oh, you mean when he runs his finger down your nose? That thing?"

"Yeah. Do you know he only does that with me?" He pulls off the highway and onto the back road leading toward the house. I shake my head, and he sees it before continuing. "I've never seen him do that with anybody else. Not Tessa, not my parents, and definitely not his mother. I don't know why he does it, but he's only ever done that with me."

I suddenly feel horrible, like I've barged in on a private Ben and Nolan bonding activity.

"I'm sorry. He did it to me when he woke me up the other day and I did it back out of reflex. I didn't know that was your thing."

"Mia, relax. I like that he does that with you. I like that that's something you and I share with him. He's only known you for a week and he's already formed this special bond with you. You'd be an amazing mom." He pauses, glancing in his rearview mirror. "You'd be better than the one he has."

"She's not good with him?"

I only have concern in my voice, but the thought of someone not being good to Nolan makes my blood boil. I keep that emotion tucked away though.

Ben shakes his head. "She doesn't spend time with Nolan because she wants to spend time with him. She does it to keep him from spending time with me. She's never been a good mom to him. When he was a baby, she refused to breastfeed him because she was so worried that it would wreck her body. I begged her to do it because I knew it would be good for him, and she still refused." His hand that is gripping the wheel seems to grip tighter. "I hate leaving him with her, knowing that he's probably being neglected. Something could happen to him because she doesn't pay attention and the thought of that . . ." His voice trails off, and I don't think, I just move.

I push up the flip console and slide across the bench seat, pulling his free hand into mine. "Nothing's going to happen to him. You can't think like that, it'll drive you crazy."

He glances over at me, our bodies pressed up against each other's.

I squeeze his hand the way he did mine when he was comforting me moments ago. "You're going to worry about him because he's your son, but you can't let that worry eat you up. Just focus on your time with Nolan. Focus on making him happy every second you're with him, because that little face back there should always be smiling."

The truck had stopped in front of the house sometime during my speech, but I have no idea when. I am purely focused on easing his troubled mind. Seeing him like this is heartbreaking.

Ben stares at me with fascination. "You've given my son more in one week than his mother has in three years. You have no idea what that means to him. What that means to me." His neck rolls with a deep swallow as he glances down at our hands that are interlocked in my lap. "How did I not see this amazing girl nine years ago?" His thumb grazes the skin of my hand, rubbing it softly.

I don't know how to answer him, so I watch him study our hands instead, admiring his features while he admires our connection—his long, dark lashes and prominent cheek bones. He seems drawn to the very sight of our hands together, but that look of interest doesn't linger.

Exhaling loudly, almost frustratingly, he slides his hand out of mine and bypasses my gaze to look at the dashboard.

"It's late. I should probably get Nolan to bed."

Friends don't hold hands. Friends don't sit this close. And Ben knows these things. I don't care what the rules of friendship are because I'm not sure I want Ben as a friend. Not when he makes me feel like this. But that must be how he's seeing me because he's breaking our contact. I slide back over to my side and open my door, jumping out of the truck. I open the back door and lean my head inside, pressing a kiss to Nolan's temple.

"Goodnight, Sir Nolan," I whisper, seeing him stir a bit. I look up front at Ben whose bright gray eyes are studying me. "Goodnight, Ben."

"Goodnight," he says with a smile that seems guarded, unlike his usual halt-me-in-my-place smile that makes me forget how to breathe.

I go to close the door but stop myself, turning back to Ben. "I'm really sorry I broke your stereo."

"What?"

I wince at the memory. "Remember the summer before I moved away? I went to your room to borrow your stereo and I knocked it off your desk, breaking it. I'm really sorry about that."

He shakes his head, his brow furrowing. "What made you think about that?"

I shrug. "I don't know. But, God, I remember how angry you were. You hated me that day."

His gaze drops briefly before returning to mine. "Mia, do me a favor. Don't apologize for stuff that happened between us before. You could've broken everything in my room and it wouldn't have justified the way I treated you back then. You don't owe me an apology. Ever. Okay?"

I smile meekly and nod. "Okay. Goodnight."

"Goodnight."

I walk inside and go straight to my bedroom, collapsing down on my bed.

Tonight was amazing. It was the best non-date I've ever been on. I loved talking and hanging out with Ben, which seems crazy considering how much I used to hate the mere presence of him. The boy I once wished never existed was now the man I wanted to spend every second with. I'm not holding on to that hate I once had for him anymore. I can't. Not when the man he is now makes me feel things I've only read about in books. I'm done trying to forget that I gave him a part of me that no one else will ever touch. I want him to have it. I want him to have every piece of me. Benjamin Kelly is becoming everything I've ever wanted, and I am finally willing to admit that to myself.

At the very moment my eyes shut, Tessa swings my door open and walks over to my bed, lying down next to me. I wait for the interrogation to start, but it doesn't come, which is shocking. Rolling over, I notice her worried expression.

"I'm late," she states, keeping her eyes on the ceiling.

"For . . ." And then it hits me. Girls only use that wording for one thing when it's paired with the look she's carrying right now. "Oh, my God. What are you going to do?"

She finally looks at me but doesn't respond. But she doesn't have to. Her face is giving away everything she needs to say.

She has no fucking clue.

ben

WANTED TO tell her she looked beautiful that night.

I wanted to wrap my arm around her shoulder and hold her against my chest when she slid next to me in my truck.

I wanted to kiss those soft full lips before she walked into the house.

But I didn't.

I couldn't do any of those things. Not when I was very clear about that night not being a date.

I'm trying to earn Mia's trust, and drilling her into my bench seat isn't the way to go about it. If I act on my impulses, it will fuck up the progress I've somehow managed to make. She's talking to me now instead of brushing me off. She's spending time with me instead of running away. Or jumping off cliffs. I can't lose what I have going with Mia. And my dick can hate me all it wants, but I am adamant about keeping things friendly with her for now.

Four days. That's how long I make it without seeing her before I find myself driving to my parents' house after work. And believe me when I say that those four days were the longest of my life. Thank Christ I have a job, otherwise I'm certain I would've gone completely mental without a distraction. Luke enjoyed my misery immensely, making sure to point out every time I brought Mia's name up in a conversation that had everything to do with work and nothing to do with her. And it was misery. Keeping my thoughts off her tight pussy and focusing on the friendship I was building with her. And if my own mind wasn't hard enough to filter on its own, she started throwing text messages at me that were becoming more and more sexual. Apparently, Mia and I were now the type of friends that joked around about sex. She was so fucking comfortable with me now that nothing was off limits to her.

And she didn't care to ask me if I was okay with that before she shifted us into that category.

> Mia: Do you think it's possible to get carpal tunnel from masturbating too much?

This was the first one she threw at me. My brain was immediately flooded with images of her touching herself, and it took every ounce of strength in me not to get off before I replied. I should've answered it with something like this:

> Me: Mia, I don't think that's an appropriate friend conversation to have. And we're friends, so let's not go there.

But no, I'm a complete shit with zero willpower. So instead, I answered with this:

> Me: If it's possible, I'd already have it.

Yup. Now she knew I was jerking off like a mad man. Which was the God's honest truth. I was hoping that this was a mistake on her part, and she'd realize her error and never tempt me with another text like this again. My dick was throbbing enough without the help from the images she was putting into my head. But apparently, she was just getting started.

Mia: What do you think is my best feature? Tessa says my legs, but I'm thinking my boobs. Thoughts?

Thoughts? Really? I was convinced that she was trying to kill me. She was an angel and a devil wrapped into one package that I couldn't refuse. One that I desperately wanted to bend over my bed and fuck into tomorrow. I couldn't ignore her. We were friends, and if this was the type of friends she wanted to be, then I could be that. I'd be hard constantly, but let's face it, being around her was already making that an issue. So I decided to just go with it and answer honestly.

Me: Tits, mouth, ass, legs. In that order.

I thought I was golden. I thought I was going to be able to handle these sexual texts and not have my dick in my hand twenty-four hours a day. And I would've been, if she didn't up the stakes.

Mia: Do guys prefer a girl that swallows to a girl that spits? I mean, isn't the general act of sucking off a guy enough to make them happy? Does it really matter what I do with your cum?

Motherfucker. This text was reread numerous times, mainly when I was jerking myself off. Especially that last sentence. The implication of it being *my* cum in her mouth was too much for me. I was weak. Weak and hornier than I've ever been in my entire life. Weak enough to give her a response.

Me: It's really fucking hot when a girl swallows. But yes, the act itself is enough to make most guys not care one way or the other.

Not a big deal. I was perfectly capable of handling anything she threw at me. Or so I thought.

Mia: I was so unbelievably horny today. Guys are lucky. They can just tuck their erections away and go on about their day like they aren't sporting wood. Girls can't do that. I had to change my panties twice before lunch.

That does it. I wave my white flag in surrender. I don't give her a response to that, not by text message anyway. No, my response is in the form of me pulling up to my parents' house like a complete dick.

I need to see her, especially after that last text. I should be seeing her to tell her in person that she can't keep sending me messages like that. But the second her body comes into view, lounging on a chair next to the pool, every thought is wiped from my brain. I suddenly can't remember why I am here, but that doesn't stop me from walking around the pool and directly toward her like a man possessed.

Her eyes are closed so she doesn't see me coming. And then she opens her mouth and begins singing along to the song that is playing through her ear buds. I recognize "Crash My Party" by Luke Bryan instantly.

It's an all right song, but hearing Mia sing it makes me really like it.

I stand in front of her, even more enthralled by the sight of her than I usually am as she stays completely oblivious to my presence. My girl can sing. Her voice is as beautiful as she is, and she's belting the tune out and tapping her feet on her beach towel as I enjoy the show.

She hums the final notes of the song before her eyes finally open, meeting the smile that's been plastered on my face since she got in my sight.

"Ben! Jesus Christ!" she yells, sitting up and placing her hand on her heaving chest. Her other hand pulls out her ear buds and discards them in her lap. "How long have you been standing there?"

"Long enough," I reply, thinking back to the night at the bar when I used the same words on her.

Her cheeks react the same way they did that night, the slight flush that causes her gaze to wander from mine temporarily until she regains her composure. But she doesn't have to hide her reaction to me. I like when I knock her off balance. And right now, I can't stop looking at her.

She's all dark hair, slightly tanned skin, and big brown eyes that regard me with curiosity after she collects herself.

"I, uh, didn't know you were stopping by today. Are you here to see Tessa because she ran out for a bit."

For the first time since Mia's arrival in Ruxton, I wish we weren't alone. I wish my sister was sitting out here by the pool. I can't be weak right now, and being alone with Mia in the insanely small bikini she is wearing is making me weak.

No, fuck that. I can do this. I focus on her eyes. Only her eyes.

"I think it's a safe assumption to make that if I ever stop over here while you're in town, I'm not here to see my sister."

Her lips part slightly as she absorbs my words. *Does she really not know that I'm here to see her?*

I glance down at the neglected book in her lap. "What are you reading?"

Her eyes follow mine and her fingers graze the cover. "Oh, um The Giving Tree. I haven't read it since I was little, but I can't really get into it." She peeks up at me slowly, taking her time to reach my face. "You didn't respond to my text."

My breath hitches in my throat uncomfortably. I reach up and rub my neck, suddenly feeling like a shitty friend. But fuck! What the hell kind of response was she expecting out of me? The memory of that text and of her wet pussy has me contemplating nailing her to the lounge chair she's reclining on. Leave it to Mia to cut the shit and just straight up call me out on my neglectfulness. Because if we are friends, why wouldn't I have responded to her? It won't surprise me if her next move is to read the damn message to me out loud and prompt a reply from me that way. And I can't have that happen. There's no way in hell I'd be able to restrain myself if she actually voiced that message. But I gotta give that daunting stare of hers something. She'll never let this go. I know her too well to try and change the subject. So a lie will have to do.

I stuff my hands into my pockets and try to seem unfazed by this. But I'm definitely fucking fazed. "I was really busy this afternoon. Luke and I got called to this domestic violence dispute and it was really intense. I'm sorry. I actually forgot about your text until just now."

I didn't. I could never forget about that text.

"Oh, okay." She begins chewing on the inside of her cheek, her eyes flicking away from mine to the pool. She seems hesitant all of a sudden. The confident girl that was just singing her heart out and ballsy enough to bring this topic up is nowhere in sight. Until I see it, something spreading over her, causing her back to straighten and her eyes to narrow in on mine with a thundering intensity that I've never seen before. "You're going to respond to it, right?"

Fuck. Me.

"I will," I promise without a single thought.

Christ, this woman has the ability to unhinge me like no other. I need to get the subject off that text. I'm going to get hard if I don't. And damn, if her persistence isn't the hottest thing I've ever seen.

She wants me to respond. She needs it. And I hate making her feel like I ignored her.

But I need to focus on something else, so I do.

"Do you know if Tessa's busy this weekend? I need to work on Saturday night and I'm going to have Nolan. I was hoping she'd babysit him for me."

"I don't know. She's got a lot going on right now," she states tensely, avoiding my eyes.

A lot going on? Tessa? Her summer plans consisted of tanning and chasing after Luke. But Mia seems uneasy all of a sudden, so I decide not to pry.

Her eyes return to mine and she smiles. "I can watch him for you if you want."

"Yeah?" I ask, completely stunned by her offer. I shouldn't be surprised at anything involving Mia, though. The girl seems to astonish me with each passing day. "You don't have to do that. I can ask the old lady that lives a few houses down from me. She's watched him before when no one else could."

She smiles wider and cocks her head playfully. "Do you think Nolan would rather spend the evening with a princess that knows her way around a wooden sword, or an old, smelly lady that probably has an absurd amount of cats?"

"An absurd amount of cats?" I arch my brow at her, finding her thought process completely amusing.

She gives me a raised eyebrow in return. "Oh, I'm sure she has them. All old women become crazy cat ladies. My grandmother did. She had eleven roaming through her house." She scrunches up her nose at the memory. "It smelled really bad in her house. You don't want Nolan to make this face, do you, Ben?" She points to herself, trying to keep the unpleasant look going but cracking into a smile after a few seconds.

I chuckle. "No, I guess not. I'm sure he'd have more fun with you anyway." She nods in agreement, smiling as if she really is looking forward to giving up her Saturday night to babysit. Could this woman get any more perfect? "I'll owe you big time for this, so start thinking of ways I can repay you."

She pulls her bottom lip into her mouth and grabs the sunscreen off the chair next to her. "Oh, I already have a few ideas." She's staring right at me, and the heated look in her eyes is hitting me where I don't need it to. "I think I'm burning. Would you mind?"

Fuuccckkk.

No. I don't mind. Not in the slightest. I'm only a man. I'm not a god. I can't say no to Mia when she's staring up at me like she wants me to do more than just rub sunscreen on her. Because that's exactly how she's staring at me. Ask my cock.

I grab the lotion and clear my throat as she spins around in her chair, offering me her back.

This is a test. A test to see if I can handle touching Mia as a friend. Because friends apply sunscreen to each other, and can do it without it being sexual.

I begin applying the lotion onto the warm skin of her shoulders, feeling the goose bumps pop up against my touch. She drops her head and moans softly, causing my cock to twitch like a fucking traitor. But I ignore it, moving down to her back. She moans again, a bit louder this time as I lift the string of her bikini, making sure to cover the area before I put it back in place. I'm only being thorough. I'd hate for Mia to burn and be in any amount of pain.

Just being thorough.

"That feels so good. I forgot what your hands felt like on my body."

Good God. I don't want to react to that. This is like her text messages, only worse. I can't hide behind the screen of my phone and jerk off with my free hand. And my cock is having difficulty *not* reacting.

I pretend like I don't hear her and run my hands down her lower back, smearing the lotion on. She does that damn whimpering sound, and all the blood in my veins rushes straight to my dick.

That's it. I have to get out of here.

I pick the bottle of sunscreen off the ground and drop it over her shoulder and into her lap.

"I gotta go. I'll drop Nolan off around three on Saturday."

I walk away from her with my hard on, thinking back to her last text message about being able to tuck it away, making it less obvious. I do just that with an agitated shake of my head.

"Oh, okay. See ya!" she yells out, but I don't turn to look at her. I can't.

Christ, the fucking sounds are filling my ears again, and I need a release.

I get in my truck, liking the distance my parking spot gives me from her, and pull out my painful hard on. I stroke it fast, keeping my grip tight to not prolong my climax. I need to do this and get the hell out of here before I fuck everything up.

"Aw, fuck."

I think of her mouth wrapped around me, those full lips teasing the head and pressing softly to my shaft. She'd take me in all the way, I know she would. Her mouth can handle everything I give her and I won't hold anything back. I'd grip her hair and thrust my hips into her eager mouth, and she'd suck me until her cheeks hollowed and her eyes watered.

"Oh, God. Yeah."

She'd swallow because she'd know that I'd love it. She'd love it, too, because she's my dirty girl. My filthy little angel that tells me her panties are soaked. And then she'd ride me, hard and fast, her perfect tits bouncing in my face. I'd suck on them until she screamed like she did the other night. I'd tell her that I'd be coming all over them soon, because I would. She'd get off on my words, my mouth, and my cock, and then she'd come perfectly around me. Her skin would blush across her chest, blooming up toward her neck as she threw her head back. The sight of her orgasm would push me over the edge. I'd come inside her, this time without a condom, because I need to fucking feel her.

I'd bury my face in her tits, my cock in her pussy, and I'd fucking give her everything.

"Fuck." My thighs tense, and I can feel my release surging through me. I open my eyes and grab a few napkins out of my console, holding them against the tip while I come by myself for the countless time this week. I wipe myself clean and then crumple up the napkins, shoving them into my cup holder.

I feel better, but not by much. I can still see her tight little body in the distance, and I want the real thing, not just the fantasy. But that isn't going to happen. It can't happen. Not yet.

I start up my truck and pull out my phone, scrolling to her last text.

> Mia: I was so unbelievably horny today. Guys are lucky. They can just tuck their erections away and go on about their day like they aren't sporting wood. Girls can't do that. I had to change my panties twice before lunch.

After I reread it six times, I finally give her the response she wants.

> Me: Even a tucked erection is still obvious. Trust me. And you aren't the only one that's been unbelievably horny lately.

I press send and get the fuck out of there before I do something I'll regret. I'm only a man, Goddamn it. She wanted me to respond to her, so I did. I can handle dirty text messages with the girl that I'm falling in love . . .

Fuck me. That's what's happening. I'm falling in love with Mia Corelli.

mia

"**O**KAY, BE HONEST. Tell me if I've completely outdone myself here."

I place my hands on my hips and survey the massive amount of babysitting supplies I picked up at the store.

"I've got chips, cookies, popcorn, ice cream, mini cupcakes that I had to get because they have little shields on them." I stand on my toes to see the rest of my purchases better. "Organic chocolate milk, organic strawberry milk, carrot sticks, grapes, and pita chips."

"He's going to freak out when he sees what you did back there. And did you just say carrot sticks?" Tessa calls out, strolling toward me from the direction of the bedrooms. "Seriously? He's three. He's more likely to use those as mini swords." Her eyes widen at the sight of my purchases. "And he's one kid. Jesus Christ, Mia. Have you ever babysat before? This is enough to feed a small army."

I nudge her with my elbow. "Yes, I've babysat before. But I didn't know what Nolan liked, so I kind of got one of everything. Ooohhh, check it out." I reach over the bags of chips and grab the two Red Box rentals, holding them out for Tessa to grab. "I got Frozen and something called Mike the Knight. I figured that one was right up his alley. The little cartoon knight reminded me of Nolan, minus the dimples."

"Wow." Tessa shakes her head and hands me back the

movies. "You're making a serious play, aren't you?" She sits on the edge of the couch, smiling widely at me. My puzzled expression gets across exactly what I'm feeling, prompting her to elaborate. "You love him," she states with a satisfactory smile.

"Sure, yeah, I love Nolan. How could you not love him?"

Tessa had already started to shake her head as soon as I said Nolan's name. "No, that's not who I'm referring to." She pauses, giving me the chance to connect the pieces on my own. It doesn't take me long.

I wave her off with my hand. "I do not love Ben if that's who you're foolishly referring to."

No. I'd know if I loved Ben. I want to bang his back out, but that's not love.

"It is, and you do. Or you're at least open to loving him now. You're not just trying to impress my nephew with all of this." She motions toward my snack pile. "And you're desperately trying to pull him out of the friend zone he so stupidly put you two in. How many slutty text messages have you sent him?" she teases.

Tessa and I never keep secrets from each other. Hell, she was the one who suggested the scandalous text message idea after I told her that I wanted Ben to see me as more than a friend. She predicted he'd drop everything and come at me hard after the first one I sent. But no, I'm either really bad at getting someone hot with my words, or he's completely immune to them.

I cover my eyes with my hand and grunt my frustration. "Not enough, apparently. I threw my best stuff at him and he barely flinched." I drop my hand and look at her. "I'm running out of ways to spell this out for him."

She stands up and walks over toward the sliding glass door. "Get naked. That'll definitely spell it out." She waves and smiles at what I assume is Nolan. "Don't tell my brother about the pregnancy, okay?"

I walk up to her, putting her hand in mine. Nolan is in Ben's arms, swinging his sword in the air as they walk around the pool.

"It's your news to tell, not mine. And the first person that needs to know about it is Luke."

After the initial shock of the possible pregnancy sank in the other night, Tessa and I stayed up for hours talking about it. She was scared, but she was also really happy about having a baby with Luke. The only problem was the two of them weren't supposed to be serious. And throwing a baby into the mix would definitely change that.

She sighs heavily. "I'll tell him. I'm just waiting for the right time."

"Like tonight?" I ask, smiling at Nolan's face as it comes inching closer to the glass. Tessa shrugs her response. "You can do it. You know he cares about you. And if you need me, I'll be right here."

She leans her head on my shoulder as the boys come up to the door, sliding it open.

"Hey," Ben greets me with a smile as he steps inside the house, placing Nolan on his feet.

I am once again stunned into silence from the sight of him in his uniform, unable to give him anything besides a goofy grin at the moment. But my God, he makes that uniform look downright sinful. I'm tempted to go commit a major felony in hopes that he'll pat me down or better yet, strip search me.

Nolan runs right at me, wrapping his arms around my legs and snapping me out of my lustful thoughts.

"He's a little excited. The maniac wouldn't even take a nap today because he was too wound up to come over here."

I laugh and rub Nolan's head, seeing him lift his face to me. "I couldn't take a nap either." I bend down and put us face to face, dropping my smile and trying to stay serious. "I tried to take a nap, but there were all these dragons in my bedroom." His eyes immediately twinkle with interest, doubling in size. "They might still be back there. Can you go check it out for me?"

"Yeah!" he yells with pure excitement, his little legs quickly taking him down the hallway.

Tessa nudges Ben's shoulder, barely moving him an inch. He smirks at her and she smirks right back before looking over at me.

"I'll see you tomorrow sometime." She gives me a knowing look and motions with her head toward Ben without him noticing. "*Get naked*," she mouths, earning herself a stern look from me before she walks out the door.

I will definitely not be getting naked unless Ben undresses me, and at the rate we're going, I don't see that happening any time soon.

"Here's all his stuff." Ben drops the duffle bag that is on his shoulder onto the couch, opening the zipper. "Pajamas, toothbrush, a few books that he likes me to read to him before he falls asleep, and this." He pulls out a stuffed dragon that looks well loved. It's worn and frayed at the edges. "He can't go to bed without this, but don't give it to him before bedtime because he'll take it everywhere and I'm afraid he'll spill something on it and I won't be able to wash it. If something happens to this thing, I'm completely screwed."

I laugh and watch him stuff it back into the bag. "What time is bedtime?"

"Between 8:00 p.m. and 8:30 p.m. He might pass out before then though, since he's running on no nap." Ben turns his head and glances over at the kitchen counter. "Wow. You are definitely prepared." He smiles at me with a teasing look. "Expecting more children?"

I shove his massive shoulder and move past him. "Oh ha-ha. This isn't all just for Nolan. I've been known to put away a massive amount of snacks when I'm entertaining."

"Take that! Leave Pwincess Mia alone!"

Ben and I both turn our heads. "What is he doing in there?" he asks. I shrug with a sly smile, and he narrows his eyes at me. "Well, now I'm curious."

I follow him down the hallway, knowing exactly what I am going to see when I look into my bedroom. I didn't just go grocery shopping today.

"Daddy. Look at all these dwagons!" Nolan is swinging his sword at the inflatable dragons that surround my bed. They range in size; some are as small as his stuffed animal and others are bigger than him. "I'm gonna kiwl dem all!"

I cover my mouth with my hand and chuckle next to Ben, feeling his eyes on me.

"Where did you get all these?"

"The party store in town. They have everything there." I watch Nolan bop one of the larger dragons in the head. He seems to be enjoying himself immensely. "Totally worth the twenty bucks."

"God, you're incredible."

Our eyes lock, and I see how much he means what he's just said. That is definitely one quality he has that I absolutely love.

Ben is honest, completely authentic when he speaks to me. I never doubt anything he's ever said and I know I never will. Of course, I'm sure he means I'm incredible in a friendly sort of way since he's not pinning me up against a wall.

We stare at each other while Nolan continues slaying the dragons in front of us.

His gray eyes are bright and filled with adoration. It is the look I want Ben to reserve just for me. The look he's given me several times before. At the dam, standing in his parents' living room after we discovered each other by the pool, and in his truck. It's the look that teeters us on the edge of the friend zone, because I've never been looked at by a friend this way before. I want Ben to say something else to me. I want to hear more of his honesty, and for a split second, it looks like he is going to give me what I want. But instead, he breaks our connection and glances down at his watch.

"I gotta go." He looks at me again with the same tender gaze. "I probably won't be back until close to 12:30 a.m., but if you need anything, just call me."

I place my hand on his arm and squeeze it gently. "We'll be fine. Go arrest some bad guys, Officer Kelly."

My voice doesn't waver at his title, but I can't deny the rush of adrenaline that spikes through me when I say it. I wink at him and move into the bedroom, scooping up a few smaller dragons.

Nolan looks at me and beams as I sit on the edge of the bed, watching him slay the biggest dragon in the room. I laugh at him and turn my head, hoping to see Ben standing there, but he is gone. And I know that I shouldn't feel disappointed because I will see him later on tonight, but I can't help it.

At least I have one Kelly boy to keep me company while I think about another one.

Nolan was like this tiny ball of energy that seemed to recharge the more he moved around. I'd never seen a kid go from one activity to another with such gusto. After he had slain dragons for a good hour, he had a snack and wanted to watch his Mike the Knight DVD. But he didn't sit still during that. He jumped around in front of the couch and swung his tiny sword in the air, mimicking the movements on the screen. We colored a few pictures, made a fort out of the extra bed sheets I found in the closet, and blew bubbles on the back patio. I saw his first yawn, the only indication he'd given me all night that he was slowing down, at 8:20 p.m. After changing him into his pajamas, I brushed his teeth and grabbed the books out of the duffle bag.

He settles under the covers in one of the spare bedrooms, holding his stuffed dragon in a death grip. "Wead that one fiwst," he says in a sleepy voice, pointing toward a book about trucks.

I prop against the headboard and hold the book out in my lap, reading in a soft voice. He closes his eyes when I am halfway through it, but I finish it anyway. After giving him a kiss on his forehead, I quietly exit the bedroom and plop down on the couch with my phone.

> Me: Little knight is down for the count. Slaying thirty seven dragons takes a lot out of a three-year-old.

I turn off the Mike the Knight DVD that is still playing and change the channel to something I am interested in. My phone beeps as I lie back on the sofa, but it isn't a text from the person I am dying to talk to, and see for that matter. This is the first time I grunt at the sight of this particular name on my screen.

> Tessa: I haven't told him yet and I don't know if I'm going to. What if he freaks out and ends it? What if he wants me to abort the baby? I'd never do that, but isn't it his decision as much as mine? We've had sex three times since I got over here and I don't even know if that's good for my current situation.

Me: First of all, why isn't he at work with Ben? Secondly, you freaking out is definitely not good for the baby, so calm down please. And third, do you really think Luke is the type of guy to ditch his pregnant girlfriend? I've only been around him a few times and I know he isn't like that.

Tessa: I'm not his girlfriend! I don't know what the hell I am, but he's never labeled me as that. Fuck buddy seems more appropriate.

Tessa: Ben is riding solo tonight. They don't always patrol together.

I chuckle and prop a pillow under my head.

Me: Just grow a pair and tell him. And I say that in my best Tessa style voice because you know that's exactly what you'd be saying to me. :)

Tessa: Speaking of growing a pair . . .

Me: Shut up.

Tessa: Just saying, bitch.

I know exactly what she is getting at.

Grow a pair. Please. I told Ben that I'm in danger of causing permanent damage to my hand from excessive masturbation, and I need to grow a pair?

I turn onto my side and tuck one hand underneath my head. My phone beeps again and this time, I can't contain the smile that spreads across my face.

Ben: I can't wait to hear all about it. See ya in a few hours.

I look at the time on my phone. Three hours and forty-three minutes to be exact.

Not that I'm counting.

⁓

"MIA? MIA, HEY, wake up."

"Hmm?" My eyes slowly open and Ben's face comes into view. "Oh, hey. Sorry. I didn't mean to fall asleep." I roll over onto my back and stretch my arms over my head, seeing Ben's eyes drop to my body and widen before he quickly turns away from me. And I mean quickly, as in, he can't get me out of his sight fast enough. I furrow my brows. "What? What is it?"

He clears his throat as I sit up, still completely oblivious to whatever it is that's making him react to me this way. He stays facing the kitchen, rubbing the back of his neck with one hand. "You might want to put something on. Your . . . breasts are really noticeable in that top."

Breasts? Oh, how formal.

I glance down quickly, seeing my erect nipples poking through my sheer tank. But I'm not embarrassed at all. I'm irritated. Really irritated all of a sudden.

My boobs are making him uncomfortable? Well, that's just great.

I stand up with a clenched jaw and walk past him, grabbing the hoodie I had taken off earlier and slipping it over my head. "Christ, Ben. You act like you haven't seen them before, or sucked them for that matter." I snap my head in his direction and see the shock on his face. "They're just tits."

"They're *your* tits," he states, his expression toughening and his voice edgy.

The sight of my chest weeks ago would've provoked an entirely different reaction out of him. Now he's desensitized to it. Awesome.

I ignore the stare he is giving me and refuse to let go of my annoyance. This is maddening. "And my tits make you uncomfortable. But I guess they should, considering how *friendly* you and I have become." I grab Nolan's books and shove them into his duffle bag.

"What is that supposed to mean?" he asks, but I ignore him. I'm too focused on getting his shit together so he can leave.

"Here. He was great. Didn't give me a bit of trouble." I thrust the duffle bag into his chest, stalking past him and grabbing my phone. "My tits and I are going to bed before we freak you out even more."

I don't turn back around as I walk toward my bedroom. I don't want to see if my words affect him, especially since my body apparently doesn't anymore. What the fuck? My boobs, that he couldn't get enough of weeks ago, are now being held hostage in his stupid friend zone against their will. And they are not happy about it one bit.

Join the club.

I rip my hoodie off and throw it in the corner of my room with a grunt.

I'm annoyed, hurt, and really horny. Three emotions that are pissing me off at the moment. I grab my phone to respond to Tessa's last text message.

> Me: *Your brother infuriates me! I'm turned on, pissed off, and sick of this stupid friend zone. I can't be friends with someone that brings me to orgasm in my dreams every night. And I'm tired of getting off on the memory of Ben. Oh, and your get naked idea wouldn't have worked. My tits were just on display for him and he acted offended by them.*

I press send and throw my phone down, reaching up and undoing the hair tie that is securing my hair in a loose bun. Just as my hair falls down my back, my bedroom door swings open and Ben stands in the doorway with that blazing look of his that leaves scorch marks on my skin. But right now, it doesn't have that effect on me. Right now, it makes me want to punch him right in the throat.

"I'm really not in the mood to talk right now."

He steps into the room and closes the door behind him. "Did you mean what you just sent me?"

I furrow my brow into a tight line. "What are you talking about? What do you mean *what I just sent you?*" I stand up off the bed and glare at him.

I'm still mad, pissed even, but now I'm confused as hell.

And then I see it, the cell phone he's gripping, and a panic surges through my system. My legs feel weak underneath me and my chest feels so tight it's as if I'm breathing through a straw.

I grab my phone and scroll to the text that I thought I sent to Tessa. But I didn't send it to Tessa.

I lift my eyes and watch as Ben reaches behind him and locks the door, never taking his bright eyes off me. I toss my phone back onto the bed and take a deep breath before responding.

"Yes. I meant it." My answer is firm and definite. This is not the time to half-ass anything. He's giving me an opportunity and I'm taking it.

He smiles that cocky grin that drives me insane. "Do you want me, baby?"

I nod.

"No, I need to hear you say it. I'll give you whatever you want, Mia. But I won't risk misinterpreting what I've just read.

Tell me exactly what you want." He stops right in front of me, keeping his body inches from mine. He's so close to me right now it's almost unbearable.

I know exactly what I want. Him. And I'm not above being forward with him right now. I understand his hesitation. He doesn't want to take this somewhere and not be positive that I want to go with him. But he doesn't know I'd follow him anywhere. Anywhere.

I blink heavily before eliminating all space between us, pressing my body against his. He doesn't tense at all, but he doesn't wrap his arms around me either. "I don't want to be just friends. I don't think I ever did." I press my hand to his chest, flattening against his heartbeat and feeling his reaction to me. "I want you, Ben. All of you. Your hands, your mouth, your . . ." I look down, pausing for the courage I need.

"Say it," he growls. God, I love the authority in his voice.

I don't hesitate at his command. Looking into his eyes, I say exactly what I want with the certainty he needs. "Cock. I've thought of you touching me constantly since we were together that first night. It's all I've thought about."

His hands come up and he cups my face. "I won't be able to hold back."

"I don't want you to."

"It's going to be really fucking intense. I don't think I can be gentle with you right now. It's been too damn long since I've had my hands on you and I'm about to start ripping shit apart."

A small laugh rumbles in my throat. He is just as frustrated as I am.

Thank you, Jesus.

I tease the buttons of his uniform, feeling his muscles clench underneath my fingers. "I don't want gentle right now.

I want you to take me."

He nods firmly, understanding exactly what I need. He keeps one hand on my face but brings the other around my neck, gripping it with that possessive hunger of his that riles me up like nothing else. "I was trying to be good, baby. I wanted you to see that I'm not that same guy you once knew. I'll never be that guy. I'll never hurt you, Mia, and I'll fucking kill anyone that does. But this is it. Once I have you again, I'm not letting you go. So you better be damn sure this is what you want, because there's no going back after this."

I snake my hands around his neck, brushing over his hammering pulse. "Good." I tilt my head up and press my lips softly against his. "Fuck me, Ben. Show me that I'm yours." My words blow against his mouth, and they're the only coaxing he needs.

My heart is his and right now, I want him to claim my body.

ben

"FUCK ME, BEN. Show me that I'm yours."

When those words escape her perfect mouth, I feel my entire body surge with power. My adrenaline spikes and the commanding need I have for Mia, that I'd dulled out with friendship, comes screaming back to life inside me. There was never any doubt in my mind who she belonged to. And after tonight, there will never be any doubt in hers either.

"If I'm too rough with you, you need to tell me," I say against her lips, backing her body up to the bed.

I'm so geared up right now, so tightly wound that I know the only way I'll be able to hold back is if she can't handle it. I'm feeling speedy, like a racehorse that's been let out of the gate, and I need her to be honest with me. I've never felt out of control before, but Mia has the ability to make me lose my shit completely.

"Baby, promise me you'll tell me if I hurt you." I push her down onto the bed, grabbing her legs and spreading them wide as I settle in between them.

She stares up at me with nothing but trust in her eyes. I'm certain with the look she's giving me, I can do anything to her right now and she won't waver.

She pulls her top over her head before saying, "I will, but I won't have to. I want this just as bad as you do. Please don't hold back, Ben. I'm not fragile."

No, she isn't. I have to remind myself that this isn't the same Mia that used to be afraid of cliff diving at Rocky Point.

I've met my match in this woman, both in and out of the bedroom.

She begins working at her shorts when I stop her, batting her hands away. "Those are mine to take off." I pull them down with her panties, tossing them somewhere behind me. She's naked, completely bare to me, and I almost forget how to fucking breathe. I take a moment to stare at her, appreciating every dip and curve of her body. Her hands drum the sheet at her sides as she allows me to have my moment. I raise my gaze to her face and she wets her lips. "You're the sexiest woman I've ever seen. And you have no idea, do you? You have no clue how stunning you are." I make quick work of my shirt, unbuttoning it halfway and pulling it over my head to get on with it.

Mia laughs softly below me, stretching her body out on the bed. "I thought you said you weren't going to be gentle with me? I don't want sweet, romantic, Benjamin Kelly right now."

I cock my head at her and she smiles. "You'll take what I give you." I pull my belt off and drop my pants and boxers, stepping out of both. "I can fuck you and tell you how crazy I am about you. I'm very capable of making you scream and worshipping you at the same time." I am about to spread my body on top of hers when she sits up unexpectedly and grabs my cock. Her eyes are blazing, filled with a stark need. I groan deep in my throat and stop her hand from moving. "Fuck, baby. I know you want to play right now, but I'm too damn wound up for that. I'm not coming in your hand, and if you touch me anymore, that's exactly what's going to happen."

She arches her brow at me. So playful, yet seductive at the same time. "I was hoping you'd come in my mouth."

Ah hell. My dirty little angel never ceases to amaze me.

I stroke along her bottom lip with my thumb. "Baby, soon, very soon I will fuck this pretty little mouth. But right now, I need to be inside you. I need to feel you around me."

And then my world collapses in on itself.

Fucking motherfucker. I squeeze my eyes tight and step back out of her needy grasp.

"What is it?"

What the fuck? I run my hands down my face and curse under my breath. "I was not at all anticipating this happening between us for a while. I honestly thought it would take a lot longer for you to see that I'm not a complete dickhead anymore, and let me anywhere near your body." I drop my hands and meet her puzzled face. She has no idea what I am getting at. "I don't have any condoms with me. And I'm not searching the house for them because that's just fucking weird. Please tell me you have some."

Her face falls in disappointment. "No, I don't. You don't have any in your truck?"

Her optimism is adorable.

I shake my head and rake my hand through my hair roughly. "No. Nolan likes to snoop around in there and I'm always afraid he's going to find one and think it's a damn balloon or something."

She giggles and pulls her knees up to her chest.

I'm about to tell her that we don't have to have sex tonight, that I'd be completely content with just holding her, because I would, when suddenly she drops the playful demeanor and looks at me with a fierce passion.

"You know I've only been with you," she says, her voice

dropping to a soft purring sound. "And I'm on birth control, so there wouldn't be any risk of me getting pregnant. So as long as you're clean, I don't see why this is a problem."

I just died. This has to be what heaven is like. Dirty little angels floating around, tempting you with barrier free sex. Is there any man on the planet that could actually say no to this?

I inhale deeply, trying to calm my painful erection that is all for driving into her wet heat without being wrapped up. "I'm clean." *And I apparently don't need that much convincing.* "I've never done it without a condom. Nolan resulted from one that had a tear in it." I step closer to her and she scoots back on the bed, reaching out for me with an eager hand.

"So I'll be your first this way? I love that."

I move toward the bed, getting up on my knees as she relaxes back onto a pillow. "Are you sure though? Baby, I could just eat your pussy for a good hour, maybe several and be fucking perfect with that. There's no need to rush this."

"But there is." She grabs my hand, and I take her other one so that both our hands are linked together. I'm kneeling between her legs, staring down into those chocolate brown eyes that hold me by the balls and could make me do practically anything right now. "We don't have forever, Ben. I'm only here for the summer. I have two months left to be with you and I don't want to waste another second not being with you the way I want to be. I love that you gave me time to get to know who you are now and I wouldn't take that back. But I don't need any more time. I just need you." She spreads her legs, dropping them on either side of mine. "You're the only man that's ever had me. Take what's yours."

This is heaven. It has to be. And we'll talk about this whole forever thing later. There is no way in hell I'm ending this with her at the end of the summer. I don't care how much distance there'll be between us.

"I don't know what the hell I did to ever deserve you, but you'll never take another breath without knowing how special you are to me." I bend down and bring my mouth to hers, needing to feel her breath in me. Needing to swallow her sounds.

She opens up and my tongue slides across hers, stroking deep into her mouth as she grips my neck with one hand and my shoulder with the other. I break the contact because I need more of her. I've gone almost four weeks without her taste and I want it running through me. I need it coursing through my system.

I scoot my body down on the bed and settle between her legs. She opens up with a soft sigh.

"You want it, don't you? You want my tongue to make you beg before my cock does."

Her hand grabs my head and she pushes me down as her response. I grin against her clit before flicking it with my tongue. She arches her hips up to meet every stroke.

Fuck, the way she tastes. Some pussies just taste better than others, and Mia's pussy is sinful. Addicting.

She pulses against my tongue as I run up her length, lingering on her clit before pulling it into my mouth.

"Oh God, Ben."

I suck hard, then harder, needing her orgasm more than I need to breathe. Getting her off gets me off, and Mia is so responsive that it's hard not to come along with her when she does it so perfectly. My eyes run up her body, over her tits that will be getting my attention very soon, and our eyes lock. I knew she'd be watching me. Her hand tightens in my hair as I move in quick circles. She whispers my name, moaning and barely making any sense as her orgasm builds rapidly. She begs me over and over not to stop. That she's right there. That she's so close. She pins me between her legs, unraveling against me as I grip her thighs and consume all of her. And then she finally relaxes her body, her legs dropping to the sides in complete exhaustion as my angel comes back to earth.

"So, so good. I love your mouth. I mean, really. I love your cock too, but your mouth?" She sighs heavily as I crawl up her body, kissing every inch of her. "It really should come with some sort of warning label."

"Mmm, and what would it say? Multiple orgasms await you if you put this between your legs?" I suck her left nipple into my mouth, pulling another low groan out of her. Releasing it with a smirk, I drop my head between her tits and inhale her scent. That berries and cream scent that completely wrecks me. "I love how you smell. Especially right here." I inhale again and growl against her, feeling her squirm beneath me. I glance up at her with a warning. "Don't you dare try to hurry me along. Next to that gorgeous view between your legs, this is where I'd want to die. Right here." I plant a kiss to her cleavage before moving up her body.

"I need you to fuck me now." She sounds urgent, needy even. As if she didn't just come all over my tongue. "Do you think you could do that?"

I slide straight into her pussy as my answer. "Holy fuck, Mia." She's soaked, her need for me is just as strong as my need for her. I groan as she arches her back and presses her tits against my chest. Nothing has ever felt like this, and I know without a doubt that there is no other woman I want to experience this with besides Mia. And I also know I'm done using condoms with her. I won't take her any other way. This is fucking perfection. I'm all the way in her, but I can't move. Not yet. I am too fucking close to losing it and I want this to last.

She wiggles beneath me, urging me on with her hands gripping my ass.

"Give me a second, baby. You have no idea how good you feel right now and I don't want to come in you just yet." I drop my forehead to hers and steady my breathing.

Her tongue darts out and she licks her bottom lip. "Why not? Can't you get hard again right away? I was hoping this wasn't a one and done deal."

I laugh, brushing against her lips with mine. "Are you challenging me? Do you want to see how hard I can fuck you and how hard I can get again just by looking at you? Just say the words and that's what you'll get."

She doesn't say any words. Instead, she clenches down on me and squeezes me tighter than a vise grip.

I rear up, grabbing her legs and pinning them against the mattress as I drive my hips into her. "Is this what you want? Fuck, baby. Is this how you want me to take you?"

I can barely get my words out before I feel my orgasm building at an impressive rate. I'm fucking her like I haven't had her in years, because that's how I feel. I'm a man deprived, and I won't stop until she can't imagine not having me between her legs.

The room becomes filled with our moans and the loud slapping sound of our bodies crashing together.

"Yes! Oh God, Ben. Please." She closes her eyes and arches off the bed, thrusting her chest into the air.

"Mia, I'm coming in you, baby. I'm coming in this sweet pussy."

I give her everything and she takes it, coming on my cock as soon as I tell her I'm filling her. Her skin flushes pink, then red, bursting across her chest and up to her neck. She reaches for me and claws down my chest, giving me the pain that she knows I need.

She's perfect when she comes, a beautiful angel underneath me.

I pull out and she sits up on her elbows, staring between my legs at the erection that is fully hard just for her.

"You came, didn't you?" she asks, her eyes full of shock. She doubts my desire for her, which she'll never do again.

I dip my finger into her and draw it to her mouth, coaxing her to taste what I gave her.

She hits me with that seductive stare she mastered the night in the bar, and sucks on my finger, releasing it with a pop.

My cock lengthens even more at the sight of her. My girl likes it.

"Mmm. I guess that answers that question. Wanna go again?"

I grab her, switching places so that I am now lying on the bed and she is kneeling next to me. "Ride me, baby. I want you to drive this time. Show me how much you want this cock that's rock hard just for you."

She straddles me without hesitation, gripping me in her hand and guiding me into her slick pussy. "Oh God." Her head falls back until I get fully inside her. Then she hits me with those big brown eyes again. "I forgot how deep you are this way. It feels like you're hitting my ribs." She moves slowly, rocking her hips in a gentle rhythm. As if I'm the fragile one.

I practically fucked her through the floor and now she's looking at me as if I'm breakable. I'm not, and she needs to know that.

I grab her neck firmly and pull her down, crashing her mouth against mine. "Do I look delicate to you? Or do I look like a man that's been starving for this pussy." I scrap my teeth along her bottom lip and she whimpers. "Fucking ride me, Mia."

Her eyes widen and she nods once, purposely. And then she reaches behind her and digs her nails into my thighs, rearing up and fucking me with wild abandon.

"Yeah, just like that. So good. So fucking tight, baby." I grunt my praise to her as my eyes wander between her mouth and her tits. I lean in and suck on them, making her scream out and ride me harder. She alternates between rocking her hips, first fast then faster, while crashing down on me. White spots blur my vision as she takes me to the edge.

"I need it, Ben. Oh God, I'm so close." She scratches down my arms and I groan loudly, loving the pain that mingles with the pleasure.

Christ, this woman knows exactly what I need and when to give it to me.

"Are you gonna come on my cock, baby?" I grab her hips and begin directing the tempo, needing that last bit of control.

I can never give it up completely, and even though Mia owns me, I need to dominate how we come together.

"Yes," she answers with a soft plea.

"Come now, angel. I'm right there with you."

I grip her tightly and begin thrusting into her with everything I have. Giving her every part of me.

Feel it. This is how I love you.

We come together, loud and wild, and she collapses on top of me. I wrap my arms around her waist and hold her close, feeling her heart hammering against my chest. Her skin is damp, glistening with sweat. We stay like this for several minutes, our breathing mirroring each other's and coming down to a steadier pace.

Being inside Mia, her body completely connected to mine, is all I'll ever need.

"Here, let me get something to clean you up with."

I slide her next to me and slip on my boxers before I disappear down the hallway. I peak in on Nolan, who is still passed out, before grabbing a hand towel from the bathroom and climbing back into bed.

"We didn't wake him, did we?" she asks as I wipe between her legs.

The sight of my cum leaking out of her makes me want to beat on my chest like a damn caveman. *Mine.* I catch a yawn that she tries to muffle as she climbs under the covers.

I toss the towel into the hamper after wiping myself off. "No, he's out cold." She curls up against my chest as I lie back on my pillow. I stroke her arm, feeling the goose bumps form against my touch like they always do. She hums softly against my skin. "Nolan's a pretty deep sleeper. He fell asleep last year at the Fourth of July fireworks display over Canyon Creek. And that shit was loud. Maybe almost as loud as you."

My girl is a screamer. I love that. I want everyone in the entire state to know what I'm doing to her. My chest expands in pride at the thought.

"I think he gets that from me, though. I can pretty much sleep through anything." Her silence has me straining my neck down to catch her closed eyes. "Mia?"

"Hmm?"

I smile. "Did I render you speechless?"

"Hmm." Her arm that's wrapped around my waist tightens as the rest of her body stays completely limp.

She's falling asleep, but she can't let go of me. It's as if she's afraid I'll slip away from her the moment she passes out. Or that I won't be there when she wakes up. She's holding on to me with everything she has, which is how I've always felt around her. Even when I was only holding on to the memory of us together.

I press my lips to her forehead, pulling the covers up over us both. "Sleep, angel. You have me. I'm never letting you go."

And with those words to her, she finally relaxes.

mia

I DON'T WANT to open my eyes.

I don't want to wake up and have this not be real.

I want to stay asleep for days, months, years even. Because this dream is different. This isn't just my typical nightly fantasy that stars Benjamin Kelly bringing me to orgasm over and over. Not that those aren't amazing. But this dream is better. Because he stayed. He is holding me like he did the first night we were together. It feels so right. So real. And I'm terrified of opening my eyes and discovering that I'm alone. That we're still only friends. I can feel his skin against my cheek. I can smell his scent, the strong masculine pheromones that are purely Ben. Is my mind completely fucking with me right now? I shouldn't be able to feel or smell anything. Right? My curiosity is piqued and I have to risk the disappointment I am sure to feel when I open my eyes.

I peek one, then both open, and I almost cry at the sight of him. I don't know if I've ever been this happy before. Forget sleeping forever. I never want to pry my eyes away from the man that is asleep right next to me.

He's in my bed.

It wasn't a dream.

His breath blows across my forehead, his legs tangling with mine under the covers. It's real. I reach up and brush my finger down his nose, seeing his lip twitch slightly. I run my finger over the tattoo that covers his shoulder, tracing over the outline of the design. It's beautiful. The way the colors blend together, the way it stretches down his arm and over his muscles. It's a scene of objects and quotes, but certain ones stand out. "Nolan" is etched on his skin in the handwriting of a child. It's the sweetest thing, and I trace over it several times with the tip of my finger. Ben stirs underneath me as my finger runs up and over the police shield that is on his upper arm. The words "Honor The Fallen" in bold ink stands out on his tanned skin. I run over the words several times as my mind drifts.

How many fallen men did Ben know? He doesn't have the safest job, and the thought of him being in danger is enough to make me want to hold on to him forever and not let him out of my sight. If something happened to him . . . no. I can't go there.

He stirs beneath me again, and the feel of his finger brushing down my nose brings my attention up to his face.

"Hey." I press my lips to his chest and rest my chin on my hand.

His eyes seem brighter in the morning, almost as if there is a light shining behind them. His hair is a bit messy and he's rocking the perfect amount of stubble. I could get used to morning Ben.

I run my finger down his nose and he catches it, bringing it to his lips.

"I like it better when you're not trying to sneak out on me in the morning." He rolls over onto his side, running his hand down my arm. "You looked like you were stuck in that pretty little head. What's going on?"

I glance from his tattoo back to him. "Have you ever been shot at?" He raises his eyebrows, seemingly unprepared for that type of question. I trace over the words underneath his shield again. "I mean, your job is really dangerous, isn't it?"

"Sometimes. But I've never been put in a situation like that. Luke got shot in the leg a couple years ago." My eyes widen, and he shakes his head at my worried stare. "The bullet barely grazed his shin, but when he tells the story, he almost died. I'm pretty sure his version has gotten him laid on more than one occasion." His hand grips my hip tightly and he pulls me against him. His eyes darken to a devious shade as I become aware of his need for me. Very aware. "Is my girl worried about me?" he asks, rolling on top of me and settling his body between my legs.

"Yes." I wrap my legs around his waist, lifting up my pelvis to grant him access.

He enters me slowly, groaning and dropping his forehead to mine. "Don't be." He kisses my lips once, then once more. "Nothing could take me away from you. You've got me, baby. This is where I belong. Right here." He braces himself on his hands, thrusting into me deeply. "Christ, there's nothing like this." His voice is strained, his eyes focused on my face, gently caressing my features as he moves inside me.

"Ben." I reach up and stroke his cheek.

The connection we share is so strong, so undeniable. I never want to break it. He's so familiar to me. Being with Ben feels like being home. And I can't imagine my life without this man in it. But after the summer is over, what will we have? Will it all just be how this thing between us started out? A beautiful memory that was never meant to last? I can't imagine how difficult leaving him is going to be, so I don't think about it. I don't allow unwanted thoughts to pull me out of this moment with him. I just focus on him.

"Oh God. You feel so good," I moan, lifting my mouth

to his. My legs grip him tighter; my arms holding our bodies together like a taut rubber band. I need every part of him touching me. I can't get close enough. I'll never get close enough.

His hips crash against mine as his hands brace my ankles on his shoulders, tilting my pelvis to that delicious angle. I reach above me and press my hands flat against the headboard, forcing him deeper. Meeting his every thrust. That familiar pull is already building in my core and I watch, mesmerized by the way the muscles of his upper body contract with each thrust.

He runs his eyes down my body and settles right where he's entering me. "Touch yourself for me," he demands with both his tone and his eyes that are daring me to refuse him.

I slide my hand down my body and stop when my fingertips feel the hard edge of his cock sliding in and out of me. "Oh, my God. I'm so wet."

"Fucking right you are. God, Mia. I've never wanted anything as much as I want this. I'll never get enough, baby."

He continues to drive into me while I rub against my soaked clit. We find a rhythm, my two fingers circling while he fucks me, and I suddenly feel drugged with pleasure. At some point, he wraps my legs back around his waist, but I don't even register it happening. I'm lost. Completely lost in the feel of him. Just him.

"I'm close," I pant, seeing a sly smile form on his wet lips.

"You think I don't know that?" He presses his thumb against my fingers and begins moving with me, directing the tempo. I reach up with my free hand and grip his neck, pulling his face down to mine. Our mouths tangle in a brutal kiss, and I feel his air fill my lungs.

We are in that moment together, so completely in tune with each other that neither one of us hear the door creaking open.

"Daddy. I can't get dis off."

Nolan's husky voice causes me to gasp and Ben to curse under his breath. The orgasm that is about to rip my body apart quickly evaporates.

I look over at Nolan, seeing a cupcake in his hand and his face covered in green icing. His big gray eyes dart between me and his father.

"What arwe you doing wiff Pwincess Mia?"

I cover my face with my hand and try to contain my hysterics while Ben slides off me, keeping his back to Nolan. I pull the sheet up to my neck.

"Buddy, can you go wait for me on the couch? I'll be right there."

But Nolan isn't having that. Instead of leaving the room, he climbs up onto the bed, causing Ben to let out a string of muffled curse words as he tries to keep his erection hidden. My entire body is shaking with my laughter as Nolan holds the cupcake out to me, completely unaffected by his father's struggles.

"Can you take dis paper off?" His dimpled grin hits me, along with his crooked smile.

I smile back at him, taking the cupcake and pulling off the wrapper. "Are you having cupcakes for breakfast, Sir Nolan?"

I guess this is my fault. I completely forgot to put all the treats away that I purchased yesterday before I stormed off to bed. But in my defense, I was more concerned with offending Ben with my tits than putting sugary snacks out of the reach of little hands.

Side note: He's definitely not offended by my tits.

He nods quickly and takes his cupcake back. I anticipate him leaving, but no, Nolan has other plans. He crawls toward me and wiggles between Ben and me, flopping down onto my pillow. "Were you and Daddy kissing?"

I look quickly over at Ben, seeing him sliding on his boxers underneath the covers. He winks at me, giving me the go ahead to answer however I want to. I turn my body toward Nolan and prop up on my hand, making sure to keep myself completely covered.

"I was kissing your daddy. When two people really care about each other, they usually kiss." My eyes meet Ben's again. "A lot."

He chews up his bite and takes another one. "Can we go swinnin today, Daddy? I wanna show Pwincess Mia how I can jump in da pool."

Apparently, Nolan is finished discussing anything involving kissing. My answer was either sufficient enough to satisfy his curiosity, or he is a three-year-old boy who has his priorities straight.

He pops the last bit of cupcake into his mouth and reaches his finger toward Ben, running it down his nose.

Ben smiles and does the same back. "Yeah, we can go swimming. But I need to take you back to Mommy's house before dinner."

Nolan sits up with a protesting grunt and pounds his tiny fist into Ben's chest. "No, Daddy. I wanna stay here wiff you and Pwincess Mia."

I haven't seen Nolan display any emotion besides pure joy, but right now, he is definitely not a happy kid.

"Don't hit me, Nolan." Ben's gentle voice he always uses with him is gone and replaced with a stern fatherly tone. Even I cower a bit at it. He grabs Nolan's fist. "If you throw a fit like that again, you aren't going swimming. Do you understand?"

Nolan nods, his face falling as if Ben had just told him that dragons don't exist.

I reach over and run my finger down his nose. He perks

up and does the same to me. "No sad faces allowed. Why don't you go grab me and Daddy a cupcake?"

He grins and scrambles off the bed, the quick tapping of his feet tapering off in the distance.

"Your son just totally cock blocked you. Are you going to be okay down there?" I quickly slide off the bed, brushing over the front of Ben's boxers.

"Not if you keep doing that I won't be," he warns. His hand grabs mine and he pulls the two fingers that I'd been using moments ago into his mouth, sucking on them as I stare with fascination. That has to be one of the hottest things I've ever seen.

I think there are two types of guys. Guys that pretend they're into eating pussy just to please the girl they're with, and guys that crave it like it's their favorite food on the menu. Ben is definitely the latter.

He slips out of the bedroom with a cocky grin and returns moments later in his swimsuit.

I dress as fast as I can, hearing Nolan's feet and animated voice coming down the hallway. I have just secured my bikini top, batting away Ben's naughty fingers, when he comes in, carrying two bright green frosted cupcakes.

"Pwincess Mia! I can jump into da pool without my fwotties!" He practically throws our cupcakes at us, his excitement uncontainable. "I'm gonna go get my bavin suit!"

"Wait a minute, buddy. It's hanging up in the bathroom," Ben yells after him. He turns to me and leans in, kissing my icing covered lips. "I should eat my cupcake off you." He licks his lips, only pulling back an inch. "My girl would look good covered in icing."

"I want to be covered in *your* icing," I tease.

His jaw twitches, along with another body part I'm sure.

He growls into my hair, smacking me on my ass before he goes off after Nolan.

I pick my phone up off the floor, laughing softly at the image of it getting flung off the bed in the heat of passion last night. I want to check in on my mom before I spend the day in the pool with my two favorite boys. She answers after the second ring.

"Hello?" She coughs before clearing her throat, the muffled sound coming through the phone.

I sit down on the edge of the bed, my entire body tensing up. "Mom, are you okay?" She can't be sick, not now. Not when things are just starting to fall into place for me.

God, that sounds awful. How selfish is my thinking right now?

She sniffs a few times, clearing her throat once again before replying. "Oh, I'm fine, sweetheart. It's just a little cold." *Cough. Cough.*

A little cold to my mom in her condition isn't something to take lightly. I am suddenly feeling panicky.

"How long have you had it? Do you have a fever? How's your appetite?"

"Sweetheart, please relax. I'm fine, really. My nose started running yesterday and now I have this little tickle in my throat. That's all. No fever. No nausea."

"So you're eating?"

It's very important for my mom to be able to keep her food down. She had lost so much weight when she started her treatments and we had finally gotten it back up to a healthy number a few months ago. I never want to see my mom that thin again.

"Yes, yes I'm eating. Soup mainly, but that's good for a cold, which is what this is, Mia. I don't want you worrying yourself to death over this. Your aunt has everything under control."

"I can't help it that I worry, Mom. You know that."

She sighs, clearing her throat again. "Yes, I know. But I'm still the parent here, and if I say that I don't want you to worry, then you need to listen to me. Now tell me, is the weather as miserable there as it is here? It's so hot outside right now that you can't even breathe. And don't get me started on the damn sand fleas."

Sand fleas. I don't miss those. They are everywhere in Georgia when the weather gets hot. These tiny little nats that will bite you and make your life miserable.

"It is really hot, but you know I've always loved Alabama summers. The air is just better here or something, I don't know. I'm getting ready to get in the pool now."

She sniffs again. "Oh, well, why are you wasting your time talking to me? Go have fun, sweetheart."

"I'm not wasting my time. I just wanted to see how you were doing."

"I'm doing great besides this tiny little cold. So please go swim some laps for me. Maybe by next summer, we'll be able to go to the pool on base together like we used to."

I stand up and smile. "Absolutely. You'll be so strong by then, Mom. I love you."

"Love you, too."

She will be stronger by next summer. I can't wait to see my mom doing everything she used to do.

But with that joy comes the heart wrenching sadness of realizing that I'll be with her in Georgia and not here with Ben.

Life can be a total bitch sometimes.

No, fuck that. I'm not going to let anything ruin my day or the rest of my time here. After brushing my teeth and pulling my hair up into a bun, I walk outside to the pool.

"Pwincess Mia! Watch dis!"

Nolan is standing on the edge at the deep end while Ben stands a few feet in front of him in the water. I walk around and watch him with excitement. He squats down ever so slightly before jumping off the side and splashing into the water. He goes under and pops back up after a few seconds, prompting Ben to grab him.

I clap for him and sit down on the edge. "That was awesome. You're such a big boy doing that without floaties. I don't even know if I'm brave enough to do that."

Ben moves closer to me in the water, holding Nolan out in front of him so he can splash around. He turns his body, putting himself between me and Nolan. His eyes do that shift from sweet to mischievous, that he seems to do better than anyone, as he rakes over my body.

"You better hurry up and put that body of yours under the water before I do very inappropriate things to you in front of my son."

I give him a disapproving smirk. *He wouldn't dare.*

He leans in and nips at my bottom lip, sending a chill up my back in the sweltering heat. "I'm completely serious," he warns with a smolder that I feel in places only he is familiar with.

"Well, I'd hate to see you put those handcuffs to use if I choose to disobey orders, Officer Kelly." I shoot him a teasing look as I slide into the water. It's warm but still cools my body off instantly.

He brushes his lips against my ear. "You'll be in my handcuffs soon enough. Disobeying me has nothing to do with that."

Good God. I was completely kidding, but by the look Ben's

currently giving me, he definitely isn't. And I am down with whatever ways he wants to use them on me.

He backs away from me and holds Nolan out in front of him. "Show Princess Mia how you can swim, buddy."

I hold out my hands to him, backing up to the wall. His little legs kick as hard as they can, splashing Ben in the process as he slaps his arms against the water. It takes him a little while, but he finally makes it to me with the biggest dimpled grin on his face.

"You're like a little fish." I wrap him up in my arms and he immediately draws me closer into a hug. He buries his face into my neck, holding on to me with all of his strength. "You give good hugs, Sir Nolan."

"I wove you," his husky little voice declares.

I lock eyes with Ben who is watching us intently. "I love you, too," I vow, never drifting from Ben's eyes. His lips part slightly as he moves closer to us. Strong arms find my waist under the water and he pulls the two of us against his chest. And we stay like that for as long as Nolan allows, Ben and I stealing kisses above Nolan's head. It's the best time I've ever had in that pool.

A perfect day with my two favorite Kelly boys.

ben

I 'VE NEVER HEARD my son say I love you to anyone besides me.

Not even to my family, and I know he loves them. He is crazy about my parents and my sister. And I'm sure he loves his mom because all three-year-olds love their parents no matter how shitty they are to them. But he's never said those words to her in front of me. Like the nose thing, those three words were something that he and I shared. Something that he kept between the two of us.

Until he met Mia.

And I can't blame him for loving her. She is incredibly easy to love. Hearing him say it to her hit me right in my soul. It was the same way I felt when he said it to me. Like I'd just been given this amazing gift. And he meant it. My son is brutally honest with his feelings. He'll tell you exactly how he feels and he won't sugar coat it. He didn't hesitate in the slightest either.

His words were strong and steady, just like I knew mine would be when she eventually heard them.

When she said it back to him, she looked right at me with those eyes that were impossible to look away from. No woman has ever looked at me the way Mia does. It was new, yet familiar at the same time. Like she's been looking at me like that our entire lives. Like she knew me better than anyone.

I was use to women staring at me because they wanted me. I was familiar with that look. That desire that was completely superficial and void of any real emotion. I could easily break away from those women. I wasn't completely pulled in by a single fucking glance. Ready to hand over my entire life because of just one look. But that's how it was with Mia.

When she looked at me, she saw me. My hopes, my fears, my future, that for all intents and purposes, belonged to her. She fucking owned me with that stare and I never wanted to look away.

I wanted Mia to come with me to take Nolan to Angie's apartment. She seemed uneasy about it at first, but Nolan turned on that Kelly charm that she'd become completely helpless against. I wasn't sure how Angie was going to take it, but honestly, I didn't give a shit. No matter how much she wanted to deny it, Angie was very aware of my feelings toward her. I've always been straight forward and honest, even when I allowed the occasional blow job. And looking back, I hate that I was weak in those moments of loneliness.

But she knew we didn't have a future, and I wanted to show off mine.

"Oh, um, I figured I would just wait in the truck." Mia looks at me with an anxious expression as I stand outside her side of the truck.

I hadn't mentioned that she would be walking inside with me, but she is well aware of that intention now. She hesitantly puts her hand in mine and allows me to help her down.

"Ben, really, I don't have to go inside."

I close the passenger door, pulling her against me and inhaling her hair. "Baby, relax. There's no reason to be nervous. You're the first woman I've ever introduced to my son's mother."

"That's supposed to make me relax?" she asks with tense-ness in her voice. "If anything, that makes me even more nervous."

I gaze down at her, cocking my head to the side. "I've also never introduced any woman I've been with to Nolan before." She seems to ease in my arms, her bottom lip finally releasing from her mouth. "That's how much you mean to me. I want you to be a part of Nolan's life as much as you're a part of mine. He loves you, and Angie's bound to find out about you eventually. We might as well get this over with now."

She shifts on her feet slightly while she stays in my arms, keeping her eyes on mine. "Is her son the only Kelly boy that feels that way?"

Wow. Leave it to Mia to put a guy on the spot. I'm certain there isn't any question that is off limits to her. But that's how she is. She isn't afraid to call you out on anything. And I'd never want her to be any different.

"No." I brush my lips against hers, teasing her with my tongue. "I'm sure my father loves you like a daughter."

She smiles against me before planting quick kisses to my lips. "Oh, is that how you're going to play this? What if I said it first, would you give it up then?" I arch my brow at her, daring her to make the first move. "I . . ." she kisses my jaw, "love . . ." her lips move to my ear, "sunflowers." She chuckles against me.

I bit back my smile, narrowing my eyes at her when she leans back.

She wipes the grin off her face and shoots me a flirtatious stare.

"You know, I carry a spare set of handcuffs in my glove compartment that I won't hesitate to use on you." I grab her wrists and pin them behind her back, bringing our chests together. Her breath hitches and she purrs against me. "Mmm, you'd like that, wouldn't you? Not being able to touch me while I have my way with you. Giving yourself up to me completely."

She nods and licks her lips.

Damn parental duties. My dirty girl wants me to take her right here, and the only thing stopping me is currently sitting in the backseat of my truck, swinging his sword around his head like a maniac.

I release her wrists and kiss her once, then once more. "Later, pretty girl."

We walk up to Angie's apartment, Nolan running ahead of us. He knocks lightly on the door and then bangs on it several times with his sword. As Mia and I walk up behind him, the door swings open.

Angie's eyes are immediately drawn to Mia, who is struggling to pull her hand out of mine.

But I'm not having that. I hold on tighter.

Angie crosses her arms over her chest in annoyance. "Let me guess. Princess Mia?" Her eyes shift to mine. "Really, Ben? Did you have to bring your latest hook up to my apartment?"

Nolan runs past her into the living room, which I'm grateful for. If we are going to have it out right now, I don't want him hearing it.

"Don't be a bitch, Angie. I'm doing you a courtesy here. Our son is going to be spending a lot of time with Mia, so I figured you two should meet."

Mia steps forward, as much as my grip on her allows, and holds her free hand out. "Hi, Angie. It's so nice to meet you. You have the sweetest little boy. I'm crazy about him."

Angie glances down at Mia's hand, refusing to take it. She turns her attention back to me instead. "Do you really think it's wise to confuse our son by introducing him to your flavor of the month? And I thought we were trying to work things out between us, Ben." She drops her hands then and wipes the irritation from her face, replacing it with a false hurt. "It really is what's best for Nolan."

"Maybe I should just go wait in the truck," Mia says softly, dropping her hand.

I shake my head at her. "No. You belong where I am."

"Oh, give me a fucking break," Angie barks out in irritation.

I look past her and see Nolan at the kitchen table with a box of crayons. Dropping Mia's hand, I step closer to Angie and she tenses up. "You're lucky he didn't hear that. And don't ever take your bitterness out on Mia. She never did anything to you, and she's amazing with Nolan."

"I'm his mother. And you should be more concerned with fixing our family than who your dick wants to play with."

"Ben, can I please have the keys to the truck?" Mia asks, holding her hand out to me, palm up.

Even though she states it as a question, she isn't asking me. But I don't want her to leave. Fuck Angie. Mia has every right to be where I am.

Unfortunately, I know now that Angie will never calm down as long as Mia is in front of her.

I reluctantly pull my keys out of my pocket and hand them to her. "Thank you." She turns her head toward Angie and offers her a smile. "I hope you realize how lucky you are to have Nolan."

Angie grimaces at her comment. I wait until Mia is out of earshot before I tear into the woman who makes my life a living hell. "Don't ever talk to Mia like that again. She doesn't deserve to be disrespected by you."

"What the hell do I care if I hurt your fling's feelings?"

I step closer to her. "She is not a fling. That woman is it for me. Do you get that? She's not going anywhere, so it would be in your best interest to accept her. Our son sure as hell has."

She inhales sharply. "What does that mean?"

"He told her he loved her today. Does he tell you that?"

Her bottom lip begins to tremble, prompting her to pull at it with her fingers. "I just don't understand why you can't at least try to make this work."

I am over this conversation. If she doesn't understand that the two of us will never work by now, she'll never understand it.

I push past her and walk over to Nolan, kissing the top of his head. "I love you, buddy. I'll see you soon, okay?"

"Wove you, Daddy. Look what I dwawed for you." He holds up the paper he's been working on.

It's three people, all looking like circles with stick limbs coming out of them. Two of them are larger than the third. He's even labeled us in his chicken scratch handwriting.

"Dats you, dats Pwincess Mia, and dats me." He hands it to me with a smile before he runs his finger down my nose.

I repeat the gesture and hold the picture against my chest. "Thanks, buddy." I rustle his hair before I walk toward the doorway.

Angie avoids my eyes, looking down at her feet instead. I don't have anything else to say to her so I walk out of her apartment and close the door behind me.

I had a feeling she wouldn't take meeting Mia very well. Angie still held on to the idea that we were going to wind up together. And considering that I've never introduced her to anyone before, I'm sure that only added to her delusion. But pining after me didn't excuse her behavior toward Mia. And I'll never let her treat my girl like that again.

I climb into my truck after folding up Nolan's drawing and slipping it into my back pocket. "I'm sorry about that. She won't talk to you like that again. I promise." I reach for Mia's hand and she places it in mine with a smile. She seems completely unaffected by the hate she just had directed at her.

"It's okay, I get it." She links her fingers through mine as I pull out of the apartment complex. "She loves you, and she's hurt that the two of you aren't together. I'm sure it isn't easy for her."

Jesus. She doesn't even have a negative thing to say about Angie after that bitchy encounter. She actually feels sorry for her.

"I don't think Angie loves me. I think she's just desperate for attention. We had one night together and neither one of us remembers any of it."

She shakes her head in disagreement. "She definitely loves you. I can tell." Her head rests back on the seat and she turns it toward me. Our eyes meet briefly before I have to put them back on the road. "Did you ever try to make it work with her?"

"Yeah, after Nolan was born. I knew Angie wanted us to be a family and I owed it to Nolan to at least try. They moved in with me after the two of them were released from the hospital. But it only lasted two weeks." Her hand tightens in mine. "We fought constantly about everything and I was fucking miserable all the time. Having a baby at twenty-three was stressful enough, and then throw in the fact that I couldn't stand my son's mother. It wasn't good. When I told her it wasn't going to work, she freaked out, threatening to keep Nolan away from me. I took her to court to make sure I'd at least get my time with him and that only pissed her off even more."

I park the truck in my usual spot at my parents' house. I help Mia out on her side, keeping her hand in mine as we walk toward the pool.

"Sometimes I wish I would've never slept with her that night, but then I wouldn't have Nolan. And I can't imagine not having that little maniac."

She laughs softly against my shoulder as we round the pool. "I can't imagine you not having him either."

I slide the door open, placing my hand on her back and moving her ahead of me into the house. Tessa is sitting on the couch, her lap completely covered in used tissues and her face in her hands.

"Tessa? What's wrong?" Mia goes straight to my sister, sitting down next to her.

"Are you all right?" I ask, moving in front of her. I haven't seen Tessa cry since we were younger, and back then, I was usually the cause of it. The older she gets, the less she lets things get to her.

If she had balls, they'd be made of steel.

She looks up at me and then back to Mia. "Oh, my God. Are you guys together now?" Mia nods and Tessa begins to cry harder. Not the reaction I had been expecting. Tessa was my biggest supporter when it came to winning over Mia. "That makes me so happy. You have no idea." She sobs, prompting Mia to wrap her arms around her.

"Do you need a girls' night?" Mia asks, giving me a knowing look over Tessa's shoulder.

I pick up on the message loud and clear. The two of them don't need me here for this. Nor do I really want to be here for whatever the fuck happens at a girls' night.

I lean down and kiss Mia's forehead. "I'm gonna head out. I'll see you after work tomorrow." She winks at me and nods against Tessa. I place my hand on my sister's shoulder. "If you say this is because of Luke, I'll go find him right now and beat his ass." She whimpers against Mia, and I would've taken that as a yes until she begins shaking her head.

Fucking women and their mixed signals. A simple yes or no would've been nice.

I exhale loudly in annoyance. "Just call me if you need me." I smile once more at Mia and get the hell out of there before I get any more cryptic responses.

mia

"**S**EE, IT'S A good thing I stocked up like I did yesterday," I say, carrying over two bags of chips and the box of cookies that Nolan and I had made a dent in yesterday.

Girls' night can't exist without some sort of junk food.

I drop them onto the coffee table and settle in next to Tessa, turning my body toward her. She isn't crying anymore, but she looks emotionally drained. I tuck my legs underneath me and place my hand on her knee. "What happened with Luke?"

She sniffs, leaning her head so it rests on the back of the couch. Her eyes are puffy and bloodshot and her nose is bright red. I've never seen Tessa cry before. Not even when we were younger. She was always the stronger one out of the two of us.

"I didn't know where Luke stood on the whole kid thing. We've never talked about it and I didn't want to just drop the baby bomb in his lap without being somewhat prepared for his reaction." She reaches up and wipes a tear from her face. "I was anticipating him saying that he'd want to wait a few years to start a family, and then I'd say something like *instead of waiting a few years, how do you feel about waiting a few months*? But he didn't say that." She looks down into her lap and begins picking at her nail polish.

"What did he say?"

"He said he didn't know if he wanted kids. He said that

every time he saw Ben and Nolan together, he never once thought that was something he'd want someday." She lifts her head and looks at me. "I got so angry. I pushed him away from me and started screaming at him. I told him I was tired of whatever the hell it was we were doing together and that I didn't want to see him anymore." She starts crying again, and I grab her hand before she continues. "I don't even know if he was fully committed to me. He could've been fucking every girl in Ruxton for all I know, and then the thought of him getting all those girls pregnant pissed me off even more. I was yelling and crying. I don't even know if I was making any sense. He tried to calm me down, but I couldn't even look at him. I told him never to call me again and I left."

I grab a tissue out of the box and hand it to her. "So you didn't tell him you might be pregnant?"

Even if she and Luke weren't together anymore, I still thought he should know about it.

She chuckles softly, which completely throws me off.

Ending things with the father of your unborn child doesn't seem humorous to me.

"The timing of this whole thing couldn't have been more fucked up. After I got home, I went to the bathroom and low and behold, there was my stupid period. That bitch really took her sweet ass time making an appearance." She shakes her head and drops it to the side, leaning it against the couch. "I keep thinking that if I would've just waited a day, that whole conversation wouldn't have happened and we'd still be screwing around. But I'm glad I didn't wait. I want a family someday. I want to get married and have kids and I wouldn't get that with him. I'd just be wasting my time."

Her words are certain, but she seems saddened by the loss of whatever it was that she and Luke shared.

I tighten my grip on her hand. "I'm really sorry things didn't work out. With Luke and the baby. I know you were excited about being a mom."

She shrugs. "It's probably for the best. I see what my brother has to go through raising a baby with somebody he isn't with. And I'm sure Luke would've ended things once I told him that I was keeping it." She grabs a few cookies and rests back on the arm of the couch. "I am going to miss the sex though. My God."

I chuckle and grab a bag of chips. "That good?" She eyes me up humorously. "Well, there's always Reed. Have you two ever gotten together?"

I really had no idea if the two of them had ever hooked up. Reed was a good looking guy, and Tessa was, well, she was Tessa.

She holds her hand up to stop me, grimacing. "Gross. That would be like sleeping with Ben. And he's got a lot of baggage. Didn't he tell you about his last girlfriend?"

I shake my head and dive into my chip bag, preparing myself for some gossip.

"It's really fucked up. He started dating this girl senior year, Molly Mcafferty, and they were like, crazy in love. Everyone thought that they'd end up married with a shit load of babies someday." She gets up off the couch and walks to the fridge, returning with two beers and handing me one before reclaiming her seat. "But that obviously didn't happen." Tessa takes a sip of her beer and licks her lips. "Molly went to college in Virginia and Reed stayed here, getting on at his dad's company. He was determined to make it work though and stayed completely faithful to her. I mean, he acted like they were married already. He wouldn't even look at other girls. He wrote her letters all the time and would take road trips every weekend to go see her, but she never came back here to see him. Not even during holidays. And after a while, she stopped calling him all together."

I have an idea where this story is going and I almost don't want to hear anymore. Reed is a sweet guy, and doesn't deserve what I fear Tessa is about to tell me.

She continues with a heavy sigh. "I voiced my opinion on their seemingly one-sided relationship and he got all pissed at me. I told him that if he was so certain that she wasn't two timing him, that he should go see her during the week when she wasn't expecting him."

"Did he?"

"Yup. He walked right in on her banging some dude in her dorm room."

I have the sudden urge to go find Reed and hug him and beat the shit out of this Molly chick. I despise cheaters. My mom's last boyfriend was one.

"Oh, God. Poor Reed. Has he dated anybody since her?"

She digs into her bag of chips, popping a few in her mouth before answering. "I wouldn't classify hooking up with random chicks as dating. He's like the king of one-night stands around here."

I chuckle softly.

It could've been Reed that night at the bar, buying me purple drinks and telling me he'd lose his mind if he didn't get inside me soon. That thought is quickly pushed out of my head. I don't want to imagine giving myself to anyone but Ben. I belong to him.

"He's just afraid of falling for some chick and then getting crushed again," she continues. "But he's never admitted that to me. He acts as if Molly didn't completely wreck him, but he didn't see what I saw. That boy was destroyed."

We both chew up our mouthfuls, placing our chip bags on the coffee table when we are finished.

I am picking at the label on my beer bottle when I feel a pair of eyes on me. I look up and meet her beaming smile. "What?"

"You got naked in front of him last night, didn't you?"

There's the Tessa I know and love. I chuckle and shake my head. "No. I sent him a text that was meant for you." I pull my phone out of my pocket and show it to her.

She arches her brow, reading over the text several times. "Damn. Well, that's definitely one way to go about getting him out of the friend zone. How did he react to this?"

"How do you think he reacted to it?" I ask playfully. I scoot over next to her so that we can rest our heads against each other's. Our legs are stretched out in front of us with our feet propped up on the edge of the coffee table. "You were right."

"I usually am. But what exactly are you referring to?"

I sigh, pausing for dramatic effect. She bumps her knee against mine, indicating that she isn't having my stalling tactics today.

"I love him."

I actually feel my heart swell inside my chest when I admit it out loud. The butterflies that only Ben can evoke inside my stomach begin fluttering about in there. I feel my love for him streaming through me as if it runs through my veins. And I know without a doubt that I'll love him fiercely and forever.

Her hand squeezes my knee. "Of course you do. And he loves you. It's ridiculously obvious and annoying now that I'm single." She yawns at the end of her observation, prompting me to do the same at the sound of hers.

I want to believe Tessa. I want to believe what my own heart is telling me. But I'll never be sure until he speaks those words to me himself. A part of me thinks I shouldn't love him, but for completely different reasons than I've ever had before. I know how hard it's going to be to leave him when I have to go back to Georgia. And leaving my heart here isn't going to make it any easier. Maybe that's why Ben hasn't said those words to me, if he even feels them at all. Maybe he's being sensible and keeping his heart out of this.

But I want him to jump off that cliff after me. I want him to feel that rush and risk the pain because I'm willing to.

I'd risk it all.

⁓

"YOU KNOW YOU'RE best friends with someone when you're willing to handcuff them, while they're practically naked, and help them get ready for a sex fest with your brother," Tessa says through a smile that I hear rather than see.

I can't see much of anything in the position I am currently in besides the headboard and the comforter.

She fastens the handcuffs to my wrists, securing my arms behind my back. "This is nuts, considering we don't have a key for these. How fucked up would it be if he got held up at work and you had to stay like this for hours? Or days?"

Shit. I hadn't thought about that. God, that would be awful. Not to mention embarrassing. I'm not sure how I'd manage to go to the bathroom like this.

I open my mouth to respond when I hear the sound of the sliding glass door opening.

"Showtime," Tessa says. "I'll be heading out for a few hours. Try not to kill him."

"Thanks," I whisper.

My entire body is buzzing with anticipation as she leaves the room, closing the door behind her. I hear muffled voices in the distance, laughing to myself at the speech Tessa rehearsed with me when I asked her to help me out tonight.

Mia was not acting like herself today. She seemed a bit on edge and a little hostile. I had to restrain her. And then the kicker. *She's been a bad girl, Ben. A very bad girl.*

I would've loved to have seen her face when she delivered that line. And his for that matter.

The floorboards in the hallway creak with his footsteps that inch closer until finally, the door swings open.

I can't see him, but I can hear him clearly with the one ear that is facing the ceiling. I am kneeling on the edge of the bed, my body angled down and my cheek resting on the comforter. My wrists are bound behind my back, and I'm only wearing a very skimpy pair of black panties. They barely cover anything and I might as well be naked right now. And by the sound of Ben's heavy panting, he isn't hating this surprise.

"Dear God. A man should be warned before he walks in on you like this. I almost came at the sight of you, baby." He moves closer and places his hand on my lower back, running it up my spine. I whimper at his touch. It's like fire melting ice. "My dirty girl looks absolutely stunning face down. And I bet you like this, don't you? I bet you're dripping right now."

"Touch me and find out."

His hand moves lower, teasing me between my legs. "Holy fuck," he grunts, sliding my panties down to my knees. His fingers dip inside me, moving in a steady rhythm as I moan against his touch. His lips press against my back, licking and kissing my skin. "What do you want, angel? Tell me and I'll give it to you."

"You, Ben. I want you."

"And you're going to get me, sweetheart. But I want you to be specific right now. Do you want me to make you come like this?"

I groan loudly into the mattress.

Jesus. His fingers are like magic. I am certain he can get me off in two seconds with them if he wants to. But I know what he wants to hear and what I want him to give me.

"I want you to do whatever you want with me. Take what you need and don't hold back. This belongs to you."

"Yes, baby." He removes his fingers, and the sound of him sucking on them nearly pushes me over the edge. And then I hear his belt loosening and I'm reminded of one more very important thing.

This needs to be said before he uses my body for his own pleasure. This is my fantasy as much as it is his.

"Leave your uniform on."

"Fuck yes." The sound of a zipper lowering is the last noise I hear before he enters me. We both moan together, his louder than mine, as his hands grip my forearms. "Christ, you're perfect. I don't think I've ever been this hard."

He moves in and out of me, taking what he needs. His power during sex is immeasurable. The way his grip tightens on me, the way his hips slam against my backside. He is fucking me with such force, such greedy need. And God, I want everything he is giving me. I want him to possess every inch of me. I am certain my body is specifically made for his pleasure and his for mine. Our sounds and his words to me ring out around us. He tells me how badly he wants me. How nothing has ever felt like this. And how he'll never get enough. I feel everything he gives me and every word he speaks. This is what being in love feels like. Raw. Honest. He makes me feel beautiful and wanted, even in this vulnerable position. When he's close to losing it, he presses his lips to my ear and his fingers find my clit. And when he tells me to fucking come, my body answers him immediately.

I'm panting into the comforter, trying to steady my breathing, as he unfastens the handcuffs. But I know we're not done. If I've learned anything from being with Ben, it's that my insatiable hunger for him will always be met by his need for me. We'll never be easily gratified when it comes to each other. Even after we've given every piece of ourselves, we'll still want more.

His hands massage my wrists, rubbing the life back into them as I turn over onto my back. My panties are finally removed and he tosses them somewhere off the bed. He pushes my one leg close to my body as he enters me again, grinding his hips against mine.

"Keep your eyes on me," he commands as his forehead beads up with sweat. He grips my other knee and pushes it against my chest, leaning his hard body into mine and stroking me deeper.

Even if I wanted to look away, which I don't—let's be clear about that—I doubt I'd be able to. Him fucking me in his uniform has gone way past any expectation I could've conjured up. I watch his eyes and the possessive gleam in them. The fullness of his mouth and how it stays slightly parted. The tease of his tongue as it licks the corner of his lips. My eyes dart up to his hair and I want to grab it, to pull it hard and bring his mouth down to me. To steal that tongue of his and hold it captive in my mouth and between my legs.

But it's his eyes that command the most attention from me. He doesn't just look at me like a man who, as he so eloquently put it, is starved for my pussy. He looks at me like a man who would do anything for it. Who would do anything for *me*. It's a look that would completely throw me off balance if I wasn't prepared for it.

But I'm prepared.

"Talk to me."

His lip twitches with that knowing smile of his and he slides out of me, grabbing me by my neck and sitting me up so we're face to face. I'm pulled into his lap, my legs wrapped around his waist, and he brings his mouth to mine.

"And say what, angel? That I could kiss you for hours. That I love the taste of you on my tongue."

He licks along my bottom lip and I open up for him, allowing him the access we both want. He explores my mouth, breathing his fire into me and setting me ablaze from the inside out. And then he breaks our kiss and presses his lips to my ear, his hands holding me tightly against him.

"You're going to have to be specific. There are a lot of things I could say to you right now." His voice is a low rumble, like thunder in the distance. He leans back and commands my attention with the storm in his eyes.

I shift in his lap so he brushes against my entrance. "I want all your words. I want to be filled with them so that when I go home, I'll never forget how I made you feel." I'm hovering over him, wet and ready when he grips my hips and prevents me from lowering myself onto him.

He brushes his lips along my jaw, nipping at my skin. "You are home," he whispers.

I lower my face into the crook of his neck, biting back the tears that sting my eyes.

He strokes my hair with one hand, his other still firmly holding me above him. "I'll always want this, Mia. I could have you every day for the rest of my life and I'd never get enough of you."

"Me too," I say, finally leaning back and letting him see my face. He reaches up and brushes the tear off my cheek with his thumb. A smile teases my lips and he gives me one in return. "Can I have it now?" I ask, shifting in his arms so he brushes against my clit. A gasp escapes my lips when he applies the slightest amount of pressure to my swollen sex.

"You want it?"

I nod, slowly, emphasizing my desire.

He eases me down onto him, grunting when I'm fully seated. I let him take the lead, moving my hips in the rhythm he wants. He keeps his eyes on my mouth, a constant of his that I love. He isn't ashamed about his obsession with certain parts of my body, and I'll gladly let him stare at me with that wild hunger of his.

His one hand digs into my hip while the other pushes on the center of my back, arching me up so he can take my left breast into his mouth.

"Ben, my God."

I watch him leave bite marks all over my chest, whimpering each time I feel his teeth graze my skin. He tilts my head, giving him access to my neck while his other hand grabs my ass and grinds me into him. I rake down his back through his shirt and he groans against my shoulder.

"Fuck. Get there, baby. I'm not coming without you."

I rock harder into him. "Bite me." His teeth skim over my shoulder and then I feel it. The sharp sting that pulls a gasp out of me, like I've been starving for a breath. "Ben." My orgasm knots in my stomach, radiating up to my chest, and I grab his face to make him look at me. "Coming. Now." I can barely get my words out as my climax takes over, burning me from the inside out.

I fall around him, a pile of embers as he gives me his release.

My eyes are already closing when he positions me on the

bed so my head can rest on a pillow. And the sensation of the bed dipping next to me and his lips on my forehead are the last thing I register before I slip into a dream.

I KNOW I'M alone before I open my eyes.

His body isn't tangled with mine, his breath isn't blowing on my skin, and I simply feel like a part of me is missing. I rub my face into the pillow before opening my eyes. And there, lying in the spot that belongs to Ben is a bouquet of sunflowers. I could cry right here. And I do.

He remembered.

ben

S HE WAS PERFECT.

No other woman got to me the way Mia did. No other woman will ever know what I need without me having to ask for it. I want control, but I also want her to take what's hers. To tell me what she needs when I might hesitate to give it to her. To demand I fuck her harder, to bite her there, and to bare my soul to her.

And I almost said it.

I love you.

The words were right there on the tip of my tongue, but I swallowed them down.

I know she is waiting for my own admission before she gives me that heart of hers that she so fiercely protects. But once I have that last piece of her, I won't be able to let her go. And how much of an asshole would I be if I asked her to choose between going back to Georgia to take care of her mother and having a life with me? Mia is mine, and she'll be mine forever, but I can't have her two hundred and forty miles away from me. And my only other option is packing up my shit and moving to Georgia with her, but that means leaving Nolan behind. Because of my screwed up situation with Angie, I'll never be able to take him with me. Which means that I am fucked.

Completely fucked.

Leaving her this morning was the hardest thing I've ever done. She was an angel next to me, curling up against my body as if she couldn't get close enough. I loved how our bodies sought each other's even in sleep. We were completely entwined, one entity instead of two. It was hard to tell where my body ended and hers began. And still, I needed her closer. I wanted her with me at all times. Every second I spent with Mia, I fell harder.

And fuck, I wanted to fall. I wanted to risk everything for something so unpredictable. Something I didn't quite understand. Loving her was wild and I wanted more of it. I wanted all of it.

Figure out your shit, Kelly. Then make her yours.

My post Mia mood was tainted by the day I was having. Everything seemed to be going to shit, and to top it off, I had a partner that was suddenly into sharing his feelings with me. By midmorning, I was very aware of the reasoning behind my sister's tears last night. And I couldn't tell what bothered Luke more; the fact that he got dumped or the fact that he had no fucking clue as to why.

"It was completely out of nowhere," he informs me for the hundredth time today as we patrol downtown Ruxton.

No matter what topic I brought up or what the hell we were doing, Tessa crept into the conversation. I can't say anything, though. I did the same shit the other day when I couldn't get my mind off Mia.

"I know you really don't care to know the details of my sex life."

"No, but that's never stopped you from sharing before."

In fact, he over-shared most of the time. Luke didn't have a filter when it came to his sex life, even when it involved my sister.

He exhales exhaustively, dropping his head back to the seat. "I just don't get it. She was insatiable that night and the next morning. I don't think I have any semen left."

"Jesus, man. I don't want to know that shit."

"Sorry. But what the fuck? She goes from not being able to get enough of me one minute, to dumping my ass the next. And she didn't even give me a reason. I could fucking work with a reason."

He starts scrolling through his phone, no doubt debating on sending her another pleading text message. I've had to stop him seven times already today from embarrassing himself.

"Do I need to throw that out the window?"

He shoves it back into his pocket with pure aggravation. "She didn't say anything to you?"

He was in deep. I knew Luke was infatuated with Tessa, but I hadn't realized until today that he was in love with her. I don't think he knows that though, and if he does, I doubt he'll admit it. Especially after getting dumped for the first time in his life.

I turn the receiver volume up on the radio before answering. "No, in the ten minutes it's been since you last asked me that same question, she hasn't said anything to me. The only thing I know is that she looked really upset."

I begin tailing a car that is going twelve over the speed limit. I'd normally let it go if we weren't currently in a school zone and I wasn't in a shit mood. Having a kid has made me stricter on certain things, and the asshole in front of me picked the wrong day to go a little heavy on the gas. We've already ticketed nine people today, all of whom decided it was in their best interest to give me an attitude. And once you argue over a driving violation with me, I'm not giving you a fucking warning.

Luke grips the back of his neck with both hands. "God-damn it. How the fuck am I supposed to fix this if she won't even talk to me?"

He turns the laptop toward him and begins looking up the license plate information.

I flip on the lights and the driver pulls over onto the shoulder, barely leaving me enough room to get behind him. That just annoys me further.

"I'm not okay with being dumped without knowing what the hell I did wrong. If she doesn't talk to me soon, I'm going to go fucking crazy."

I grab the bottom of the mount that holds the laptop and turn it so I can see it. "Give me the fucking thing. Do you realize you just looked up my sister's information in here, dick?"

Luke leans over, looking at the screen that displays every past address and speeding ticket Tessa's ever had. He flinches before falling back into his seat. "Fuck me. I'm in deep, man."

"No, you're in love, asshole."

And when he doesn't argue with me, I don't feel the need to say anything more. He'll have a hard enough time dealing with that realization himself without me fueling the fire. But I do owe it to him to at least try and get some information out of Tessa. And I silently vow to do that.

I didn't dare mention my sister's name again while we finished patrolling. Luke had dropped all conversation involving her after he looked to see if she had a record accidently. And I wasn't a glutton for punishment, so my conversations with him stayed as far away from that topic as possible. I didn't even mention Mia, because I knew that would just trigger him. And not talking about Mia was more difficult than I had anticipated.

I am mentally exhausted by the end of the day.

The only thing I want to do is hold Mia against me and

fall asleep with her. So you can only imagine the surge of disappointment that runs through me when I arrive at my parents' house and she isn't there.

I grab my phone and dial her number, needing to at least hear her after the day I've had.

"Hello?" she answers in that voice that can drop me to my knees.

I smile against my phone and sit down on the couch, aimlessly flipping through the channels. "Baby, I'm at the house and you're not. It kind of sucks here without you."

"Oh, God, is it after six already? I'm so sorry, babe. Tessa wanted to get our hair and nails done today and I completely lost track of time."

Muffled voices come through the phone, and I can tell she's in a crowded place.

"You called me 'babe'," I state.

She's never called me anything besides Ben, except for some profanity that I'm sure she labeled me with when she first discovered who I was. Or multiple profanities.

"Oh, yeah, I guess I did." She laughs softly. "Is that okay? You call me so many different nicknames and I wanted to try one out. I liked babe."

I shift on the couch, resting my feet on the coffee table. "I like it too." My phone beeps, indicating that I'm getting another call. "Oh, hold on a second, angel."

"Okay, babe," she responds, the obvious smile in her voice.

I press a button and answer the incoming call. "Hello?"

"Hey, Ben. It's Rollins." Phil Rollins is another officer that works in my precinct. I don't see him or his partner much, considering that they worked nights. "Listen, man. You're gonna need to come down to the 14th block of Canton Street. I just pulled Angie over for drunk driving and she's got Nolan with her."

I am on my feet and moving toward the door as soon as I hear Nolan's name.

"What? Is he okay? Rollins, fucking tell me if he's hurt!"

My entire body tenses up, and I feel my heart pounding in my head.

"He's fine, man. I'm about to arrest Angie though. She's way over the legal limit and she seems to be on something besides alcohol."

That stupid cunt.

I sprint to my truck, not being able to make my legs move fast enough. "Don't arrest her until I get there. Do you hear me? I wanna see her fucking face before you take her away."

"All right, just promise me you won't be joining her in the back of my car. Keep your shit under control, Kelly. Your son needs you."

"I'm on my way. Tell him Daddy's coming. Don't let him think I'm not coming for him."

I start my truck and hang the phone up, startling at the sound of it ringing again. *Shit. I forgot about Mia.*

"Baby, Angie was just pulled over for drunk driving and Nolan is with her."

My voice cracks at the end. Something could've happened to my son. She could've killed him.

"Oh, my God. Is he all right? Where are you going? I'll meet you there. I'm leaving right now just tell me where to go."

Now it's her voice that is quivering. I hear movement and the sound of a set of keys jingling.

I need her. Nolan will need her. I clear my voice and keep it steady.

"He's okay. He wasn't hurt, thank God. If he was, I wouldn't be responsible for what I might do to that bitch.

They're at the 14th block of Canton Street."

"Okay. Tessa and I are on our way. Babe, just try and stay calm, okay? Nolan's probably really scared with all that commotion and he's going to need you to be strong for him."

God, I loved this woman. She knew exactly what to say to keep me composed.

"Just meet me there, angel. I need you."

The sound of a car starting comes through the phone. "I know. I'm coming."

THERE ARE THREE cop cars at the scene, and an ambulance.

People are starting to gather on the street outside their homes, but I don't pay attention to any of that. The only face I see is Nolan's as I scramble out of my truck and run up to the back door of the ambulance. He is in Rollins' arms, getting checked out by the paramedic. As I rush up to them, Rollins takes in my terrified state.

"Just a precaution, man. He's perfectly fine."

I nod in relief, smiling at Nolan who finally registers my presence. My son grins at me the way he always does.

"Daddy! Wook at all da powice carws!"

The paramedic gives me the go ahead to grab him, having finished with the examination. I pull him to my chest and hold him gently. "Are you okay, buddy? You aren't hurt anywhere?"

He looks completely unharmed, but I feel like I am cradling a wounded animal against me. I can hear Angie's hysterical voice in the distance but I try to block it out. I don't want to get angry in front of Nolan. I pull him away from me and look all over his face, his arms, and his legs. I'm scanning every inch of exposed skin for some sign of injury, but I find none.

"Nolan, you don't have any boo-boos?"

He shakes his head and looks past me over my shoulder. His face lights up. "Daddy, Pwincess Mia and Aunt Tessa arwe herwe!"

I turn my body and feel a rush of calmness run through me.

Mia's face is streaked with tears, but she quickly shakes off her sadness when she sees Nolan. She is either relieved or she doesn't want him to see her like this. Tessa, on the other hand, looks murderous.

"Here, can you take him for me while I go handle this?" I hand Nolan over to Mia and he can't seem to get into her arms fast enough. She leans into me and kisses me on my jaw before walking toward my truck, her lips pressed to Nolan's forehead.

Tessa waits until Nolan gets several feet away before saying, "Where the fuck is that stupid bitch? She doesn't deserve jail. She deserves to eat my fist."

"Calm down, Tessa." Luke's voice startles us both, Tessa more than me. He walks past her and joins my side, keeping his eyes on her. "How would you going to jail help out in this situation?"

She glowers at him, crossing her arms over her chest as we walk toward the first cop car behind the red Altima.

I can feel the blood rushing in my ears as Angie's face comes into view, her lower body hanging out of the back of the cop car. Her hands are obviously bound behind her and she is crying hysterically. She seems to cry harder when she senses my presence. And now that Nolan is out of ear shot, I don't have to remain calm.

I push past the officer that is standing right outside the door, not even bothering to register who he is, and bring my face a breath away from hers. I can smell the booze on her and that just fuels my anger. If she was a man, I'd rip her throat out.

"You fucking bitch!" I feel the hands on my shoulders, trying to pry me away from her but they aren't strong enough. I stay right where I am and she feels every ounce of hate I have for her. "You're a fucking disgrace. I hope you've enjoyed your three years with him, because you'll never see my son again." The hands multiply on me, and I am slowly being dragged away from a regretful looking Angie. But I don't care how sorry she is or if she's sorry at all. There is nothing she can say to make me feel a shred of remorse for her. But the dumb bitch speaks anyway.

"I'm sorry. Ben, I'm so sorry. But you gave up on us." Her tears come harder. "You gave up!"

I lunge forward and fill my lungs to the max. "There is no us! And I don't give a shit if you're sorry! You could've killed him! You could've killed *my* son!"

She is delusional if she thinks any amount of apologizing is going to help. And the fact that she thinks it will help only enrages me further.

"You're a fucking piece of shit!"

"Ben, that's enough," Luke strains in my ear.

He has the main hold on me and I am now a good fifteen feet away from the cop car. I see Tessa's wide eyes and realize I need to calm down. I can't be like this when I get back to the truck. I've said all I wanted to say to Angie, and I don't want to see her face again.

"All right. I'm fine." I shrug him off me and walk over to Rollins, who is watching the scene.

"Can't say I blame you for that outburst. I would've re-acted the same way."

"What are my chances of getting sole custody of my kid now?" I ask him.

Rollins' wife is an attorney that we work with frequently, and he in turn knows more about the system than I do. He also has an ex-wife that took him to court years ago over a custody battle.

He puts a hand on my shoulder and applies mild pressure. "Pretty damn good, man. Especially if the test results come back with more than just alcohol in her system. That on top of the class E felony she's getting charged with should give you full custody."

I knew under law, she was facing up to four years of jail time for having a minor in the car with her. And I figured I'll have a damn good chance of getting full custody of Nolan. But I wanted to hear it out loud. I needed to hear those words. I wanted certainty.

I nod at Rollins, thanking him before walking back toward Luke and Tessa.

She is watching me while he is watching her. And by the look on both their faces, they still aren't talking.

"I'm going to stay at Mom and Dad's tonight with Nolan. Did you drive here or did Mia?"

"I did. I'll meet you at home." She turns on her heel without giving Luke a glance.

"Tessa, come on. Will you at least talk to me for a minute?" Luke calls out.

She hears him, but she doesn't respond, not even with a look over her shoulder.

He runs his hands down his face and lets out a grunt behind them. "I'll see you tomorrow, man. I'm glad Nolan's okay." He walks away looking defeated, which is not a look he wears often. Especially pertaining to women.

I feel bad for the guy.

I talk to some other officers before finally walking to

the truck.

Mia is holding Nolan against her chest in the front seat, both of them asleep. I open her door and pry him out of her hands so that I can put him in his car seat. She stirs at the loss of his weight on her.

"Hey." She places her hand on my cheek after I settle into the driver's seat. "Are you okay?"

I turn my face into her palm and kiss it. "I am now."

She doesn't ask me any questions on the drive back to my parents' house. It's as if she knows I need the silence right now. My brain is working out the possible scenarios that could've transpired tonight. All of them involving Nolan injured somehow. My grip keeps tightening on the wheel, and every time it does, Mia tightens her hold on my hand. She keeps her other hand on the back of my neck, massaging it gently and relieving the tension that is beginning to permanently set in.

When we get to the house, I carry Nolan inside and lay him down in the middle of the bed he sleeps in when he spends the night here. I can't leave him. Not yet. So I sit on the edge of his bed and watch his chest rise and fall.

I could've lost him.

I'd never be able to watch him sleep again. I'd never hear his husky voice ringing throughout the house or see him slaying invisible dragons. I'd have three years of memories to live off of for the rest of my life, and it wouldn't be enough. He is my world, and now because of his mother's reckless decision, he's all mine. I'll never have to miss another moment with him. I'll never have to beg to see my son on days that aren't technically mine. And I feel like a complete shit for feeling slightly grateful for the events that unfolded tonight.

What the fuck is wrong with me?

I have no idea how long I sit there, but when I eventually

get up and turn around, Mia is leaning against the doorframe. I walk over to her and she wraps her arms around my waist, pressing her face to my chest.

"You know if you want to talk about it, I'm here." She turns her face up and I kiss her forehead.

"I'm glad it happened. How fucked up is that?"

Her hands grab my face. "You're not glad it happened. You'd never want Nolan to be in any sort of danger. The fact that you'll probably never have to split your time with him again because of Angie's poor judgment is a small silver lining. But Nolan's well-being is the only real thing that matters to you. You'd give up all your time with him if it meant keeping him safe. I know you would."

I love you.

The words burn the back of my throat, aching to be released.

I have no idea how long it will take to get Nolan's custody arrangement sorted out. And I can't take him to Georgia until that happens. The legal system takes its fucking time when you want it to hurry the hell up. And Mia may have to leave me before I can take him out of the state. Plus, I'll need to get a job lined up out there. It could be weeks, months before I'm with her again. And I won't make this harder on her. So I swallow those same three words again, not letting them out. Not yet.

I bend down and lift her by her ass, prompting her to wrap her legs around my waist. "I need you," I whisper against her lips.

"You have me."

I carry her into her bedroom and drop her in the middle of the bed. "Take all of that off." She sits up and pulls her dress over her head, revealing herself to me in only a pair of white panties. "Fuck. I need to be inside you, angel."

She sits back on her hands, pushing her perfect tits out and teasing me with them. "I'm waiting."

I practically rip my shirt off, and when I start loosening my belt, she lies back and slips her hand into the front of her panties.

"Jesus, Mia."

I step out of my pants and move over her, letting my cock drag up the length of her body.

"Get in me," she pleads, her hand still working between us and her eyes rolling closed.

"Not yet. I need to taste you first."

Her eyes shoot open with that flirtatious glint and her hand wraps around my cock. "So do I."

Her panties are torn from her body before I pick her up and position her over me so that she's straddling my face. I feel her warm breath tickling my cock as I nip at the soft skin of her inner thigh. "Those pretty lips of yours better find themselves wrapped around my dick in two seconds."

Her soft laugh fills the room. "And if they don't?"

I lick up her length, not being able to hold out any longer. Her taste fills my mouth and her moan vibrates against my lips. I savor her with my tongue, letting everything fade out around me. I'm a junkie getting his fix. But instead of the hit dulling out my senses, I feel my pulse quicken and my bones begin to vibrate. I'm a fucking king between her legs, and when she finally swallows my cock, I grab onto her hips and bury my face into her pussy.

She releases it with a pop and presses down on my pelvis with her hands, her back bowing in pleasure. "Oh, my God. I'm not going to be able to focus if you keep doing that." Her voice breaks with another moan when I don't let up, and her hand takes over where her mouth was.

I groan against her clit before biting down on it gently. She gasps and I release it. "Bend down and suck my dick, Mia. I'm coming in that mouth tonight."

"Then you're going to have to let up a little."

Yeah, that's not happening.

I smile against her. "Nothing could pull me away from your pussy, angel. Put my dick in your mouth and don't be fucking gentle about it. I want to feel the back of your throat when I'm coming."

I feel her weight shift and her tongue licks the head of my cock. I'm about to tell her not to tease me when she deep throats me like a fucking champion and scraps her teeth along my shaft.

"Mia!" I grunt out, digging my fingers into her ass.

She sucks me like her life depends on it, and I flatten my tongue against her clit, stroking it in a rhythm that makes her lips vibrate against my cock. And then it's about getting her off before me. I alternate between sucking on her clit and fucking her with my tongue, pulling her hips down so hard I'm practically being smothered. I feel her pulse against my tongue, and when she releases my cock and digs her nails into my hip, I know I have her.

She rocks against me, fucking my face and riding out her orgasm while she softly chants my name. I press my lips once more to her clit before she collapses on top of me, her face now resting on my thigh.

"Sorry. Just give me a minute," she pants, sliding off my stomach and settling between my legs. She glances up at the smug face I'm wearing and wraps her hand around my cock. "Still want to come in my mouth?" she questions before pressing her lips to my shaft.

I groan as she slides down. "Stop talking and suck my cock, baby."

Her cheek twitches with a smile. "Yes, Officer Kelly."

mia

THE BED IS jolting underneath me, bringing me out of my dream. A tiny laugh fills the room and prompts me to open my eyes.

Nolan is jumping on the bed and giggling at himself, and when he sees my eyes on him, he hops over toward me and collapses on my stomach.

I grunt as his elbow connects with a few of my ribs.

Jeez. How can such a tiny body inflict so much pain?

After recovering, I rustle his hair with my hand, rubbing his back with the other. "You are a little ball of energy in the morning. Are you hungry?"

He slides off me and scoots off the bed. "I want pamcakes."

His husky little voice is hoarser in the morning. That and his crazy hair are the only things giving away that he has just woken up. He certainly isn't moving as slow as I know I will be. Even off the bed, he is jumping around like a jack rabbit.

I sit up and rub my eyes with both hands. "Go wake up Aunt Tessa and I'll meet you in the kitchen."

His little feet quickly take him out of the room and down the hallway while I get dressed for the day. My phone beeps on the nightstand just as I am pulling my hair back into a pony.

Ben: Is the maniac awake yet?

Me: *Are you kidding? He's running on full speed already. :)*
We're getting ready to make pancakes.

Ben: *He's probably psyched out of his mind getting to spend*
the day with you. I'm jealous.

Me: *You'll get me tonight, don't worry.*

Ben: *Bet your ass I will. I'll see you around six.*

Me: *Can't wait.*

I tuck my phone into my pocket and walk out into the kitchen. Tessa is rummaging through the cabinets while Nolan is playing with her phone on the couch. I snicker at the sight of him browsing iTunes like he's done it a million times.

"Crapola. We don't have any pancake mix," she says, closing the doors she had opened and turning toward me. "My parents really should have stocked up before they decided to take a six month trip to Europe. I'm extremely disappointed in them."

I chuckle and grab my keys off the counter. "Yes, how dare they not provide you with food for half the year while they go on vacation."

She scowls at me playfully, pulling the orange juice out of the fridge.

"I'll run to the store and get some. Do we need anything else?"

"We'll need some more milk with Nolan here. Other than that, I think we're good." She walks over to the couch and plops down next to him. "Can you not buy apps please? How do you even know my password?" She leans her head into his and monitors his actions on her phone.

I laugh under my breath as I walk toward the door. "All right. I'll be back in a little while. Hold down the fort, Sir Nolan."

He shoots his dimples at me before returning to purchasing apps on Tessa's phone.

I'M WAITING IN the checkout line at the grocery story after having grabbed the pancake mix, some milk, and a dragon coloring book I found near the greeting cards when my phone starts ringing. I pull it out of my pocket and place my basket at my feet, seeing my aunt's name flashing on the screen.

"Hey, Aunt Mae."

"Mia, sweetie, you need to come home." She sniffs loudly, and my heart immediately drops to the floor next to my basket.

I'm out the door, running across the parking lot within seconds. "What's happened? Is it that stupid cold she had? Does she have a fever now or something?"

I knew it was more than a cold. *Fuck!* My tires screech as I pull out of my parking space and drive toward the exit for the highway.

My aunt sobs through the phone.

"Aunt Mae, tell me what's going on. Can I talk to her?" I hear a faint beeping sound through the phone in between my aunt's cries.

She's in the hospital. That's what that sound is.

"She was fine. I don't know what happened. I went to wake her up this morning and she wouldn't respond to me." Her voice cracks and she starts crying harder. "She won't wake up, Mia. The doctors are waiting for you to get here. Oh, sweetheart. I'm so sorry."

I'm crying now, sobbing uncontrollably. I have to keep

wiping my eyes to be able to see the road in front of me. The hand holding the phone to my ear is shaking so badly, my aunt's cries are fading in and out.

I know what she means. My mom has a DNR. The doctors are waiting for me to get there before they take her off the machines. My mom is dying and I'm not there.

I haven't been there for her.

"I'm on my way. Tell her I'm on my way!"

"Honey, she's unconscious."

"Tell her I'm coming!" I hang up the phone and drop it somewhere, anywhere. I don't give a shit about my phone right now.

My attention is on the road and nothing else as I fly down the highway. The speed limit means nothing to me. Nor do the other cars on the road. I swerve in and out of traffic, taking the median occasionally when I can't get around someone. The only thing I care about is getting to her in less than four hours.

Four fucking hours. Why the hell did I leave her?

I knew in my gut that I shouldn't have left for the summer. I was selfish. I was more concerned with having an amazing summer with my best friend than taking care of my own mother. And now she's dying and I'm not there. I wasn't there when she got that fucking cold. I wasn't there last night when she probably started feeling bad, and then the bad turned to worse sometime in the middle of the night. She probably called out for me in her weak voice, too weak to alert my aunt. And now I'm two hundred miles away from her and I can't get to her fast enough.

The world blurs in front of me.

The image of my mother in a hospital bed fills my thoughts as I speed down the highway. I only stop when I absolutely have to, and it's only to pump gas. I don't even run inside the gas station to use the restroom. But I do grab my phone that had slid underneath the back seat. I have a few missed calls from Tessa, but I ignore them for now. I dial Ben's number and it goes straight to voicemail.

"Babe, my mom is dying. I'm on my way to Fulton now." I pause and take in two shaky breaths, wiping underneath my eyes. "I know you can't be here with me, but can you at least call me? I just, I need to hear your voice right now. I'm not ready to say goodbye to her. I don't really know how I'm going to get through this." I blink, sending the tears streaming down my face. "Please call me." I end the call, keeping my eyes on the pump. As soon as the numbers stop rolling over, I yank it out of my car and get back on the road.

How I manage to get to Fulton in two and a half hours, I'll never understand. But I do by some miracle. Of course, I did break the speed limit by a long shot the entire way here. I pull my phone out of my pocket as I run up to the entrance. I need to tell Tessa where I am. She's probably worried sick right now, and I can only imagine how hungry Nolan must be. After four rings, her voicemail picks up and I curse under my breath.

Is nobody answering phones today?

"Hey, it's me. I'm so sorry I missed your calls, but I'm in Fulton at the hospital. It's my mom. She's dying, Tessa." I bit my lip to stop myself from crying. "I got the call from my aunt when I was at the grocery store and I just drove straight here. Can you tell Ben to call me? Or text me or something? I tried calling him but he didn't answer." I remember the groceries I left on the floor by the checkout counter. "Oh, and tell Nolan I'm sorry about the pancakes. I'll make him some the next time I see him."

I tuck my phone away and run into the hospital, stopping

at the information desk. I'm directed toward the ICU, and as
I run off the elevators, I see my aunt.

She's pacing outside the room, glancing down at her
watch repetitively when she turns toward my footsteps. She
wraps her arms around me and I cry against her shoulder.

"Oh, sweetheart. I'm so sorry this happened. I swear to
God she was fine yesterday. I would've called you if I thought
it was serious."

I pull away from her and look into the room. "Do the
doctors know what happened? She was doing so well. I just, I
don't understand. She was beating it. She was going to beat it."

I watch as the nurse jots something down in my mom's
chart, her eyes shifting from the monitor to her clipboard. Just
then, a man walks over to where my aunt and I are standing
and holds his hand out to me. He's wearing a white lab coat
and an apologetic expression.

"Miss Corelli? I'm Dr. Stevens, the attending that's been
looking after your mom."

I shake his hand weakly, my eyes straining to look at him
because they want to stay glued on my mom. Now that I'm
here, she has my full attention.

"I'm sure you're aware of how sick your mom was. The
treatments seemed to have been working, but these things
can happen. The slightest infection that wouldn't affect a
healthy person can really be detrimental to someone with
her condition."

I start crying again. "She told me a few days ago that she
had a cold, but she said it wasn't a big deal. But I knew it was.
I should've been here."

My aunt's arm wraps around my shoulder as I blink heavily, sending the tears streaming down my face.

Dr. Stevens puts his hand on my shoulder. "Darling,

there's really nothing you could've done. The cancer was just too strong and your mom couldn't fight it anymore. She's not in any pain now." He looks into her room briefly before turning back to me. "You take as much time as you need, okay?"

I nod and give him a weak smile before walking into the room.

My aunt stays outside, giving me the privacy I need, and the nurse steps out as well. I sit down in the chair and grab my mom's hand. She's pale but her hand is warm, and she looks peaceful. Content. Like she's ready to let go. I bend down and press my lips to her knuckles.

"Hi, Mom."

I stay with her for hours, listening to the monitors and the light chatter of the people out in the hallway. I never once let go of her hand, not even when the nurses come in to take her vitals. I talk to her like she's awake and watching me, listening intently to my voice. I tell her all about Ben and Nolan, and how I've fallen in love with the boy that I'd once hated more than anything. I tell her that I wished she could meet the man he is now, because I know she would love him. And I tell her that I want to have babies just like Nolan with him. Dimpled little versions of Ben with maybe a few of my features, but mostly his. The tears come back when I realize she'll never see me on my wedding day, or meet any of her grandchildren. But I promise her that my children will know all about their grandmother and how beautiful and kind she was.

My aunt joins me after a while and we talk about the last several days she spent with her and what they did. She fills me in on every tiny detail, making me feel like I was there instead of miles away. I keep checking my phone but never hear from Tessa or Ben, and I can't hide the sadness that overwhelms me when neither one of them contact me.

Especially Ben.

I need to hear his voice. I need him with me, but he doesn't call me or text me and I don't understand why. And as time drags on, the hurt in my heart grows to the point of being agonizing.

Maybe I had imagined what we had together. Maybe he didn't love me. Maybe this was all just some game to him, tricking his sister's annoying best friend into loving him. And when Dr. Stevens comes in to ask if we're ready to say our goodbyes, I lose it.

I drop to my knees and cry harder than I ever have before. I cry over losing my mom to this bullshit disease that doesn't care whose life it ruins, I cry over my selfishness and the fact that I chose a summer with Ben over my last summer with my mom, and I cry because the man I love doesn't care enough to comfort me over the phone.

I know he can't be here with me. He has to work. But he could've called. And as I stand outside my mom's room, watching them cover her up with a white sheet, that familiar hate I once reserved just for him comes right back up to the surface.

"You know, I think it's really amazing that your mom wanted to donate her body to science. She could be the reason they find a cure for that fucking disease."

I can't help but laugh at my aunt's use of profanity. She never cusses around me.

Her hand tucks a piece of hair behind my ear that has fallen out of my hair tie. "Are you going to stick around here for a while or are you heading back to Alabama?"

I glance down at my phone again. Still nothing. "I don't have any reason to go back to Alabama."

"Isn't being in love a good enough reason?" she asks.

"Not when it's one-sided." I look down at my phone and squeeze it tightly, willing it to ring. "He didn't even care about me enough to text me. You really can't get more impersonal than a text, and that was still too much for him." I meet my aunt's pitiful gaze. "It's fine. I'm used to hating Ben. It's not very difficult. I can get my stuff mailed to me, that way I don't ever have to go back there."

The thought of never seeing Nolan again makes my stomach churn. But seeing Nolan meant seeing Ben. The Ben that doesn't care enough.

She takes a sip of the coffee she's been nursing for the past hour. "Why don't you step outside and get some air. It'll be good to get out of this stuffy atmosphere for a few minutes. Clear your head a little."

I nod in agreement and take the elevators down to the main level, walking out of the entrance I came sprinting through several hours ago.

As soon as I step onto the sidewalk, my phone starts beeping like crazy in my pocket. Startled, I pull it out and watch as the number of missed calls from Tessa's cell phone rack up. But still nothing from Ben.

How the hell did I miss this many calls?

And then it hits me—there isn't any cell phone reception in the hospital.

I begin listening to the voicemails she left me. The first several are wondering where I am, telling me that Nolan is driving her nuts with his impatience. Then she tells me that Nolan was messing with her phone again and she noticed that he turned the volume down and that's why she missed my call. She tells me she'll call Ben, and I can't help the aggravation I feel at that statement. She cries in the next message, asking me to call her so she can find out what's going on with my mom. As soon as she starts talking about Ben not answering his phone, I delete the message and go on to the next one. If she had any excuses for him, I didn't want to hear them. He obviously didn't love me, because if you loved someone, you'd take five seconds out of your day to send them a text when their mother is dying. One fucking word could've been sent to me. A simple "sorry." But no. I needed him and he didn't care. He doesn't love me. And that realization stings my entire body with a discomfort I've never felt before. But just when I think my world can't crumble anymore, I reach the last voicemail in my inbox.

"Mia, Ben's been shot. He's been fucking shot. I don't know anything except that they're taking him to St. Joseph's hospital. Please call me. Please."

I can hear the restrained panic in Tessa's voice.

I fall to the ground, my knees hitting the sidewalk and causing a shooting pain to ride up my thighs. But that's not the pain that has me struggling to breathe.

"Oh, no, God. Please no." I push myself up and begin running toward my Jeep when I remember my aunt.

"Fuck!"

Running faster than I ever have, I take the stairs because I don't want to wait for the elevator. My aunt is where I left her and she startles when she sees me, meeting me halfway next to the nurse's station. I'm crying and I can barely take in any air, but I manage to speak.

"Ben's been shot. I have to go. Right now. Do I need to do something? Is there anything I need to do here? Please, can I just go?"

My chest is heaving from my run and my legs are burning, but I don't care. And if I have paperwork or anything I have to do, it will have to wait.

She squeezes my hand, shaking her head with concerned eyes. "No, sweetie. Go. I'll take care of everything. Call me when you get there."

I run back down the stairs, nearly falling in my hurried state. Once I get outside, I dial Tessa's number as I sprint to the Jeep. It goes straight to voicemail.

"I'm on my way. Oh, my God, please call me back and tell me he's okay. Tell him I love him, Tessa. Tell him I'm going to say that to him every second for the rest of his life. He'll never go another day without hearing those words from me."

I wipe the tears from my eyes so I can focus on the road in front of me as I whip through the parking lot.

"Please don't take him away from me."

I whimper my plea to God, and to Tessa, not knowing if either one of them will hear me. If Tessa is in the hospital, she probably won't get this message until she walks outside. And if Ben is dying, why would she leave him? I wouldn't leave his side if I was there. The man I spent the last two hours bitterly hating was the man I loved more than anything in the world. He was my life, my family, and my future. I couldn't lose him. I wouldn't lose him. I've never believed in fate before, but I did the moment I saw Ben in that bar. He was always the one for me. We were always meant to end up together.

And the two hundred miles that are separating us now will be the last thing to ever keep us apart. I'll make damn sure of that.

tessa

"I WANT PAMCAKES! I want pamcakes!" Nolan yells, jumping up and down on the sofa. "Pamcakes, pamcakes, pamcakes!"

I love my nephew, but I'm about to stick him in the dryer.

I grunt my annoyance, looking for any sign of the red Jeep out the window. "Nolan, relax please. Mia should be back any minute."

"It's Pwincess Mia," he corrects me, causing me to narrow my eyes at him.

I snatch my cell phone from his little grubby fingers and dial her number. It rings four times and then her voicemail greeting comes through the phone. I wait for the beep. "Oh, my God. Please tell me you're on your way back. The little monster is getting unbearable to be around. Oh, and if you're still at the store, can you pick me up some mountain dew?" I hang up and watch as Nolan rips all the pillows off the couch and jumps on them like stones in a creek. "How about some Fruit Loops to hold you over?"

He jerks his head up and connects with my eyes. "Gwoss. I hate fwuit woops. I want pamcakes." His little menacing body flies into the air with each leap he takes. "Pwincess Mia pwomised me."

I turn away from him and look out the sliding glass door, praying that Mia's body will come into view any second. But it doesn't. And my impatience begins to grow right along with Nolan's as the time ticks by. I dial her number again.

"Hey. You do remember how to get to my parents' house, right? Nolan's about to start eating the furniture."

And again.

"Which grocery store did you go to? There are some in Alabama. I'm about to start making pancakes out of cornmeal, and I'm not sure how those are going to go over, so you might want to speed it up a little."

And again.

"Sweet Jesus! Would you call me and let me know that you're still alive!"

Nolan's voice grows louder and louder, more urgent as the minutes drag on.

I silence him with my phone when I think my head is going to explode, and raid the fridge myself. I don't need to wait for pancake mix to eat breakfast. I am perfectly happy with Fruit Loops, unlike my hot meal loving nephew.

"Nolan, don't buy any more apps. I will be looting your piggy bank to pay for the seven that you bought already."

He doesn't respond as I clean up my dishes, most likely browsing the hottest games on iTunes. Another hour goes by before I grab my phone and really start to worry. There's no way in hell it should take Mia this long. Not unless she really did go to another state to grocery shop. I notice the missed call from Mia on my screen.

"Nolan, damn it. You turned my volume down."

He gasps softly, and I look up at his wide-eyed stare.

"You said a bad wowrd."

Shit. I hold my phone up to my ear to listen to her voice-mail, turning the TV on as a distraction. Hopefully he'll find something amusing and will forget all about my potty mouth.

I really don't feel like getting my ass handed to me by Ben for my language usage around his son.

"Hey, it's me. I'm so sorry I missed your calls but I'm in Fulton at the hospital. It's my mom. She's dying, Tessa. I got the call from my aunt when I was at the grocery store and I just drove straight here. Can you tell Ben to call me? Or text me or something? I tried calling him but he didn't answer. Oh, and tell Nolan I'm sorry about the pancakes. I'll make him some the next time I see him."

"Oh, God." I exit my voicemail and quickly dial her number again, cursing under my breath and moving into the kitchen. She doesn't pick up and I begin to cry. "Oh, my God, Mia, I'm so sorry I missed your call. Nolan was playing with my phone and turned down the volume." I try to muffle my cries, but I'm one of those loud criers and it's useless. "Jesus, I should be there with you. I'm going to call Ben right now and let him know what's going on. Just call me when you get a chance, okay? I love you."

I wipe my eyes and dial Ben's number. Nolan jumps around on the couch cushions, completely oblivious to me and anything else that isn't the cartoon he's watching. Thank God, I got his mind off those pancakes.

"Goddamn it."

Ben's voicemail message begins playing. I wait for the beep and slip farther into the kitchen, trying to get out of earshot of Nolan.

"Is nobody answering their phones today? Mia's mom is dying, Ben. She needs you. She's already in Fulton and you better call her or get your ass there. I'll take care of Nolan. And answer your phone when I call you, please."

I dial Mia's number again.

"Hey, it's me. I called Ben but had to leave him a message.

God, I wish I was there with you. I hate that you're dealing
with this alone. Just call me as soon as you get this and let me
know what's going on. I'll keep trying Ben."

I dial his number again.

"Answer your fucking phone. Mia needs you, asshole."

I hang up and walk over to the counter, grabbing the box
of cookies that is almost empty. There is no way in hell I am
going to inform Nolan that he won't be having pancakes any
time soon. I've seen some of his temper tantrums.

I pick up the couch cushions and re-situate them before
plopping down on the end.

"I feel like having cookies for breakfast." I take a bite of
one of the chocolate chip ones as he scrambles up next to
me, his crazy, gray eyes flicking from my mouth to the box.
"What about you?"

He nods eagerly and dives for some cookies. He then
stretches out, lying sideways on the couch with his head at
the other end while he eats and watches his cartoon.

I dial Mia's number several more times, hoping to get a
hold of her, but get her voicemail each time. I also call Ben a
few more times, and I'm sent straight to his voicemail with
each dial. I'm hurting for Mia and want to be there with her.
Ms. Corelli was always so sweet to me when I was younger.
She would do anything for anybody, a quality my best friend
acquired. I think about throwing Nolan into my car and beginning the drive to Fulton, but I'd never do that unless I
made Ben aware. And since my dumbass brother isn't liking
his phone today, I can't make him aware of that plan.

Nolan and I devour the cookies while watching several
of his favorite shows, and just as I'm about to grab us both a
drink, my phone finally rings.

I lunge for it, hoping and praying that it's either Mia or

Ben, but it isn't. Luke's name flashes on my screen, and I hit ignore with my middle finger before turning it up in front of my phone as if he can see it.

He is the last person I want to talk to.

He calls again, and again, and each time I hit ignore with an irritated grunt. Until I realize, like a complete dumbass, that I need to talk to Luke. Because talking to Luke means getting through to Ben.

"Shit." I frantically hit redial and stand from the couch, walking around the back of it.

Nolan giggles at my choice word before turning back to his cartoon.

"Jesus fucking Christ. Finally!" Luke barks into my ear. I open my mouth to cut him down to size, and to remind him that we're not together, so I don't have to answer his calls, when his voice halts me. "Ben's been shot, Tessa. They're taking him to St. Joseph's hospital."

His words are like a kick to my diaphragm. I feel the air leave my lungs, and I don't register anything else coming through the phone. It's all white noise. Background gibberish from a guy that I don't really want to talk to anyway. The bones in my hand ache as I grip the phone tighter and stare at the back of Nolan's head.

Ben's been shot. Nolan. Mia. I somehow manage to take in a breath and find my voice.

"I'm on my way. I'll meet you there."

I hit end and run down the hall toward my bedroom, dialing Mia's number. I'm not even surprised at this point when it goes to voicemail. I try to keep my voice as calm as I can for her.

"Mia, Ben's been shot. He's been fucking shot. I don't know anything except that they're taking him to St. Joseph's hospital. Please call me. Please."

I hang up and grab my keys before sprinting back into the living room. "Nolan, come on. We gotta go."

He continues jumping on the couch. "I wanna watch dis." I grab him and feel his body tense in protest. "Noooo!" He flails in my arms, but I just hold him tighter as we head out to my car.

"Stop it, Nolan. We need to go see Daddy."

He immediately stops fighting me, and I immediately regret telling him where we are going. If something were to happen to Ben and Nolan doesn't get to see him, I'm not sure how I will handle that. Not only for him, but for me as well. And Mia. God, no. I can't think about that. Nothing was going to happen to him.

I fight back my tears and buckle Nolan in before peeling away from the house.

St. Joseph's hospital is thirty-five minutes away, but I get there in a little under twenty. I wanted to call my parents, but I couldn't inform them of Ben's situation with Nolan and his sonic hearing listening in, so I resorted to a text message. I knew I'd get an earful once they saw that this was the way I'd decided to fill them in, but it was my only option at the moment.

I manage to keep myself calm when I collect Nolan from the car and carry him into the hospital. But once the lady at the reception desk tells me Ben's room number, I sprint toward the elevators.

I don't know what condition I will find him in. He could be unconscious. Unrecognizable. Dead. I have no idea. I don't know the extent of his injuries, and I am willing to risk Nolan seeing his father in whatever state he is in, because I need to see him.

Once the elevator stops on my floor, I clutch Nolan against my side as I maneuver between the people in the hallway.

319. 319.

I'm scanning for Ben's room number as I pass every doorway. Finally, after what feels like a lifetime, I pass room 317 and know his room is next. I stop just before reaching his door, my heart pumping so loud it's causing tremors in my field of vision. I let out an unsteady breath and shift Nolan on my hip before filling the doorway.

I'm prepared for blood.

I'm prepared for the annoying constant beeping of machines and the sight of my brother bandaged up.

But this? I'm not prepared for this. Not after the multitude of emotions I've felt today.

My heart thunders in my chest at the sight of Ben, sitting up in bed while a nurse tends to his shoulder. He looks completely unharmed except for the deep gash that the nurse is stitching up. Luke is sitting next to him in a chair beside the bed, and as I step into the room, both pairs of eyes fixate on me.

"Daddy!" Nolan scrambles out of my arms and runs over to the bed, climbing up on it.

"What the hell is this?" I gesture with my hand toward my brother, getting a bewildered expression in return. "I thought you'd be dying. Or at least severely injured." I snap my head toward Luke who leans back in his chair in response to the anger behind my glare. "Jesus Christ, Luke. You think you could've mentioned that Ben was only suffering from a flesh wound! Do you have any idea how scared I was! How scared I've probably made Mia!"

"Where is Mia?" Ben asks, but his question goes unanswered when I continue contemplating how I'd like to inflict pain on the idiot in the room.

Luke's eyes shift from Ben's to mine. "I told you he was wearing his vest, thank Christ, and only took one to the arm. If he hadn't been wearing it, he'd probably be dead. Look at this thing." He reaches down and lifts Ben's police vest off the ground, numerous holes visible through the chest plate.

I put my hands on my hips. "You didn't say that. You only said he got shot and was en route to the hospital. Thanks for keeping the important details to yourself, asshole."

I don't want to admit to Luke that I had tuned him out sometime during our conversation. He could've told me that Ben was okay, and the thought of me not hearing it instead of him not saying it was maddening. I've freaked everyone out for no reason. This was all me. But he doesn't need to know that.

Ben grabs Nolan's head and covers his ears. "Really, Tessa? Could you not cuss around him? And where the fuck is Mia?" he harshly whispers, keeping Nolan completely oblivious.

Luke stands up and drops the vest on the bed. "God, I'm so sick of this shit from you. You break up with me for no Goddamned reason at all, and now you act like a complete bitch." He bridges the gap between us, bringing his face inches from mine. "Why did you end it? You owe me a reason and you're going to give it to me right fucking now."

"I don't owe you shit."

"Tessa!"

Luke and I both turn toward Ben's frantic voice.

The nurse who is working on him grabs his shoulder and pushes him back so he's reclining on the bed. He's still covering Nolan's ears, which is a good thing.

"Sir, you're going to have to keep still so I can finish this. If you yell like that again, I'm likely to stick this needle straight into your arm."

"Sorry," he says to her before looking back at me. "Where is she? Nothing else comes out of your mouth until you tell me where she is."

I ignore Luke's closeness and feel my stomach drop at the thought of my best friend. "Her mom was dying. She went out to get pancake mix for Nolan and got a call from her aunt. She's in Fulton."

The words come out like rapid fire, and as soon as I finish talking, Ben tries to get up. The nurse firmly pushes against his shoulder again. "Sir, I'm not finished."

He shrugs her off and shifts Nolan in his lap. "I don't care. I need to go."

"Mr. Kelly, you can't leave with an open wound. You're likely to get an infection. A nasty one at that. Let me finish stitching you up and we'll see if the doctor will release you."

He grunts and leans back, both fists clenching on his sheet. "Hurry. Up," he firmly directs her. His eyes pierce into mine. "Why didn't you call me? Why didn't she? She shouldn't be there, going through this, without me. One of us should be with her."

"I know that. I haven't been able to get a hold of her all day. She left me a message and asked me to try and get a hold of you because she couldn't reach you. And then I couldn't reach you. Where the hell is your phone?"

He looks at the vest on the bed and reaches for it, pulling out a barely held together phone. "Shit," he whispers, looking quickly at Nolan, who is now playing with the TV remote at the foot of the bed. He winces while the nurse continues to stitch him up. "Call her. Find out where she is and tell her I'm coming to get her."

I pull my phone out and notice the nonexistent reception I'm currently getting. "I have to step outside. Do you want me to take Nolan?"

"No. But I'll need you to watch him when I leave. I'm getting to Fulton in under four hours." He turns and watches the nurse, undoubtedly willing her to hurry the fuck up.

I nod and exit the room, hearing footsteps behind me. I turn, and Luke runs straight into me, grabbing me before I topple over. "Christ! What? I don't have time for this. I need to call Mia."

He keeps his grip on my arms. "Tell me why you broke up with me."

I'm sick of this. And I know Luke. He won't let this go until he gets what he wants.

Persistent little bastard. Just like when he has to get another orgasm out of me.

The nerve.

I pull my arms out of his grasp and grit my teeth. "I thought I was pregnant, you prick."

He leans back as if I've just slapped him across the face. "What? You did? When? Are you?" His voice is softer, the heat that was in it moments ago completely vanished.

I feel my body remembering that day and the pain I felt when I delivered the blow that broke us. The agony burns like acid in my mouth, coating my words. "No, I'm not. But I thought I was."

He holds his hands out in front of him, still seemingly clueless to why I ended things.

"I asked you if you ever saw yourself having kids someday and you said no. You said you never wanted what Ben had. And I want that." I bite my tongue to distract me from the pain of the memory.

His nostrils flare and he steps closer to me. "You broke up with me thinking you were pregnant? And you didn't think I should know about it? Do you know how fucked up that is?"

"You wouldn't have wanted it. You said . . ."

He steps into me and brings his face so close to mine; his breath tickles my eyelashes. "Don't tell me what I would've wanted," he growls. "Was there a chance it wasn't mine? Is that why you didn't tell me?"

His words are like venom coming out of his mouth. I gasp, stepping back and putting some distance between us. "No, there wasn't a chance it wouldn't have been yours. But since you're bringing it up, how many other girls were you sleeping with besides me? I should probably go get myself tested while I'm here."

He shakes his head and comes up beside me, stopping when his arm brushes against mine. "You should've told me," he snarls down at me.

He's never looked at me like this before. I can practically feel the revulsion coming off him. And then he's gone, moving down the hallway in the direction I was originally heading.

He chose not to satiate me with an answer to my question, but I suppose his silence answers for him.

I walk outside and quickly dial my parents' number after my phone beeps with a voicemail alert. My mother's casual voice throws me off, until she informs me that she hasn't read my text message due to the fact that they've both been asleep. However, that doesn't prevent the earful she gives me about not feeling the need to call her with that kind of information. She calms down eventually after I tell her Ben's okay, and only keeps me on the phone for a few minutes. After hanging up with her, I dial Mia's number. She picks up on the second ring.

"Oh my God. Is he okay? Please tell me he's okay."

Her panicky tone makes my heart shudder in my chest cavity. It's my fault she's so worried.

"Sweetie, he's fine. He's not really hurt at all. Just a minor cut on his arm."

She cries through the phone, her whimpers mixed with the noise of traffic. "Tessa, I thought . . . I thought I'd never see him again. I never got to tell him . . ." Her voice breaks apart in sobs, and it kills me.

"Shhh, Mia, it's okay. He's okay, I swear. He's fucking pissed as hell about not being there with you. And so am I. Are you okay?"

She pauses, taking in a few deep breaths. "I'm okay, I guess. She wasn't in any pain when she died. It was very peaceful, and I got to say goodbye. My last memories of her are of when she was healthy, so I have those to hold on to."

"I'm so sorry I wasn't there. And Ben's torn up about you going through this alone."

"I actually thought that maybe he didn't care about me. That he didn't care enough to call me when I needed him. And then when I got your message telling me he had been shot, God, Tessa, I almost died right there. I've never been that scared before."

I wipe the tear that had worked its way down my cheek. "Oh, sweetie. How could you think he doesn't care? He loves you. Hasn't he told you that?"

"No, not yet. It doesn't matter. I'm telling him as soon as I see him. I can't wait another second." Her voice sounds steady now, full of determination. When my best friend wants something, she goes for it. "I better get off here though before I get pulled over. I'm about two hours out, so tell Ben I'll be there soon."

"He's coming to you, Mia. I'm telling you right now, as soon as he's discharged, he's leaving here."

She sighs heavily. "Well, tell him to stay put."

"You've met him, right? I can't tell him anything when it comes to you."

She laughs slightly, sniffing at the end of her subdued chuckle. "Yeah. Just have him call me when he's leaving. I guess I'll meet him somewhere."

I walk toward the entrance to the hospital, having worked my way along the side during our conversation. "All right. I love you."

"I love you, too."

I end the call and pull up the voicemail, crying again when I hear her voice. And then she says it, "Tell him I love him, Tessa." And I stop the message.

This isn't for me. It's for him.

ben

I KEEP MY eyes on Nolan as he fumbles with the TV remote.

I need a distraction, and he's the only thing keeping me from jumping out of this bed and not giving a shit about my stitches. Every time I watch this nurse work the needle in and out of my skin, she seems to slow down. So I don't look. Because I need to get the fuck out of here.

I wasn't with her when she needed me.

It kills me to think that Mia couldn't get a hold of me. And worse than that, that there was a moment I considered not putting on my vest before that raid. Something could've happened. One of those bullets could've been fatal, and I'd never hold her again. I'd never see her face light up with her smile or the playful glint in her eye that teetered on seductive. My chest is on fire where the welts are forming, but the pain I'm feeling right now, being without her, is excruciating. I feel like a part of my soul is missing.

She's the best part of me, my entire future, and as soon as I see her, I'm saying it.

Tessa walks into the room, wiping underneath her eyes before giving me a nod. "I talked to her. She knows you're okay. And she seems okay now. Her mom wasn't in any pain when she died. She's on her way here."

Fuck. I wasn't there for her. Her mom died and I wasn't there.

The pressure forming in my chest intensifies. and I scoff at the nurse who seems to be taking her good old fucking time on my arm.

Tessa walks over to the bed, holding out her phone. "Here. You need to listen to this."

I take it from her with apprehension. "What is it?" She doesn't answer me as she walks over toward Nolan, and I place the phone up to my ear. Within seconds, my angel's voice fills me.

"I'm on my way. Oh, my God, please call me back and tell me he's okay. Tell him I love him, Tessa. Tell him I'm going to say that to him every second for the rest of his life. He'll never go another day without hearing those words from me." I hear her quivering breath before she pleads, "Please don't take him away from me."

The desperation in her voice nearly guts me. But those words, the words I've held off saying, have my heart slamming so hard against my sternum I'm certain it'll snap it in half. But I don't care if it does. I never want it to stop beating like this. I'd do fucking anything to keep feeling this way.

I need her. Now.

I start to move off the bed when the nurse slams her hand on my shoulder. "I have one more stitch. And then you'll have to wait to see if the doctor will release you. You have a lot of bruises from those bullets and you'll be in a lot of pain. You might want to think about going home with some medication."

I turn my head and make sure she is looking right into my eyes. I don't want to have to repeat myself.

"I don't care about the pain. I'll endure anything to get to the woman I fucking *breathe for*. She needs me, and as soon as you're finished with that last stitch, I'm going to her."

Her eyes widen slightly, and she steadies the needle against my shoulder. "But the doctor will want—"

"Tell him that I'm not waiting to get discharged. Say I went against orders. I don't give a shit." I look at my shoulder and then back at her. "It doesn't need to be pretty. Just finish it so I can get out of here."

She gets to it, and I hold Tessa's phone out to her.

She waves me off with her hand. "No. Take it. You'll need to call her so you two don't pass each other on the highway." She looks down at Nolan and smiles before looking back at me with a saddened expression. "Her message kind of killed me."

I rest my head back on the bed. "Yeah. It kind of killed me, too."

The nurse stands and pulls off her gloves after placing a bandage over my stitches. "All finished. I'll go grab the paper-work you need to sign."

I'm out of bed before she leaves the room and my speed startles her.

"Uh, you're not going to stick around and sign anything, are you?"

"Nope." I turn to Tessa who is scooping up Nolan as the nurse utters something under her breath while leaving the room. "You got him?"

"Yup. Go to her. But please be careful. I've suffered enough stress today."

I give Nolan a kiss before I sprint out of the room and down the long hallway to the stairwell. I'm out the door and running toward my truck that thankfully, Luke had made sure would be here for me when I was released. But it didn't matter. I'd fucking steal a car at this point to get to her. As soon as the bars register on Tessa's phone, indicating the reception, I dial Mia's number.

"Hey, I'm still like an hour and a half out. This traffic is ridiculous! Does nobody work anymore?"

I start up my truck and pull away from the hospital, the sound of her voice sending an ache throughout my entire body. "Baby," I whisper, my voice a strained plea. I hear her soft gasp, and then her staggered breathing fills my ear.

"Ben," she says through a soft cry.

My name on her lips blankets the pain I'm feeling right now. The pain that I've felt for the past several hours. Hope and pure need flood my senses, and I push my foot down on the gas pedal until it touches the floor.

"Oh, God, babe. I'm so happy to hear your voice. I was so worried."

"Angel, where are you? I'm getting on 215 right now."

"I'm on Route 7. Why don't you just wait there for me? We might pass each other."

I laugh slightly, my first laugh since yesterday. "There's no way I'll let you pass me, baby. Just keep driving to me and I'll find you."

She pauses for a beat, and I can almost see her fidgeting through the phone.

"Ben, I have to say it. I can't go another second without saying it to you."

Christ, I needed to say it, too. But not like this. Not fucking yet.

"Don't say it, Mia. I want to be looking into your eyes when I say it to you. And then you can say it back. Okay? Just hang on for me."

She sniffles several times. "Okay. But you better say it the second you see me or I'm saying it first. I've waited long enough for you, Benjamin Kelly. Don't make me wait anymore."

I shake my free hand out of the fist that is beginning to

permanently set in. Knowing Mia is this close to me feels like having an itch I can't scratch.

"No more waiting, baby. I promise you that."

"Good." She pauses and a muted grunt fills the phone. "Shit, babe. My phone's about to die. I should get off here in case we completely miss each other and I need to call you. I'm actually betting on that happening."

"Don't doubt me, Mia. I'd find you anywhere."

The possessive hunger in my blood yearns to prove her wrong on this one. She won't need that phone again. I'm drawn to her like a fucking honing missile.

She laughs slightly. "Yeah, you better."

I KNEW I'D run into her on Route 7 somewhere.

It's the longest stretch of highway that connects Alabama and Georgia. I'm only looking out for one vehicle across the grass covered median that separates east and west bound. And as soon as that cherry red Jeep comes into my line of sight, I feel like someone plugs me into an outlet.

My entire body stiffens in anticipation as I cross the three lanes and drive my truck across the median. My back end fishtails several times given the speed I take it at, but it doesn't slow me down. I drive toward the direction of the traffic, still in the median, and the red Jeep darts off the highway in between cars and skids to a halt in the grass.

Christ, baby. If you got into an accident right now . . .

I slam on my emergency brake and jump out of my truck, leaving it on. She swings her legs out of the Jeep and hops down, steadying herself before taking off running in my direction.

Mia. Mia. Mia.

She slams against my chest, a whimpered moan escaping both of us as I cradle her to me. The pain she's causing against my welts is ignored. I can't let her go. Not yet. But I do ease her away from me and take a hold of her delicate face with both my hands.

She looks at me with desperation. To hold me. To talk to me. To fucking hear what I've kept from her. And I don't make her wait.

"I love you. I can't remember a moment when I didn't love you. I'm so sorry that I wasn't there for you when you needed me, but that'll never happen again. I can't be without you, angel. Please tell me you'll stay with me." I drop my forehead to hers and close my eyes. The magnitude of my love for her is crippling. "I can't say goodbye to you."

Her hands grab my wrists with a gentle squeeze. "I love you, too. And you'll never have to say goodbye to me. It was always supposed to be you in the bar that night, Ben. You were always meant to be my first, and my last. I can't imagine giving myself to anyone but you. Not now. Not ever."

I open my eyes when I feel the tears falling down my face.

She reaches up and wipes them away. "This is where I belong. Wherever you are. Always."

Her declaration has me struggling to stay upright. My knees feel weak enough to drop me. But she has me. She wraps her arms around my waist and places her head against my chest. I bury my face in her hair.

"We'll come back for your car. I'm not driving home in separate vehicles when I've been without you for this long."

She giggles against me, her face turning up and knocking me out with that smile. "It hasn't even been a whole day."

"Felt like a whole year. Come on."

I move her along the grass and help her up into my truck

after securing her vehicle. There's no space between us, not anymore. And there never will be again.

She's against my side the entire drive home. Her head against my shoulder and my hand in her lap with both of hers holding on to me. I let her scent fill my lungs, feeling it calm me like a damn drug. Pain killers? No. I won't need any pain killers. She has me completely relaxed, every muscle in my body loose, until I feel her lips press against my neck.

She squirms against me, wiggling my hand down so it settles between her legs.

"Remember when you were so close to pulling over and taking me in your truck?" Her breath heats the skin below my ear, sending a jolt straight to my cock. "I want that. Right now." And then her hand is pressing on my massive erection, the one that is threatening to rip through my zipper.

I hiss through a moan as she works me through my shorts. "You want me to throw you in the back and fuck you on the side of the road?" I feel her nod against me as her teeth scrape against my ear. "Fuck. How wet are you right now?"

"Very." She grabs my hand and slips it under her dress, pressing my fingers against her panties. My cock becomes painfully hard at the feel of her arousal, and she moans when I press a finger against her clit. "Ben, please," she pants, digging her nails into my wrist as I twist my hand.

I slide underneath her panties and dip one finger into her. Her head falls back onto the seat with a shuddering gasp.

"Jesus Christ. Hold on, angel."

She protests with a whimper as I slip my finger out of her and pop it in my mouth.

I pull off on a back road that breaks into a secluded wood-ed area, parking my truck between the trees. I turn the truck off and unbuckle my seatbelt as she does the same.

"Climb over the seat and take that dress off. I want you naked and ready for me."

She complies with a gleeful chuckle, giving me a gorgeous view of her ass as she crawls into the back.

I step out of the truck and glance around. We're completely isolated. Good. Nothing is interrupting this. Opening the back door, I pull my cock out of my shorts before I climb inside. She's slipping off her panties, her dress discarded somewhere. Her hungry eyes focus on my dick that I'm slowly stroking while I watch her.

"You're so hard for me," she states with a fascinated tone. She reaches for me but quickly pulls her hands back. "Do you want me to do that? Or should I touch myself while you watch?"

Christ. That is tempting as hell. My cock jerks in my hand at the thought. But I'm suddenly hectic with the need to feel her around me. Nothing else will suffice right now. I grab her leg and pull her toward me, keeping my other hand on the base of my cock.

"Straddle me. I want those tits in my face."

I guide her over me, sliding my hands up her thighs as she grabs my cock and rubs it against herself, slicking the head. "Fuck, you feel amazing, baby," I grunt through a tense jaw. I lean in and lick her taut nipple, teasing it before drawing it into my mouth.

"Ben," she whispers urgently, shifting her weight forward and guiding me to her entrance. She grabs my face with both her hands, pulling me away from her breast, and locks eyes with me. "Watch me." Her mouth parts slightly as she lowers herself down, taking me to the hilt. "I love you."

I lean my head back and smirk. "Me? Or my cock?" Before she can answer, I grab her hips and lift her up, slamming her down on top of me five times with brute force. "You. Love. This?" I ask with my thrusts.

"Yes. God, yes."

When I finish, she takes the lead and digs her nails into my shoulders as she rocks against me.

"Easy, baby," I warn her when her hand presses against my stitches.

Her eyes go to the spot on my arm, and she raises the sleeve of my shirt. Her brow furrows with pain, maybe guilt. I'm not sure. She leans in, pressing her hand to my chest as she kisses the bandage. I wince at the pressure she puts on me and she notices. Her hands grab the bottom of my shirt. "Take it off."

I stop her from lifting it farther than my upper abs. "I'm fine. Just a little sore."

"I want to see it." She pulls with determination and I comply, shifting so she can lift it over my head. She inhales sharply, her eyes taking in the nine welts and the bruises that have formed around them. Her hand lies gently over the one welt that sits right in the middle of my chest. I see her lip tremble and reach up, cupping the side of her face. Her eyes meet mine with agony. "I could've lost you."

I pull her face toward me. "No. You'll never lose me. I told you that nothing could ever take me away from you." I brush my lips against hers and taste her tears on my tongue. "Don't cry. Not now. Be here with me, Mia."

She kisses me gently after wiping her tears away. "Make love to me. Just like you did that first night."

"You want me to be gentle?" I ask, snaking my arms around her waist. She nods before sliding off my lap and lying out on my back seat, legs spread. I shove my shorts and boxers down to mid-thigh before getting between her legs.

"Guide me in, baby."

She smiles and reaches around me, pulling me straight into her.

I thrust my hips slowly, letting her feel every inch of me as I brace myself on my elbows. Her eyes flutter close and she arches against me, brushing her chest against mine with a deep inhale. I can feel her heart knocking against my chest, mimicking my beat. I kiss her jaw, her nose, her cheeks. Every inch of her face is touched by my lips. She lets me worship her body like it's the first time. My hands caress every part of her, my lips sliding along her skin. I commit her to memory. Her scent. Her taste. The way her body shudders against mine. The feel of her right now, beneath me while I drag this out, while I prolong this moment with her, this, fucking *this* is the reason for my existence.

With every breath I take, I take one for her.

She moans loudly and grabs my face, pressing her lips against mine. "I'm so close."

I move in her at the same pace. Not speeding up. Not taking her the way she's become accustomed to.

"Oh, God, Ben," she says against my lips, raking her nails down my back. "Please."

"I know, angel. I've got you." I slide my hand between us and press my thumb against her clit. She answers with a whimpered cry and I get her there. Right there with only a few strokes.

Her eyes open and she wraps her legs around me. "I don't want to come without you." She barely gets her sentence out before her body tightens around me. "Ben . . ."

I groan loudly and feel my orgasm burning up my spine. "Holy shit." I watch her lips part with a silent cry, eyes closing as the pleasure builds, and push her knees back, needing to get deeper. My breath is stolen from me as I go off inside her, driving into her to the point of exhaustion. Giving her every piece of me. And even though I was tender and unhurried, it rocks me with a blinding intensity.

The kind I've only ever felt with Mia.

I collapse on top of her, resting my head on her chest. Her arms wrap around me and hold me tighter. Closer. Never close enough. I can't imagine loving her any more than I do right now, but I know I will. Because every second I'm with her, I fall harder. It's how it's always been between us. Even when I held myself back. I loved her when she became my best friend. And given the chance, I'd never change the way it happened. I'd never take back those weeks I suffered in silence, wanting more than she was willing to give me. I'd give her that a thousand times over if she needed it. A future with her was more than I'd ever deserve.

And I'll cherish her like the gift she is until I draw my last breath.

mia

"YOU KNOW, BEFORE this whole thing started between the two of you, you technically were mine for the summer," Tessa says as she helps me pack up my stuff in the bedroom I've occupied for the past two months. "I mean, I don't see the harm in you finishing out your time here with me and then moving in with Ben after the summer's over."

"Because he'd be so quick to agree to that arrangement," I state with a soft chuckle.

I knew there was no way in hell he'd go along with me prolonging my move. It's all he's talked about for the past five days. I'm actually surprised he's given me this long.

"And you act like I won't be right around the corner. You do realize I'm here permanently, right?"

She smiles over her shoulder as she grabs the clothes that are hanging in the closet. "That's not the point. I love that you two are together, but he's a horrible sharer. He always has been."

I take the clothes from her and pull them off the hangers. "Have you talked to him?"

"Who?" I give her a knowing look and she rolls her eyes. "Why would I talk to him? There's nothing to talk about. It's over."

Her words are final, but I know Tessa. She's hurting.

She'll never admit it, but she misses him. "Isn't tonight going to be weird? Seeing him at the concert?"

She shrugs once before taking the hangers back to the closet. "There's going to be like, five thousand people there. I can avoid him in a crowd that size. Plus, I plan on getting shitfaced, which is sure to help with the situation." She closes the closet door before dropping her forehead, hitting the wood with a soft thud.

"Tessa . . ."

"I don't want to talk about it." She lifts her head and turns toward me, her eyes giving away exactly what she's feeling. "Okay?"

I nod. "Okay."

We finish packing up my room in silence. I know when she's ready to talk about it, she'll open up. And she knows that I'm here whenever that time comes.

My aunt is taking care of selling my mom's house for me, allowing me to stay in Alabama during the process. Ben and I will be making a trip to get the rest of my things soon, but to be perfectly honest, I have everything I'll ever need. I never imagined moving back to Ruxton, but now I can't imagine not living here.

This was always my home. Wherever he was.

After loading my stuff into my Jeep so that I can take it straight to Ben's after the concert, Tessa and I head over to the field.

Ben somehow managed to snag tickets to see Luke Bryan. Lawn seats, which allows us to park in the field overlooking the stage and sit in our vehicles while we enjoy the music. I spot Ben's truck after weaving in and out of the crowd and park next to it, watching as he jumps out of the bed and walks over to my door.

"Hey, baby. You all packed up?" He opens my door for me and I hop out, waving to Reed who Tessa is making her way toward.

I take his hand and let him lead me to the back of his truck. "Yup. Everything's in the Jeep. Your sister's not too happy about it."

He stifles a laugh as he drops the tailgate down. "Like that would stop me from moving you in with me. Here. Up you go."

I climb up into the back of his truck, spotting the pillows and the blankets spread out for us. I turn to him with a smile. "Am I getting lucky during this concert?"

He wraps his arms around my waist and kisses my bare shoulder. "I'm always prepared, angel. My girl seems to be a bit insatiable lately."

"You're like a dirty little boy scout," I add, hearing Tessa's laugh get louder behind me. I turn in Ben's arms and spot her walking over toward us with Reed.

"Hey. I'm really glad you guys worked your shit out. You sucked as friends," Reed says through a teasing smile.

I flip him off over Ben's shoulder and he throws his head back with a laugh. Just as Tessa opens her mouth to speak, another truck pulls up alongside Ben's and catches her attention.

"Oh, perfect. He couldn't have gotten lost on the way here?"

Ben's chest shakes with laughter against my back as his hands splay across my abdomen. "We've been here a thousand times. I doubt he'd get lost."

Tessa's body goes rigid suddenly, and I turn my head to see why.

Luke isn't the only one emerging from his truck. A tall, leggy blonde is at his side as he joins the group, stopping just a few feet short of Tessa and Reed.

He shifts his gaze from Tessa to Ben and then to me. "Guys, this is Brandie. Brandie, this is . . . everyone." She waves her delicate hand, the one that isn't currently roaming freely over his chest. Luke wraps his arm around her waist. "We're going to head closer to the stage. We'll catch up with you guys later."

As he walks away with little Miss Handsy, Tessa slams the tailgate of the truck up and startles the three of us. "Well, she seems lovely. He's really scraping the bottom of the barrel now, isn't he?"

Reed shrugs once. "I don't know. She's pretty hot."

She glares at him and he steps back a bit. "Yeah, she's really got that street corner look down. And could her name be any more whorish?"

"You'd think that if her name was Mary," Ben says. "Stop being jealous, Tessa. You broke up with him."

She waves him off and grabs Reed's hand. "Whatever. Let's go get several hundred beers. You guys want any?" she directs toward us, her face still tense with bitterness.

"I'm good," I say, looking back at Ben who is situating the pillows and spreading the blanket out.

"Me too," he adds.

Tessa and Reed disappear into the crowd.

I turn around just in time to see Ben reach through his back window and pull out a picture frame. He smiles at me and sits down on the blanket with his back against a pillow. He reaches for me with his free hand. "Come here, angel."

"Whatcha got there?"

He pats the spot between his legs. and I sit with my back against his chest, drooping my arms over his legs. He places the frame in my lap. "Don't cry," he whispers against my ear.

I tilt the frame up and look at the drawing. Three figures, undoubtedly drawn by Nolan, depicting our family. My family. He even labeled me as Pwincess Mia Mommy. And the tears come instantly. I can't help it.

"Your artistic skills are horrendous." I reach up and wipe underneath my eyes as Ben laughs against me. "God, he is the sweetest, isn't he? Can we hang it up at your house?"

"Our house," he corrects me. He presses his mouth to my hair again. "Don't cry, baby."

I open my mouth to tell him that I can't not cry at seeing our first family drawing, but he wipes every word from my vocabulary when he places a small box in my lap.

You know, the kind of box that every girl recognizes.

I gasp softly, holding the frame tightly against my chest while my eyes stay glued to the box.

His steady hands open it. "Do you know how much I love you?"

I nod and clutch the frame harder, feeling the tears well up in my eyes. I blink them away and focus on the ring that he's holding between his fingers. "As much as I love you," I choke out.

"No, angel. No one has ever loved anyone as much as I love you. I got you beat there, I'm afraid." He motions for my hand and I place it in his, allowing him to slip the ring on my finger. "You're my best friend, Mia. I want you every day, for the rest of my life. I will always cherish every moment you give me. Marry me, baby."

I'm nodding and whispering "yes" before he even finishes. And then he's turning me and cradling me against his chest, worshipping me with kisses all over my face. "Thank you," I say against his lips.

I feel them curl up into a smile. "For what?"

I kiss along his jaw up to his ear. "For being at the bar that night. For being the guy that you are. For giving me Nolan." I pull back and cradle his face in my hands. "Can we have more babies?"

He brings my hand up to his lips and kisses the back of it. "Can we start right now?"

And then I'm on my back, his body covering mine. I laugh against him as he brushes my hair away from my face. "We're in the middle of a field."

"Don't care. Nobody can see us anyway. Look how high up we are."

"Yes, but I've been told I'm rather noisy," I tease as he kisses my neck. He grunts once and nips at my sensitive skin there. "I love you."

"Love you."

"I want lots of babies."

His head comes up and he smiles widely. "Lots." He shifts his weight and lays his head on the pillow, pulling me so I'm lying against his chest.

And we stay like that long after Tessa and Reed return. Long after the concert starts and ends. Until we're the only vehicle left in the field. He makes love to me under the stars, his tenderness breaking into a wild frenzy when we both need it. It's perfect. And I'm right where I belong.

Where I always will be.

ben

Mia: Meet me at our spot.

STARE DOWN at my phone, reading the text message for the second time.

Our spot. What spot? As far as I'm concerned, every spot I've taken Mia to has become our spot. And we've racked up a lot of spots over the past four months.

I go to reread her text again when my phone beeps.

Mia: The bar, Ben.

I shake my head with a laugh.

Me: I would've figured it out. What have I told you about doubting me?

Mia: Just hurry up before one of the other men in here takes me home.

Me: Mia . . .

Mia: Kidding. Hurry though.

I'm in the parking lot within ten minutes, pulling up next to her Jeep. It's about as crowded as it was the night Mia became mine, but I spot her on that same stool she occupied all those months ago. I don't go to her though. Instead, I go to the side of the bar where she can't see me and watch her without her knowing.

She's tapping the bar anxiously with her fingers, looking over her shoulder every few seconds toward the door. Her hair is down, and she's wearing a shirt that has my eyes going from her chest to her face and back again. I motion for the bartender.

"Can you send one of those purple drinks to that girl right there for me?"

He nods and gets to work on her drink while she pulls her phone out with a scowl. My phone beeps.

Mia: I mentioned today, right?

Me: You're so fucking beautiful. Do you know that?

Just as my message goes through, the bartender sits the drink down in front of her. She smiles at him, looking at the drink and then glancing at her phone. Her eyes immediately find mine across the bar, and I make my way to her. My hand brushes along her back, and I claim my spot.

"You looked thirsty from where I was standing. Thought I'd help you out," I say with a smile.

She places her one hand on my knee. "I need to talk to you about something."

I tilt my head and push her drink closer to her. "And what is that?"

"We need to move the wedding up." She grabs the straw between her fingers and dunks it in and out of her drink.

"Why? I thought you wanted a summer wedding? I mean, I'm all for stealing you away right now and making you my wife, but you seemed pretty dead set on the date."

She smiles and pushes her drink away, motioning for the bartender. He stops in front of us and gives me a friendly nod before looking at her. "I'm sorry. Can you make this nonalcoholic? I can't drink this."

"Sure thing," he says, taking her glass away.

She hits me with a smile and grabs my hand, laying it across her stomach. "Ben."

"Hmm?" I'm still trying to piece together why she suddenly doesn't want the drink that she so eagerly consumed our first go-around. It takes me a minute to focus on my hand. My eyes meet hers and she smiles. And then it clicks. "Baby, are you pregnant?" The hope in my voice dominates over the sudden anxiousness that begins to brew in my gut.

"I really don't want to be the size of a house when I'm walking down the aisle to you. So, I was thinking maybe a spring wedding instead? I'd be five months by then."

"Angel." I'm on my knees in the middle of the bar, pressing my face against her stomach. "Please tell me I'm not hearing you wrong."

She giggles against me and turns my face up. "You're not hearing me wrong. Nolan's going to be a big brother."

My senses are flooded with a need to protect this woman and my baby that she's carrying. "We need to get out of here."

"Why? This is our spot."

I shake my head and stand, grabbing some money out of my wallet and paying for the drink she won't be consuming. "There's people smoking. And it's really loud."

She laughs and puts her hand in mine, allowing me to lead her outside. "Babe, I don't think the noise level in here is going to hurt the baby. He's barely the size of a peanut right now."

I stop in the middle of the parking lot, spinning around. "He?"

She smiles up at me and places her hands on my chest. "Just a gut feeling I have. It's too early to tell."

I wrap my arms around her, staring down at the woman that I'll give my life for.

"You're going to put me in a bubble for the next nine months, aren't you?"

I kiss her forehead, pulling her against my chest. "I'll do whatever's necessary," I say.

And she doesn't argue with me. She allows me to hold her right where we stood that night. Before I knew she'd change my life. Before I knew I was holding the woman I was going to marry.

My future. My forever.

All mine.

The End

Read on for the first chapter of
four letter word

chapter one

Sydney

I HAD BEEN sitting in the same spot for an hour.

Well, at least it felt like an hour. I honestly had no idea what time it was. I couldn't look at the clock to verify how long I'd been immobile. I couldn't look at anything besides the hand resting in my lap.

No, not resting. It shook violently, no matter how hard I pressed it flat against my jean- covered thigh.

My skin all over was clammy and frigid at the same time. Sweat tickled my palms, pooled at the base of my neck and in the hollow dip of my throat. It was quite possible I was running a fever.

I should feel sick. This *was* sickening.

The house felt eerily quiet, desolate, though I knew Marcus was in the other room. I hadn't heard the evidence of his departure—the front door closing or the low rumble of his truck starting up.

He hadn't left. And why would he? Why would *he* be the one leaving in this scenario?

You should be leaving, Sydney. Get up. Run. Grab your stuff and get the hell out of here.

I exhaled a trembling breath. I couldn't move. I couldn't stop shaking. I could barely remember how important oxygen intake was in the matter of staying alive. Long seconds stretched out before I would inhale in a panic, allow my lungs to taste the air in the room I shouldn't still be sitting in, then expel that breath all too quickly.

I needed to go. I needed to react somehow, because I hadn't thus far.

I felt numb. And this . . . this felt like a dream.

A paralyzing dream.

The kind you didn't wake up from.

My phone rang from my bag on the floor somewhere, but it sounded miles away. I couldn't lift my head to the noise. I couldn't even remember where I had tossed it after I endured the one-sided conversation with Marcus.

Endured. Not participated in.

Him, doing all the talking, all the explaining, and none of it sounding the least bit apologetic, his voice cold and distant, detached, final . . . having made the decision, *his* decision, while I stood there frozen.

Frozen.

Marcus turned on his heel and swiftly left the room. I collapsed into a pile of heavy limbs on the floor, where I'd remained, and where I had every intention of remaining.

That was my reaction. It was the only reaction I was capable of.

Until the phone rang . . . *again.*

Something felt off. It was a miracle I felt it, whatever it was, considering my deadened state.

Like a whispered warning against my ear.

My spine stiffened in an instant. I turned my head in the direction of my muffled ringtone, scanning with what felt like new eyes.

Fresh and alert.

I was up to count six of Taylor Swift singing about being

young and reckless. I knew who was calling, and I contemplated ignoring my best friend again, slouching over and righting myself to my previous position, until I realized . . .

Shit.

Shit.

My already tight chest grew tighter.

Tori never called me that many times in a row. If I didn't answer her, I was usually in the middle of a shift at work, and she'd leave her standard "call me when you get a sec" message.

She never rang me up like this. Urgently.

Was something wrong?

I found my bag halfway under the bed and tugged it out by one of the straps. Palming my phone, I answered the call just before the last words of the verse sounded.

"H-Hey, what's up?" I asked, voice strained and anxious, stumbling brokenly through my greeting.

My head hit the side of the mattress as I resumed my location on the floor with my knees pulled in close against my chest.

"Syd." Tori's voice cracked with a whimper. "Hon . . . hey, hey, are you busy right now? Do you have a minute to talk? I need to talk."

I blinked rapidly at her distressful tone.

I suddenly couldn't remember the last hour, or however long I had been in this room. I couldn't remember the bomb Marcus dropped in my lap before he dismissed me with a curt nod and went about his business doing God knows what.

My hands no longer shook. My breathing was even. Focused.

I had never heard my best friend cry. Never. Not once in the twelve years we'd known each other. And we'd been through some shit, let me tell you.

But she was now.

I was right. Something was off.

Worry consumed me. My blood ran warmer as I began to pace along the length of the bed, pressing the phone to my ear as I quickly collected myself.

"I have as much time as you need, sweetie. What's going on? Why are you upset?"

"Wes," she hiccupped.

Wes.

Tori's boyfriend of six months and serious enough he was obviously worth shedding tears over.

I hadn't had a chance to meet the guy yet, due to my busy work schedule and the three-hour drive time between Tori and myself. But I felt like I knew him. Ninety percent of Tori's and my conversations revolved around what amazingly sweet thing Wes did for her that week.

He seemed perfect.

My attention snapped back to the phone at my ear when I heard a crash, the sound of glass breaking, followed immediately by my best friend's livid but still distraught high-pitched voice.

"*Married.* He's fucking married, Syd! Can you believe that? That son of a bitch has a wife!"

I stopped pacing and stared openmouthed at the wall.

Married?

Oh, *God* . . .

Tori took in a shuddering breath and I started pacing again, needing to either move or hit someone. And I wasn't jumping at the chance to confront Marcus just yet, so option two was out.

Tori's voice shrank to a more vulnerable decibel when she finally continued.

"God, Sydney, how stupid am I? How did I not see this? His weeknight rule with being too busy to see me Monday through Friday, always sending my calls to voice mail only to return them minutes later, which I'm imagining now was enough time for him to make up some bullshit story to appease his wife so he could sneak out and call me back. *Asshole.* God . . . that stupid, *fucking* asshole. How? How did that not set off alarms in my head? Was it that obvious? Was I that blind, Syd?"

I didn't know if it was from my frantic pacing, or from Tori's confession sinking in, but suddenly I needed to steady myself with a hand on the wall.

The room began to spin.

I blinked everything into focus before finding my own voice, which I kept quiet.

"Oh, my God, Tori. My *God*. How did you find out? What happened?"

"Saw him with her at the mall, pushing a damn stroller through the food court," she answered, sounding equal parts disgusted and destroyed. "They looked so fucking perfect together, I didn't know whether to throw up or scream."

She groaned, and I heard more things rattling in the background.

I pictured Tori testing the weight of different glass objects before she chose one to hurl against the closest wall.

"I walked right up to the son of a bitch. I saw her ring. I saw *his*. I was ready to confront him then and there. You know me. But you know what that bastard did?"

She sniffed loudly through the phone.

It broke my heart to hear her like this, but I didn't get to tell her that before she continued.

"He . . . he threw his arm around her, smiled at me, and

introduced us. He actually *introduced* his wife to me, Sydney. Told her I was an old friend from high school. Can you believe that? A *friend*."

She chuckled derisively at the word.

"I've done things with him I've never done with other men. I've talked with him . . . you know? That kind of talking where you just share yourself with someone for hours and hours and you can't think of anything else you'd rather be doing. I don't know if I loved him, but I could've. I know I could've."

"What did you do?"

She breathed through a tight laugh.

"I know what I should've done. I should've called him out on it. Stomped his balls out. His wife deserved to know. *I* would want to know, but I couldn't do anything. I couldn't. I stood there like some *freak*, staring at him with my mouth hanging open. I probably looked psychotic. I couldn't believe what I was hearing. After God knows how long they walked away and I . . . I just kept standing there until a security guard came up to me and asked if I was okay." She paused, then whispered, "I wasn't. I'm not."

I moved to the bed and sank onto the mattress, elbows on my knees, and rubbed my palm across my forehead.

I couldn't believe what I was hearing either. I couldn't believe people could be this malicious as to openly hurt someone this way, even though I was suffering from a pain similar to what Tori was experiencing. But at least she was acknowledging it. Admitting the effect it had on her and even going as far as confessing it to someone.

I couldn't do that yet. I wasn't feeling anything.

Until now.

The change was swift. I suddenly felt everything, as if

someone had taken a book filled with the range of human emotions and chucked it at my head. I was overwhelmed. Alive with reaction. I wanted to cry. I wanted to scream. I was full of rage and bitterness, pain . . . God, the pain was undeniable now. It felt like a cancer eating away at my bones.

Tori let out a strangled yell. Something else shattered through the line.

I closed my eyes and imagined doing the same thing.

I knew her adoration for Wes ran deep and threatened to run deeper the more time she had spent with that man.

She saw him as her future.

He already planned one out with another woman.

Are all men complete pieces of shit?

My eyes flashed down at my left hand, lifeless on my leg. One particular finger felt foreign to me. Irritating. Like an itch I couldn't reach to scratch.

I couldn't remain still anymore.

My skin pricked at the base of my neck as I stood and pulled my suitcases from the walk-in closet, dragging them to the bed.

I knew my best friend better than anyone. I knew that sometimes she simply needed me to listen instead of offering my assurance or advice. Just knowing someone was there for you spoke louder than a lot of words.

So that's what I gave her. Silence.

She cried softly into my ear as I threw my entire life into two suitcases and one duffle bag. I ransacked the bathroom, not caring how I left it as I packed away my toiletries. I wiped away every memory of myself from that room.

Every photo. Anything tying me to Marcus. Everything personal.

I wanted them gone. But more important, *I* wanted to

be gone.

I stripped the ring from my finger and held it tight in my fist, the blunt edge of the diamond threatening to break skin.

Tori dragged out an edgy breath, then told me quietly, "I'm sorry, hon. I just needed to get that off my chest. You're probably busy, right? Are you at work? It's cool, I'll let you go."

Work. That was another thing I had to deal with. Immediately. Sooner the better.

"Yeah, I'm kind of in the middle of something," I replied, which wasn't entirely a lie. I knew she would assume that meant I was at the hospital, when in reality I was in the middle of letting go of the life I thought I was meant to have.

The one I wrote vows for.

I had to get off the phone. The sooner I finished this, the better.

"All right. I gotta go anyway. There's glass everywhere. I should probably clean it up before I step on it. Call me tomorrow if you have a chance."

The call disconnected.

I chuckled, which seemed so strange given the reality of the situation.

My current, completely fucked-up situation.

Tori never waited on the line to hear anyone's good-bye. I knew that about her. I'd overheard many conversations she held growing up, but every time we spoke, I still readied myself with a response.

It was habitual, and the normal thing to do.

I envied her ability to cut the world off like that. To dominate life.

It wasn't too late for me to become a wrecking force. I had absolutely nothing to lose anymore.

I had nothing at all.

Securing the duffle strap over my shoulder, I lifted the suitcases and marched down the hallway.

Noise from the television grew louder as I descended the stairs. Marcus was continuing on with his night as if nothing had been revealed. As if we were still an "us," and he hadn't taken all of that away from me.

I briefly glanced in his direction when I moved past the living room.

He was sitting in his favorite chair and nursing a beer, his feet crossed at the ankles and propped up on our coffee table. His eyes glued to the game.

Typical.

He was a creature of habit, and he had already come to terms with a world we were no longer facing together. He chose it willingly.

Why should my departure affect him? He'd already let go of me.

Marcus didn't speak. I knew he wouldn't, but what surprised me was my silence. I had so much to say, to scream, in his face or from this distance, it didn't matter, but more than anything I wanted to get on the road before darkness blanketed the sky. I hated driving at night.

And most important, I wanted to get to my friend.

I didn't need to free up a hand to open the door. Our storm door never latched properly, and with a swift kick at the base, it would swing free and open, creaking at the hinges.

For the first time since we'd moved into that house, I was grateful for the minor imperfection.

I didn't need to free up my hand, but I did need to open it slightly. Two fingers letting go of the weight burning against my flesh.

The last noise I heard before I stepped outside and

welcomed the damp air on my skin was the ping of gold striking the wood beneath my feet.

I RODE WITH the windows down the entire drive to Dogwood Beach. I reveled in the clean scent of grass and earth, the sweet warmth of a May evening. Everyday things, beautiful things that would normally calm my restless mind, but not tonight. I kept the music off and just let myself *think*, piling on sign after obvious sign I had been too stupid or too disconnected to notice over the past three months.

It was all so clear now. Every color of our corrosion.

The naive veil had finally been lifted, and the longer I drove, the more I hated myself for becoming one of those women who allowed deceit to slip past them. Who stayed too detached and okay with little changes that should've been red-hot alarms, blaring with an incessant warning.

Our growing silence with each other, leaving our only conversations to be ones we needed to have, not ones we wanted to have. The indifferent way he began to look at me, or the late nights when he'd claim he was too tired to drag himself to bed and instead chose to camp out on the couch.

A couch I knew from experience wasn't the best for sleeping on.

I regretted every whispered word I uttered into the dark late at night when I wrapped myself around a cold pillow and reached with a seeking hand for a body I knew wasn't next to me.

What was I reaching for?

And why? Why didn't I see it? Where had I been?

Tori's questions from earlier became a mantra.

Was I that blind? How stupid was I?

With each passing minute, my hands formed tighter to the

wheel until a crack of pain shot up my forearms. I adjusted and readjusted, flexing until my shoulders began to shake. I was a bottle of pent-up aggression, a warrior in a cage, watching as a threatening figure inched closer . . . closer until I saw the intimation radiating off them in heated waves. Until I felt it on my skin. The warm bite of hunger scratched the back of my throat. I wanted to bare my teeth and sink them into flesh. Draw blood. I couldn't remember ever feeling this alive before, but I was ready.

Ready to release my anger onto someone who truly deserved it.

It was after nine when I finally arrived, parked my car behind Tori's Volvo, and grabbed my duffle, leaving my other bags in the backseat.

The smell of salt water soaked into my lungs as I climbed the stairs to the porch, and for a brief moment I thought about how peaceful my new life was about to become.

Living at the beach was a fairy tale to me. A pipe dream that was about to become a reality . . . at least I was hoping it would.

I was showing up at my friend's house, unannounced, seeking refuge.

Bag in hand, I held my breath and knocked three times.

Seconds passed before the door swung open.

Tori stood before me in her pajamas, a pair of pale blue linen shorts and an oversized T-shirt that hung off her shoulder.

Her jaw hit the floor as she looked me over with wide, startled eyes.

"Syd! What are you . . ." She paused, gaze lowering to the duffle in my hand. "What's going on? Where's Marcus? Is he with you?"

She glanced behind me in the direction of the driveway.

Explanations were in order. This was the boldest move I had ever made in all of my twenty-four years, aside from getting married straight out of high school.

I never visited Tori without planning out my trip, and she always knew about it well in advance.

This wasn't simply a visit, though. This was a permanent relocation.

But explanations could wait. I had to deal with something, or someone, to be specific, before I revealed anything.

I pushed past her and entered the house.

"No, he's not. And he won't be joining me either. I hope that offer you made me last year still stands. I know you were just joking about us ditching our men and starting a lesbian life together, but as long as we keep it purely platonic, I could swing it."

I tossed my bag on the couch in the large sitting room and spun to face a very, very confused-looking Tori.

Rightfully so.

She tilted her head, motioning around the room as if the house, and not the woman standing in front of her, had just magically appeared.

"What's going on here? What are you doing?"

"I need that asshole's number. Let me handle this first, and then I'll explain everything. I promise." I tugged my phone out of my back pocket. My hand shook ever so slightly. "What is it?"

She slowly inched closer.

"Who? Wes? Why? You're not going to call him, are you?"

"Tori," I growled. "Give. Me. His. Number."

My words, and the tone behind them, acted like a fire lit to blaze under her ass. She gasped, then moved with purpose through the tiny but lavish beach house.

Tori came from money. Her family came from money. You didn't live this close to the water and in digs like this without either having connections or a stacked bank account.

"Okayyy." She spoke with uncertainty, her tongue clinging to the word as she walked back into the room. "Okay, um, seriously, I have no clue what's going on right now, but I'm almost afraid you might choke me if I don't do what you say. You're a bit scary right now, Syd."

If I'd had it in me, I would've smiled at that.

But I didn't have it in me to smile.

Tori dug the heel of her hand into her eye while her other scrolled through the contacts on her phone.

Her long blond hair was haphazardly pulled back into a loose pony, with several pieces falling onto her shoulders and curling there.

She looked unkempt and exhausted, but still unbelievably gorgeous, because she always looked unbelievably gorgeous no matter how unkempt or exhausted she was.

Tori was a natural stunner and the definition of small-town beauty queen. She grew up in the pageant circuit, won every competition she ever entered without even caring enough about them to try, it was all her mother's doing, putting her in those pageants and exploiting her daughter's beauty, and Tori went through the motions to make her mother happy, but that didn't mean Tori didn't know when to put her foot down and that occurred when she was approached by some agency to do shampoo commercials when she was fourteen.

My best friend wasn't interested in the kind of attention appearing in a shampoo commercial would bring a fourteen-year-old who had developed a lot earlier than the rest of her peers.

So that offer was the end of Tori's pageant days and,

subsequently, the beginning of her mother's descent into the world of plastic surgery.

If her daughter wasn't going to bring her attention, Mrs. Rivera would find her own way to grab it.

I watched another strand of hair fall out of Tori's messy, yet still utterly perfect pony.

I imagined after she destroyed God knows how many breakables in the house, she probably tossed about in her bed, praying for sleep and dreams involving Wes's unfortunate but highly deserved demise.

Bastard.

Keeping her eyes on her phone, Tori shook her head then finally spoke.

"He probably won't answer you. That's his thing. But whatever. Ready? It's 919–555–6871."

I opened up the keypad on my phone and moved my thumb furiously over the numbers.

He would answer. I'd hit Redial until my fingers bled if needed.

I placed the phone to my ear and waited.

I felt anxious and slightly dizzy. My pulse was racing. I knew I probably needed to sit down, take a breath, but the second that motherfucker's deep voice seeped into my ear with a tired yet undeniably sexy "yeah," which pissed me off to no end seeing as I hated this man with every fiber of my being and had no businesses thinking his "yeahs" were sexy, I was on high alert and once again found myself pacing the room like a strung-out junkie.

"You," I growled, voice vibrating low and sore in my throat. "Stupid, worthless piece of dog shit."

Tori gasped behind me.

"Excuse me?" Wes sounded put off. "What the fuck—"

"Who the hell do you think you are, huh? And in what universe is a douche bag tool like you able to bag a wife? Is she *also* a fucking idiot?"

I heard his heavy breathing on the other line, but nothing else. His silence boiled my blood.

"Hello! Remove the dildo from your mouth and fucking speak!"

I spun around, shocked at my own coarse words, and looked up at Tori, curious to see her reaction.

She stood frozen between the couch and the wall, her eyes swollen and red from her earlier tears, doubled in size now that I'd let my mouth loose on this dipshit.

A light, amused chuckle hissed in my ear.

I pulled in a breath through my nose.

"Jesus Christ," he mumbled. "Think you might have the wrong number, Wild. I don't normally suck on dildos after six o'clock on Tuesdays."

I blinked at the floor.

Wild?

Was he making fun of me?

He was. He was making a joke, out of me, out of this, out of my best friend's pain.

I flattened a hand to my chest, feigning regret.

"Oh, I am so, so sorry. I forgot. You're into ass play. Hard and deep, right? Tori told me all about it. My mistake. Is that something your wife enjoys? Do you take turns fucking each other?"

"Fuck," he groaned. "You serious?"

"You hurt her," I bit out through clenched teeth. "You hurt my best friend. And you better pray to the God of assholes like you that I don't ever see your ugly, motherfucking face. Jail doesn't scare me, loser. I will cut your dick off and make you eat it in front of your mother."

He laughed again, only this time it was bold and straight from his belly. One of those laughs I knew had his head thrown back and tears brimming his eyes.

My feet stuck to the carpet. The hand at my side curled into a tight fist with nails threatening to break skin.

"You're . . . *wow*," he said, his voice floating with another soft laugh. "Damn. Just slow down a minute, all right? Quit yelling for a second." He cleared his throat. I heard the creak of the mattress. "Look, I'm not going to deny that I partake in a little ass play on occasion, but no joke, I'm the one delivering it. There is no other scenario. As for my dick? I really need him to stay attached. We're close. You get me?"

Did I *get* him?

"I hate you," I whispered, closing my eyes, my heart pounding.

Suddenly, I forgot who I had dialed and could only picture Marcus standing in the doorway of our bedroom.

Marcus, telling me it was over.

Marcus, digging his nails into my chest and clawing out my heart.

Marcus, my husband, who had stopped loving me and wanted out.

He didn't look remorseful in that moment. He looked . . . relieved.

There was no need to lie anymore. No need to pretend he was happy. He was free, and I was falling.

Down.

Down.

Into the unknown, where I had to find the person I was without him. I didn't even know where to begin looking for her.

Wes hesitated responding, finally giving me a quiet, "Don't even know me," followed by a heavy sigh. "Again, you got the wrong number. This guy who you *think* I am, he screwed over your friend? Right? Do me a favor and check the number you were supposed to dial. I'm betting you're only off by one."

"Fuck you," I spat.

I was sick of hearing his denial, but then strangely found myself pulling the phone back and studying the screen.

There was something in his voice when he dropped the enjoyment of my verbal lashing. A concealed sadness, and I didn't think the man who had shamelessly introduced his wife to his girlfriend had the ability to feel anything that deep.

You had to have a heart first. Wes clearly didn't.

I couldn't remember what number Tori had given me. It could easily have been the number lit up on my phone, but I wanted to be certain.

I lifted my head to look at her.

"What was that number again?"

Tori narrowed her eyes, her mouth dropping open. She then glanced down once more at the phone in her hand and slowly repeated, "Uh, 919–555–6871."

Shit.

Exactly one number off. I'd dialed 6872.

"What's going on?" Tori asked, stepping forward.

I knew the man on the other end of the line heard the confirmation he was betting on. By the time the phone touched my ear again, he was finishing the last subtle notes of a throaty chuckle.

"Sorry you're going to have to go through that epic speech again, Wild. You nailed it, though, if that helps."

Wild.

His voice was smooth and low, wickedly playful.

Sexy.

I was ready to dig a hole in the sand and bury myself in it.

God, I am such a shit.

I slapped a hand over my eyes, groaning.

"Oh, my God. I am so, *so* sorry. This . . . was clearly a call not meant for you. I'm sure you're not a douche bag tool."

"Who sucks on dildos and gets fucked by his wife?"

He chuckled again.

I could feel the heat burn across my cheeks and down my neck.

"Yeah," I said through a wince.

"Not really my thing."

Tori nudged my elbow, then held her hands out, silently questioning what was going on.

I shook my head. I needed to get off the phone with this guy. I'd abused him enough already.

I held up a finger to Tori and spun around, facing the large bay window at the front of the house.

"Right. Um, again, I'm very, *very* sorry I cussed you out and accused you of enjoying . . . those things. I don't normally go off like that. It's just been . . . one of those days. You know?" I blew out a quick breath. "Sorry again. Take care."

Quickly, before he had the chance to respond, I slid my thumb over the End Call button.

My body slumped into the nearby recliner and I curled into the leather, dropping my head back with a sigh.

That felt good. Even if I hadn't spewed that hatred at my intending victim, something in my chest felt lighter. It was bizarre. Maybe I didn't need to dial the correct number to chew out Wes, or face my new reality and lay into Marcus.

Speaking of douche bag tools.

Marcus had gotten off too easy. He pulled the pin on our relationship and walked away without any refusal from me. I'm not a wallflower. Far from it, actually. I would eventually face him and give him every word I was meant to say in that bedroom. He deserved to know how I felt, but more than that, he deserved to feel it.

"What . . . the *hell* was that?" Tori appeared in front of me, her hands stuck to her hips. "Did you seriously say all of that to a wrong number?"

I nodded.

"Holy shit, you badass. Way to commit." Her smile faded a second before her eyes went soft. "Are you going to try Wes again? Because really, Syd, you don't have to do that. I'm not asking you to fight my battles, and to be honest . . ." She trailed off, swallowing heavily as her eyes lowered. "I think I'm okay. I mean, I'm completely done with men for the time being, but I'm not chasing a bottle of pills with some hooch. I'll get over it. He was just another mistake."

After I was silent for a few seconds, she bent down and placed her hand gently on my knee.

"Hey," she whispered.

I rolled my head to the side until our eyes met, and before she spoke her next words, I knew from the look on her face what she was planning on asking me.

I decided to beat her to it.

"Marcus told me tonight he wants a divorce."

She sucked in a breath.

"What? Why? What happened?"

Before I could answer, she shot up abruptly, holding her hand out to keep me quiet.

"Wait. We need wine for this discussion, and all of the chocolate in this house. Give me a minute."

She turned to take a step, but halted, spinning back around and pointing at the floor.

"You will be living here."

My mouth lifted in the corner.

"Thank you."

She disappeared down the hallway in a blur of blond hair and long limbs as I tucked myself into a ball, staring off into the quiet house.

My new home.

Four Letter Word is available now

acknowledgements

MY FAMILY, THANK you to my family for your continuous support. To my ridiculously amazing husband. You, YOU are my favorite thing in the entire world. I'm a bit crazy about you. Heads up.

To all the amazing blogger friends I've made so far, thank you. SERIOUSLY, I can't even express how much you all mean to me. Beth Cranford, Kylie McDermott, Smexy, Lisa Jayne, Maree Hunter, Karrie Puskas, and countless more. Did I just name drop? Oh, fuck yes I did. You all have showed me so much love ever since I published Sweet Addiction and I will never be able to thank you enough. To Give Me Books for everything you've done for me. I heart you girls. Now, all of you come to Maryland so I can hug you. Now. Do it.

R.J. Lewis, for always being there. Even when I'm stressing out. Even when I'm really stressing out. My cell phone bill has reached a new high due to our international text messages and I love it. However, if I don't get a new book from you soon, I might become hostile. :)

Trish Tess, thank you for showing me so much love. You, my little friend, are the sweetest.

To the best readers a little indie author could ask for, thank you for taking a chance on me and for all your kind words. Your support means the world to me, and I wish I could hug each and every one of you.

Thank you again,

J

books by
J. DANIELS

SWEET ADDICTION SERIES

Sweet Addiction

Sweet Possession

Sweet Obsession

ALABAMA SUMMER SERIES

Where I Belong

All I Want

When I Fall

Where We Belong

What I Need

Say I'm Yours

DIRTY DEEDS SERIES

Four Letter Word

Hit the Spot

about the author

J DANIELS IS THE *New York Times* and *USA Today* bestselling author of the Sweet Addiction series, the Alabama Summer series, and the Dirty Deeds series.

She would rather bake than cook, she listens to music entirely too loud, and loves writing stories her children will never read. Her husband and children are her greatest loves, with cupcakes coming in at a close second.

J grew up in Baltimore and resides in Maryland with her family.

follow j at:

www.authorjdaniels.com

Facebook
www.facebook.com/jdanielsauthor

Twitter—@JDanielsbooks

Instagram—authorjdaniels

Goodreads
http://bit.ly/JDanielsGoodreads

Join her reader's group for the first look at upcoming projects, special giveaways, and loads of fun!

www.facebook.com/groups/JsSweeties

Sign up to receive her newsletter and get special offers and exclusive release info.

www.authorjdaniels.com/newsletter

CPSIA information can be obtained
at www.ICGtesting.com
Printed in the USA
BVOW04s1329160317
478605BV00024B/58/P